Clergy Hustle

OTHER TITLES BY EARLIECIA J EBRON

COMPLICATED LOVE
REGRESS
CHURCH VIXENS
RESCUING DESTINY

Clergy Hustle

Earliecia J Ebron

Library of Congress Control Number:		2016912852
ISBN:	Hardcover	978-1-5245-3190-4
	Softcover	978-1-5245-3189-8
	eBook	978-1-5245-3188-1

Print information available on the last page.

Rev. date: 08/05/2016

To order additional copies of this book, contact:
Xlibris
1-888-795-4274
www.Xlibris.com
Orders@Xlibris.com
747769

THANK YOUS:

First, I would like to thank God for continuing to bless me in my gift of writing. I couldn't have made this 5th novel without His help. God has shown me so much talent within myself and am excited about this journey and next phase in my life.

Next, I want to say thank you to my son, Michael, for continuing to believe in me and making sure I stay on task. I love you and am so proud of you.

I want to say thank you to my wonderful parents for supporting me. You've been there from the very beginning and always encouraged me to pursue my passion. Thank you for always being in my corner. I love you.

I also want to thank Isaiah. You have been beside me every step of the way. I have never met anyone who makes me feel safe and complete. Thank you for loving me and listening to me rant about my characters. You've been holding me down for years and I am appreciative of it. It's your turn now. The world is now awaiting your debut.

And to my readers, I want to say thank you so very much for reading my work. You don't see many people reading books anymore which is why I try to keep you entertained and wanting more. It's been a long road and many of you have been with me from the very beginning. And I just want to say thank you for your constant support. My Corinda series is coming soon. Her world is still turned upside down.

You can follow me on:

Twitter: @ejebron

IG: ejebron.

Website: ejebron.com

And when you can't get enough, check out my blog: delicioustalker.blogspot.com

And as always I dedicate my novels
to my grandparents Mr. Earlie and Jestine Lucas.
Until we meet again RIHP
REST IN HIS PEACE

Scriptures were taken from the Message Version and New International Version.

Jeremiah 5:30-31 (MSG)

"Unspeakable! Sickening! What happened in this country? Prophets preach lies and priests hire on as their assistants. And my people love it. They eat it up! But what will you do when it's time to pick up the pieces?"

Chapter 1

Proverbs 13:11 (MSG)

"Easy come, easy go, but steady diligence pays off."

Daniel Sanders and his wife Nicole Sanders has been married for four years. They have a daughter name Simone who is five years old. Daniel and Nicole were high school sweethearts who was so much in love that they eloped after they graduated from high school. Their parents wanted them to graduate from college and get successful jobs. But Daniel wanted to prove to his parents that he didn't need a hundred-thousand-dollar college degree debt to have a lucrative career. A couple of months after he and Nicole were married, Daniel found work at a local used car dealership. He didn't have the experience in sales, but he was hired because of his fast talking and underhanded negotiating skills. He knew how to say the right things to make people spend their money on faulty warranty packages and lackluster insurances. For instance, he would have potential buyers assume they were purchasing full coverage insurance, but the full coverage insurance that the car dealership has is only covered under a three-month warranty. After three months, their insurance drops to partial coverage but the buyer continues to pay the full coverage amount. One time he had sold a used twelve-thousand-dollar car that CD player was broken and had a malfunction sunroof to an older couple. Daniel knew that when it rained the sunroof wouldn't open, so he purposely showed the old couple the car when they had sunny skies for six straight days. His average look helped a little too. Daniel appears to be the average hard working man trying to support his family. He always keeps his hair neatly cut, he wears dress pants or jeans with a dress shirt and he went to work every day, never missing a day. And his smile enhances the deep devil pits on the side of his cheeks. A lot of women find him irresistible and charming. Sometimes he would have women come to the dealership just to make small talk with him, hoping that he would delight them in their waiting bedroom. But he is faithful to his wife, Nicole. Then again, what man wouldn't be faithful to a five-nine slim, long luscious legged wife. Everything about Nicole was perfect. Seeing her, you would assume she's one of those angels on the catwalk. Her perfect 36 D cup breasts compliments her size 8 curvy figure. Her short pixie hair cut is perfect on her small oval face. And when she looks at you with her soft gray eyes and smiles, flashing her white teeth, you get a taste of summer and is mesmerized by her beauty. When she was pregnant with their daughter Simone, she barely put on weight and lost the extra pounds that she did gain within three months. Nicole works in an office at a Christian school in the city. She always looks out of place there. You would expect her to work at a high end retail store or somewhere lavish where she can be seen and signed as a model immediately. Nicole was always told that she has a face that should be on television. But her priority is her family. She wants to be home to cook dinner, spend time with Simone, and make sure their tiny apartment is kept clean so when Daniel comes home from work, he will have all of her attention and more. For two people who have only high school diplomas, they are doing better than most. Nicole's steady salary is about twenty-five thousand a year and Daniel's salary fluctuate pending on his car sales for the year. The lowest he made one year was thirty thousand and the most he made was forty-five thousand. But what they are making isn't enough. With the cost of living going up and inflation on the rise, it is hard to save money. He refused to go to church because he didn't want his hard earned money given away. But he prayed. He prayed every day and evening. Even Nicole would pray with him. Daniel and Nicole knew the Word of God. Both of them grew up in the church. But as they got older, like everybody who grew up in the church, they drifted away. Every so often, Daniel would crack open the Bible on his down time at work or early in the morning and begin to read. He couldn't understand why the Bible speaks about prosperity so much because he hardly sees him and his family prospering. He refused to believe that not having the hundred-thousand-dollar college debt is the cause of him not having a lucrative career. He was tired of waiting for God to make a move. There are millions of people without a college degree who are banking money. Why not him? He is tired of diligently waiting. He wants his prosperity that he hears about from numerous pastors, and the Bible itself, right now. Their daughter Simone always said she that wanted to be a doctor when she grows up. He thought it was the typical phase that she was going through. Every child wants to be a doctor. But when she walks around with a stethoscope every day, even to school, researches body aliments, and has a list of questions at every doctor's visit, Daniel knew she will be bound for medical school. He knew he needed Med School money. He didn't allow his frustration to be seen by anyone, including Nicole.

After coming home late from work sometimes, he would meet his childhood best friends Darryl and Marshal at the bar for a drink. His friends Darryl and Marshal always seem to make him laugh and keep him in the know of things. They are bouncers at one of the hottest clubs in the city. Like Daniel, they chose not to go to college either. Darryl and Marshal are cousins, but are more like brothers. Marshal's mother took Darryl into their home when he was five years old after his mother was killed by a drunk driver. Marshal is a tad bit taller than Darryl, but the enormous muscle structure on them over powers their six-six height. Surprisingly, they didn't try out for the football team when they were in high school. They were more interested in going to parties and hooking up with various girls. But they were also the class clowns. One year they caught and bought hundreds maybe thousands of crickets during the summer vacation. One week into the new school year they released the crickets throughout the school. It was extremely funny when a teacher would ask the class a confusing or mind provoking question and the quietness of the classroom was interrupted by the chirping sounds of free crickets. They eventually had to close the school for a couple of days to fumigate the entire three level building. But there were still some lingering crickets to keep the sounds going. So Daniel knew he could always count on them for a laugh and for protection. Daniel stands at six-two. No one wanted to mess with Daniel or even tried to because not only was he a nice guy, but Marshal and Darryl intimidated people with their rough thug-like appearances. Marshal and Darryl has never been in a fight, but they have a lot of bark that would make you think twice before taking it to that level with them.

But no matter how much Darryl, Marshal and Daniel have a good time together, Daniel is always thinking about what his next financial move could be.

Chapter 2

John 8:44 (MSG)

> "You're from the father, the devil, and all you want to do
> is please him. He was a killer from the very start...."

Another day, another dollar. Daniel woke up wanting to sleep a little longer. He's been working three days straight from nine in the morning until nine in the evening. His body is run down with constant working, but he must support his family. In those three days that he worked he sold six cars. That's good considering many people would rather go to those big name car dealerships to buy a used car instead of going to the rink-a-dink used car dealership that he works for. Daniel wiped the dried mucous from his eyes ready to start another day. He can hear Nicole and Simone in the kitchen getting ready to leave the house. He turns to look at the glowing red digits on the clock that is sitting on the night table next to the bed. It reads 7:36. He has to be at work in an hour. He has to clock in at 8:30, a half an hour earlier, before the dealership actually opens. He tosses the comforters off him getting out the bed to get the day started. The small bedroom that he and Nicole sleep in is big enough for a queen size bed, one-night table and a dresser. He let Nicole have the closet and some dresser space. Daniel doesn't mind folding his clothes and keeping it in the dresser. He occupies the bottom two draws and Nicole has the top two dresser draws for her undergarments and pajamas. Daniel keep some clothes hung in the closet in the living room. Before going into the kitchen, he makes a pit stop in the bathroom to relieve himself and wash his face and brush his teeth. Daniel admires himself in the mirror. In his eyes he can still see the same guy from high school, but only he appears to be wiser and stressed out. He stretches his arms onto the two corners of the sink, allowing his muscles to flex a little. He put his head down to take a deep breath wanting to get rid of the stress. It's always about money, it'll always be about money.

"You better get moving Danny," Nicole says as she came up behind him. She wraps her arms around him tightly and lays her head on his back.

"I would rather stay home and sleep," he says, now looking in the mirror.

"You can stay home tomorrow on your day off," Nicole responds.

"I can't wait. I can really use the rest."

Nicole releases her arms from around him to turn him around to face her. "You're going to be looking forward to your day off tomorrow," she says. Daniel can't help but smile as he looks into Nicole's dazzling gray eyes. "Why, do you have something planned for me?"

"Yes I do. You're going to sleep and rest all day lying next to your wife."

"Don't you have to go to work tomorrow? Is it a holiday or is it some kind of special Christian day?"

Nicole began to giggle. "No silly. I'm taking the day off to spend it with you. I'm going to put on that French maid costume that you love so much and I'm going to tend to your every need and desire."

Daniel kisses Nicole on her lips. His body is beginning to react. "You better leave before you make the both of us late for work," he said.

They can hear Simone walking down the hall, getting closer to the bathroom, "Mom, we need to go before I'm late for school."

When Nicole turns around and Daniel stared in the bathroom doorway, Simone is already standing there with her coat on and her book bag on her back.

"Good morning Simone," Daniel says smiling at their daughter.

Simone zips down her coat so she can show her dad that she has on the stethoscope around her neck.

"Oh excuse me," he says putting his hand on his chest, "Good morning, Dr. Simone."

"Good morning daddy."

"Come on let's get out of here," Nicole said turning around to kiss Daniel quickly, "I'll see you later. Have a good day." Nicole headed out the bathroom. Daniel bent down to hug and kiss Simone good bye.

"Have a good day in school.

"I will," Simone says leaving.

Daniel knows he has less than an hour to be at work. He quickly turns on the shower so the water can warm up. He quickly walks in the bedroom to get his underclothes. The digits on the clock now read 7:45.

Daniel sped in the parking lot, quickly parked his 2005 car, and jumped out, as he walks quickly to the dealership door. He is twenty minutes late for work. He already knows he is going to hear his boss, Al, complaining. As soon as he walks into the office, Al peaks his head from his small office.

"You already know it's almost nine and you were to be here at eight-thirty," he belts out in his raspy old voice.

"I know Al. I overslept. Those last three days wore me out. Didn't you hire someone last week," Daniel asked. At the current time, it's just him and Al who works at this small used car dealership. Al wants to work as hard as the other car dealers, but he's burning out his only employee.

"Yeah I did, but the guy turned down the offer two days before he was to start. He got hired at that new car dealership that opened not too far from here."

Daniel takes a deep breath. Working from nine to nine is becoming too much. Daniel pours himself a cup of coffee. This will be his first cup out of five that he will have today.

"Daniel, I need to talk to you," Al says coming out of his office.

Daniel watches Al closely as he appears to be moving slower every day. Al has been in and out of the hospital because of his failing health. Daniel tells him that he needs to lose some weight and eat healthier, but Al is an old timer. He feels that young people shouldn't tell people his age what to do. Al thinks it's out of order.

"Did somebody try to return a car," Daniel asked.

"No, no, I'm going to cut down the hours. I'm going to start closing the dealership at five."

"What! I'm going to get more pay right," Daniel asked trying to keep his frustration in control.

"It's not that easy."

"What do you mean it's not that easy? You're the boss, increase my pay!"

"As far as your pay is concern, it will remain the same for now."

"Al, I've been working for you almost four years now. You hired me as soon as I graduated high school and I never asked for an increase but if you cut my hours you have to compensate me somehow."

Daniel only stayed at his job for so long because he got comfortable. He has good health insurance for his family and doesn't have to work as hard to sell cars to the stupid young and old people that come in to buy a used jalopy.

"Have you stopped to look around to realize that the world has changed in the last four years? I'm surprised you stayed this long! You're lucky I didn't tell you at five 'o clock at closing time. But just know that I'm not going to have this place open for too long. I'm closing it at the end of the year."

Daniel slams his fist on the counter in frustration. This is how his day at work is beginning. First Al tells him that he's cutting his hours then to tell him that he's closing the dealership in a couple of months. Daniel storms pass Al nearly knocking him over. He is through with playing nice. He is ready to make some real money. Al turns around shocked at Daniel's behavior. He wants to call out to him but Daniel is already in his car pulling off.

Daniel's foot is hard on the gas. Something has to give. Everywhere he turns, people are getting promotions on their jobs, raises and living the life he's been struggling to provide for his family. He wants to know when will his time come? "*Baby, you need to get in church,*" is the only thing his mother keep saying. She thinks that church solves everything. The church can't do anything for him. He tries to slow down when he sees a police car up ahead. The last thing he needs is a speeding ticket, more money going out the window. But it is too late, he is going too fast pass the cop to slow down. He looks in the mirror and see the flashing red and blue lights behind him. He takes a deep breath knowing that he can't escape the inevitable. He pulls over slowly putting the car in park. Today is going to be a bad day he thought to himself. He reaches inside the front compartment in his car to get his information only to hear the police sirens speed by him with the flashing lights now ahead. Daniel takes a deep sigh of relief. He leans his head back onto the heads rest, closing his eyes, breathing more relief. Daniel knows that he needs to get into another line of work that will support his family.

"It's time to stop settling," he says out loud, "I don't need a degree to make money. And I'm about to find that perfect job."

He put the car into drive, did a quick U-turn heading back to Al's dealership. "I got this," he says over and over. "I'm going to find something."

Within twenty minutes he pulls back into the parking space that he sped out of. He can see Al standing behind the counter reading the morning paper. Daniel got out the car with anticipation as a light bulb went off in his head.

"So you decided to come back," Al said to Daniel as he walk through the same door he stormed out of almost a half an hour ago.

"Al, why don't you sell me your dealership? I know everything that needs to be done. I can run this place." Daniel never thought about owning his own business before, but if Al is thinking about closing the dealership, he should be the one to take over.

"Ha," Al laughs out loud, "What do you know about running a business?"

"Not much, but you can teach me."

"And what's in it for me; how much are you offering to buy this place?"

Daniel didn't think about the money he has to put up to get the place. He and Nicole created a college fund for Simone that barely has two thousand dollars in it.

"You let me figure that out. Did you have any offers on this place," Daniel asked curiously.

"Of course I had offers! I have offers all the time. The most that was offered was two hundred and fifty thousand dollars. Can you beat that," Al asked looking at him bluffing?

"If you show me how to run this business, I'll give you what you ask for."

Daniel watched Al as he began rubbing the stubble gray hairs on his fat face. "If you do this, you know there's no going back. This place will be all yours. You will have to deal with all the issues that comes with running a business."

"I know."

"Let me think about it. Give me some time to consider it."

What Daniel wasn't going to tell him was that he is going to flip the place to make a profit.

After Daniel got off from work for the first time at five, he called Darryl and Marshal to tell them to meet him at the bar nearby for happy hour. When Daniel walked into the bar, it is already packed with people off work drinking and laughing their work issues away.

"Hey Danny baby, what are you doing here," one of the local hood rats asked, "Don't you work at that car dealership till nine?"

"Are you my wife," he responds sarcastically.

"I can be your second wife," she replies holding a beer in her hand.

He ignores her comment and heads toward the back of the bar where he knew Darryl and Marshal is playing pool, hustling people out their money.

"Red ball, corner pocket," a man called out aiming the stick at the red ball.

"Nigga, you aren't going to make that shot," Darryl said.

"Fifty bucks say I will," the man says.

"An extra two hundred bucks say you won't," Darryl says putting two hundred dollars on the table.

"A hundred bucks extra says that he'll make it," Marshal said putting another hundred on the table.

The man stood up in amazement, "If your boy is against you, then I know it's a sure shot." He reaches in his wallet to take out an extra two hundred dollars. Five hundred and fifty dollars is lying on the table. Daniel leans against the wall looking at the money on the table. If he knew how to play pool too, he would hustle people out their money so he can make an easy five hundred in ten minutes.

"Yo D, you want in on this," Darryl asked looking at Daniel.

"I'm strapped," he responds folding his arms watching the play that's about to unfold.

"I got you son," he says winking at him.

The man went back into position. He steadies the stick aiming it at the red ball. The stick glide slowly back and forth. Daniel can see the concentration on the man's face. He knew either way the man is going to lose but can lose more if the bet went against him. The stick hit the ball. The ball rolls across the pool table hitting the side just missing the corner pocket. The man drops the stick and began cursing violently.

"That's seven hundred and fifty dollars you owe me. I have five hundred and fifty dollars; now where is the two hundred," Darryl said.

"Hold up! How the hell do I owe you seven hundred and fifty dollars," the man yells?

"You originally put in fifty dollars, I put in two hundred, my boy put in a hundred, you then put in an extra two hundred."

"That's only five hundred and fifty bucks. Where did the extra two hundred dollars come from," the man yells.

"You forgot that my boy put in two hundred. You lost to him too," Darryl said.

"I don't have two hundred dollars on me," the man complained, "I'm not paying an extra two hundred dollars! Your boy never put in his two hundred dollars!"

Only this time the man got in Darryl's face or at least tried to. He barely reached his neck.

"I don't think you want to do that," Darryl said deeply. Marshal is already standing behind the man ready to fight if need to. But as always their size and height speaks for itself.

"I got to go to the ATM," the man said as he looks at both of them. Darryl took the man's wallet and took out his driver's license. "You got a half an hour," and hands the wallet back to the man, "Or you will see us at your house," he says holding up the man's license.

The man scurries out the bar in a hurry. Marshal and Darryl began laughing, happy that their hustle paid them off lovely.

"So, we're going to split the money right," Daniel asked.

"You only put in two hundred dollars that *I* put in for you," Darryl laughs, "*You* don't get anything. You're lucky you're my boy, cause technically you owe *me* the two hundred just for putting it in for you."

How can Daniel forget that Darryl has a way with words too, but Daniel already hustled Darryl and Marshal by not backing down off the bet.

"Actually I get part of the money. So, that seven hundred and fifty dollars has to be split three ways instead of two. I never backed out the bet nor involved myself. You volunteered me."

Marshal and Darryl stopped laughing and looked at Daniel.

"You can't hustle me," Daniel says, "Darryl, you let me in, therefore, I'm part of the grand prize. Thanks brother, you've made my day so much better, Daniel says placing a tight grip on Darryl's shoulder.

"Well at least you can finally buy your wife some new shoes. She wears the same worn out shoes for the past two years," Darryl joked.

"Well at least I have a wife who can wear shoes. I saw that amputee chick you had in your car the other day," Daniel joked back.

About three days ago while, Daniel was at work, he saw Darryl drive by with a woman who has a prosthetic leg. The woman was in a bad accident almost six years ago. The accident almost took her life.

"Well handicap people need love too," Darryl joked back.

The three of them went up to the bar to get a couple of beers before going back by the pool table.

"So, did you guys hear about that preacher who preaches at the church in the south," Marshal asked drinking his beer.

"Yeah, my mother goes to that church," Daniel said, "It holds like eight thousand people."

"And the pastor is getting crazy paid," Marshal added, "He just bought a sixty-five-thousand-dollar car the other day, paid in full."

"Word," Daniel is shocked, "I thought preachers are poor. The ones I see around here drive broke down cars worse than the ones I sell. That pastor, uhm, Pastor Donald Knight at Love Overflow Ministries, car broke down off the freeway. I gave him a jump before I went to work one day."

"So what are those rich preachers doing that these poor ones aren't," Darryl asked.

"It's all about business," Daniel said, "You run the church like it's a business."

"But here's what you don't know," Marshal said, "Everything is tax-free."

Daniel and Darryl nearly choked on the beer they are drinking. They couldn't believe that the funds that churches get are tax-free.

"That's why you see a lot of these store front churches popping up all over the place," Daniel said.

"Yeah, but the ones with the power are the ones who got the game down pack," Marshal said.

"Then we are in the wrong business," Darryl said to Marshal, "We need to have a church."

Daniel starts laughing hard. That is the funniest thing he has heard.

"What's so funny," Darryl asked Daniel. He looks at him with a confused stared.

"Man, can you really picture you and Marshal on the pulpit preaching? That's really funny," he says still laughing, "You two aren't preaching material. You need to be slim or fat with less or no muscles. You two look like grizzly body builders. No one would take you seriously." Daniel began to calm down, wiping his tears from his eyes.

"But people would take you seriously right," Marshal added sarcastically looking at Daniel.

Daniel just looks at him still laughing a little bit but he began to think. What *if* he became a preacher? He knows the Word. He has his quiet time when he feels like it. Why not preach and make a living off of it like everyone else. This is what is going through Daniel's mind.

"Now that's funny," Darryl said, "Daniel on the pulpit. He's pretty boy. Can you picture him in a robe?"

"They don't wear robes anymore," Marshal said, "They wear suits. One guy wear a different color suit every Sunday, looking like an extra-large Skittle."

"What's wrong with that," Daniel asked.

"Have you ever saw a black man in a fuchsia suit."

"Only the pimps from back in the day."

"Well this pimped out preacher's suits are from high designers. I would rock a yellow suit too if they made it in my size."

"Nigga, you wouldn't wear a suit. You wore a suit only once and that was for Daniel's wedding," Darryl said to Marshal, "And even that came with a price."

"My point exactly," Marshal said, "With the right price I would wear a suit. Preachers get crazy money! The pastor I was telling you about gets a salary of a hundred and twenty thousand dollars a year and that doesn't include offerings he gets at his church and preaching at other churches. The church even pays for him to have extensive health insurance. They even have him and his family stay at a five-bedroom mansion that the church pays for.

"How do you know all of this," Darryl asked.

"You remember Frankie that use to live around the corner, well, he works security for the pastor. Frankie gets paid nice too and he gets to travel around the world with him."

"Damn and all that is tax-free," Darryl asked for reassurance.

Marshal nods his head yes. Daniel heard enough. He is drinking his beer, listening to Marshal talk about the inside deeds of the church life. The more Marshal talked, the more Daniel was interested. He wanted a way in to that world.

Daniel came walking into the tiny apartment with Nicole's amazement on her face. He's never been home this early. She was about to start cooking dinner when he walked in. He came into the kitchen with a dozens of red roses in his hand. Nicole was ecstatic to see the roses and gave him a big juicy kiss. He got his cut of the money Marshal and Darryl had hustled from the man, a nice two hundred and fifty dollars.

"What are you doing home so early; it's six-thirty," Nicole asks kissing Daniel again.

"I got off early. Al will be closing the dealership at five instead of nine so I hung out with Marshal and Darryl for a little bit."

"Oh yeah, what are those two up to," she asked placing the roses in a vase filled with water.

"Nothing new, still hustling. I made two hundred and fifty dollars out the deal."

Nicole laughs and shakes her head. People will never learn to stop betting from them.

"Why is Al closing the place so early now," Nicole asked.

"Business is slow. Honestly, I'm surprised he didn't do it sooner." Daniel purposely left out the part when he stormed out the job and how upset he was. Daniel never wants to tell Nicole how angry or stressed he got. He wants her to feel and know that he will take care of everything. He doesn't want his wife stressed. Besides, no matter what kind of crazy day he had, once he gets home she captivates him every time.

"How was work today," Daniel asked taking a water bottle from the fridge.

"It was okay," she says putting some spaghetti in a pot of boiling water. "The school's enrollment is low for next year. I'm not going to wait to see if they have enough funds to pay us."

Working at private schools, everyone is paid based upon the tuition payments. So if parents don't pay, no one gets paid.

"So, are you looking for another job," Daniel asked sitting down at the table.

"Yeah, there's a couple of secretary positions that are opened in a couple of schools. And now since the country is trying to open more charter schools, I have nothing to worry about. Besides, the jobs that I applied for, the secretary gets paid about forty-five thousand."

"Seriously!" Daniel is surprised that secretaries make that much.

"Yeah, I was shocked too. That's an extra twenty-five thousand a year for me."

"Well it looks like we both may be getting a raise, you sooner than me."

"Did Al say that he is giving you a raise," she asked shockingly, "It's about time."

"We'll talk about that later."

Daniel has his mind made up. He is going to go into the ministry. It's time for he and his family to prosper as the good book says.

Nicole pours a little olive oil into the water with the spaghetti. Daniel admires his wife from behind. He is always thankful to come home to a beautiful and caring wife like her. Ever since they've been married they never had an argument only disagreements. He walks behind her grabbing her waist and began to kiss her gently on the neck.

"Where's Simone," he asked.

"She's in her room doing her homework," she replied enjoying her husband's touch.

He wants to tell Nicole about the change in his career, but he doesn't know how she will take it. But at this moment that is the last thing on his mind. All he wants is to make love to his wife.

"Want to meet me in the room for a moment," Daniel asked softly breathing in his wife's scent on her neck. Her scent always drives him crazy. She smells like a hint of sweet vanilla and wildflowers.

"I got to get this dinner done." Nicole then turns around to wrap her arms around Daniel's neck and kisses him. "I think you should save your energy for tomorrow," she says seductively.

"I can't wait until tomorrow. A man has needs," he jokes back, grinding on her a little.

"Well you know little Miss Nosey will be in here soon. So your needs will just have to wait like mine."

She pushes him away playfully so she can continue to cook dinner. Daniel taps her on her behind before leaving the kitchen. He takes the tablet off the living room table, flops on the couch and began to research, "*How to start a church.*"

The next afternoon Daniel and Nicole laid lazily in bed after a mind blowing passionate morning. Her maid costume that she loves to wear for Daniel is laying on the floor next to a couple of pillows and a sheet.

Daniel embraces Nicole in his arms as she is sleeping peacefully. He takes pride in his wife. *I'm going to have the best looking First Lady*, he thought to himself. Once Daniel's mind is made up, there's no changing it. He figures running a church isn't hard. At this point, Daniel is feeling a little cocky. He is going to enjoy being the boss for once. A sneaky smirk came across his face. For the first time he's taking control and will be calling the shots. If people want to give money away, give it to his church. His church, he thought. The smirk now turned into a devilish smile.

"Man, I'm so ready for this," he whispers. Nicole stirred a little, letting out a soft moan.

Now is the time he should talk to her about his decision.

He shakes her lightly, waking her up.

"Nicole, I need to talk to you," he says softly. She buries her face in between his arms, enjoying the sleep that she needs.

"Nicole," he pleads gently.

"What," she answers.

"I need to talk to you about something."

Nicole sighs deeply wanting to be left alone so she can sleep, but she knows it must be important if Daniel is pleading with her.

"Are you awake," he asked.

"I'm listening." Her eyes are still closed.

"Well, Al is going to show me how to run his business because he is talking about closing the dealership at the end of the year. I asked him if I could take over. He didn't give me an answer, but I'm thinking about doing something else. I'm thinking about beginning my own ministry."

Nicole sat up quickly, quickly dismissing the want of her sleep. She could not believe what she is hearing. Her silence then turns into laughter, "Danny, you play too much."

"I'm not playing. I'm really going to do this."

"You are serious aren't you," she asked looking at him intently.

"Yeah, I would like to give it a try."

"But Danny, preaching isn't a normal job. It consists of a lot of studying and preaching. We don't even go to church. How did you come up with this?"

"Yesterday, Marshal, Darryl and I were talking."

"Oh boy, here you go." Nicole says now getting out of bed. "I knew you had to get this brilliant idea from them somehow." She began to pick up the pillows and her maid costume off the floor.

"It's not like that. We were talking about how preachers get paid. Marshal was telling us how a pastor, who is my mother's pastor, from the south makes about one hundred twenty thousand a year tax-free dollars and that doesn't include offerings and extra pay he gets from preaching at other churches."

"Tax-free, are you sure that's even legit," Nicole asked now sitting on the bed still naked.

"It's legit. I researched it last night. I mean, there are some taxes involved but there are ways around it. I figure, I read the Bible, I know what's it's all about. It even talks about us being prosperous."

"I hear those TV preachers talk about it all the time especially that white man that come on," Nicole added.

"Exactly, so we can prosper by me preaching! I was going to call my mother's pastor so he can help me get started. With his eight thousand congregation, the sixty-five-thousand-dollar car he just bought and his hefty salary, I know he's doing *something* right."

"But you said something about running Al's business. What's that about?"

"So, I was going to get a loan from the bank, buy it from Al then flip it to a buyer doubling or tripling the cost of the place."

"Does Al know about this?"

"Once he sells me the business, it's my call. I can do what I want with it."

Nicole sat quietly on the bed thinking about what her husband said. She always seemed skeptical of preachers but envious of the lavish lifestyles they have. They appear to have the perfect life and the First Lady is treated like royalty. They dress in the flashy clothes, always have their hair done, getaways with their husbands when he has to preach in tropical or fun places. A smile came across her face as she looks at Daniel intriguingly.

"Let's do it," she says, "We are no different from them. We deserve the best like those preachers too. Only don't expect me to wear those funny looking hats or dress like those old First Ladies."

Daniel leans forward pulling his wife's naked body toward him, "No, as long as you keep it tight for me I don't care what you wear."

Daniel kisses her passionately. He is happy that she decided to support him in his decision. They have a great marriage that everyone looks up to, a perfect family, intelligent daughter and everyone knows how hard he works to support his family. A perfect devil in disguise.

Chapter 3

2 Corinthians 11:13-14 (MSG)

"I'm giving nobody grounds for lumping me in with those money-grubbing preachers, vaunting themselves as something special. They're a sorry bunch - pseudo-apostles, lying preachers, crooked workers-posing as Christ's agents but sham to the core! And no wonder! Satan does it all the time, dressing up as a beautiful angel of light."

5 YEARS LATER......

Another day, more rest; Daniel woke up feeling refreshed and relaxed. He stretches fully in the King size bed, smiling from ear to ear, like he does every morning now. He rolls over to cuddle Nicole, the First Lady of his church Abundant Overflow Ministries. Daniel came up with the name to the church. He wanted the name of the church to represent the type of life he was living and what everyone should live, a prosperous life, an abundant overflow of prosperity life. When he took that hour and half drive to his mother's rich pastor's church to meet him, that day changed his life. Bishop Wilkens is his name. Daniel had to play it cool. He didn't want Bishop Wilkens to know that he wanted to go into the church ministry just for the money. When his meeting was confirmed for him to meet Bishop Wilkens, he was ecstatic. It's extremely hard to meet Bishop Wilkens because he is always traveling all over the world preaching, doing seminars, conventions, revivals and maintaining his own church. Daniel knew his mother would know when the Bishop would be available. She's one of his most avid members and sometimes assist in the Administrative Office. He didn't explain to his mother as to why he wanted to meet with the Bishop. Nor did she pry. She was just happy to know that her backslid son wanted to see the Bishop.

When Daniel pulled into the massive parking lot, he was in awe at the massive church that was in front of him. He sat back in his seat and took in the sight. *"One man runs all of this,"* he thought to himself, out loud. He got out his car walking toward the magnificent architecture. He straightened his jacket and made sure his shirt was tucked in his pants. He knew he looked good in his seventy-five-dollar suit that Nicole bought for him at the men's superstore. When he told her about his scheduled meeting, she surprised him with a new suit the next day. He had a hard time leaving the house because she couldn't keep her hands off him. It's not every day Nicole got to see him in a suit. When Daniel walked through the doors of the church, the sight literally almost took his breath away. He wasn't sure if he walked into a church or the entrance to a stadium. The marble floor sparkled and was met with clean large white walls that met a glass ceiling. With the sun shining outside, the entire stadium-like foyer lit up. You would have thought God himself lived there. Daniel's cemented awe looked ahead and saw four wide double doors about fifteen feet ahead. He knew that had to be the sanctuary. He wanted to go inside but hesitated. *I can't just go walking into a church without being seen or greeted by someone,* he thought to himself. But it's a Wednesday. Daniel wasn't sure if there was some kind of protocol he had to follow, but he wanted to see the sanctuary. He wanted to see what it was like behind those four double doors. He then understood why his mother was a member there. Who wouldn't want to be a member at a church like that? He proceeded to take slow steps to the sanctuary only to be called by a gentleman approaching him to the left.

"Hey brother, do you need help with something," the man asked.

As the man approached closer, Daniel realized it was the church's security. The man had on a black shirt and black pants, with the church's logo on the upper right sleeve that read *Abundant Love Security*. "This Bishop must really be banking money to have his own security," he said to himself.

Daniel extended his hand and smiled greatly ready to put on some acting skills. "Hello, I'm Daniel Sanders. I have an appointment to see Bishop Wilkens," he said giving him a firm handshake.

"Right, right, the Bishop said that he was expecting you. I'm Brother Brown. I'm on the security team. I'll take you to his office."

Daniel began following Brother Brown while still taking in the magnificent sight.

"So, *you're* Sister Sanders' son. Your mother helps in the office from time to time. She's a great lady," Brother Brown said as he was making small talk with Daniel.

Daniel was listening, but he was busy looking at everything around him. They walked past a large book and clothing store. It was closed, but Daniel can tell it was large as a regular size store in a mall.

"Yes, my mother is a great lady. I have to tell you though; this church is breath-taking. I'm listening to you but I'm taken back by everything I see."

"Is this your first time here," he asked with a shocked tone. Everyone who lives in the state has come to Abundant Love at least once.

"Yes it is. I live about an hour and half away and work on Sundays," he said lying. On Sundays the dealership is closed. But he didn't want the man to know that he doesn't go to church, especially since he was about to start his own ministry.

"I feel you man, it's hard for a lot of people to get here but every Sunday at both services, the sanctuary is packed."

"People will go where they need to be spiritually fed."

"Everyone gets taken back when they first come to Abundant Love. We have a coffee shop down the other hall and a basketball court downstairs with a gym."

"Are you serious," Daniel exclaimed.

"Yeah, it helps keep the young people busy and off the streets. It's locked up on Sundays though or whenever we have service."

Brother Brown stopped in front of an elevator, pushing the up button. Daniel had seen everything, a church with an elevator. He was getting even more anxious to meet Bishop Wilkens. He seen his pictures and billboards throughout the state, but he wanted to meet this man in person. They walked onto the elevator going up to the second floor.

"So what church do you attend when you are able to go," he asked.

"I attend a store front church around the corner from where I live. It's called Living Waters Baptist Church."

"I've never heard of it. It must be new."

"No, it's been around for a couple of years," Daniel said.

Daniel visited the church quite a few times. The pastor, Pastor Bradford Smalls, always tried to get him to join the church, but for some reason Daniel always declined because he didn't want to join a church, and give away his hard earned money.

The elevator finally opened onto the second floor. When they stepped off the elevator, Daniel realized that he was on the Administrative floor. He looked around at all the cubicles wondering if his mother was there. He knew there was no way his mother would miss him being in a church.

He saw a couple of people at their cubicle hard at work on the computer or on the telephone. They approached a closed white door that had a secretary sitting at a huge desk next to it.

"Hey Vanessa, is the Bishop ready to see Brother Sanders," Brother Brown asked.

"Let me call him. Mr. Sanders, you can take a seat over there," the secretary said pointing to an empty seat.

Daniel went to take a seat, as he tried to keep himself calm. That was the first time he's been in the offices of a church. He sat back looking at everything going on behind the scenes. He even noticed Brother Brown hovering over the secretary, Vanessa, whispering something naughty to her while she's on the phone. She's trying to speak professionally on the phone to the Bishop, but her soft playful giggles are something he is too familiar with. Nicole sounds the same way whenever he messes with her when she's on the phone.

"Mr. Sanders, Bishop Wilkens said you can go in," she said hanging up the phone. "You're going to get me into some trouble one day," she said as she gave Brother Brown a love tap.

"You're already in trouble; wait until you get off work," he said to her.

Daniel was surprised to know that church folks were freaks too. He got up straightening his suit, ready to pick the Bishop's brain.

He opened the door to Bishop's office, leaving the secretary and the security in their own lustful world. As he entered, he closed the door behind him trying to keep his amazement to a bare minimum. His office has a plush gray carpet and the walls are covered with awards, plaques, pictures he's taken with celebrities and a couple of degrees.

"Mr. Sanders," the Bishop belted out, "It's nice to meet you." The Bishop was at a desk which was around the corner from the door.

Daniel turned around to see a tall stature man approaching him in jeans and a polo shirt. This couldn't be the Bishop he thought. He was dressed in jeans. But when Daniel looked down and saw the high priced designer shoes he had on, he knew that, that was the head nigga in charge.

"It's great to finally meet you too," Daniel said as he shook his hand firmly.

"I hear about you all the time from your mother," he said.

Oh crap, he thought. He hoped he would still be able to play this off. He doesn't want the Bishop to know that he doesn't go to church.

"I hope it's all good things," he answered back keeping his rising nervousness suppressed.

"It is, but you know how mothers are, always bragging about their children. Take a seat," he said pointing to a chair.

Daniel took a seat in the chair in front of the desk. He noticed that the office extends further back. He has a leather sofa set, an enormous coffee table in the middle of the room and right in the middle of the wall is an eighty-inch flat screen. The walls have a gold trim around the border.

"So what can I do for you," he asked sitting behind his desk.

"I'm looking to start my own church. And you're the man who can show me how and where to begin."

"Is that right," he said as he leaned back in the chair.

"I'm a simple car salesman who goes to church whenever I can, but lately I've been feeling that God wants me to preach. I tried to ignore the feeling, but the more I run from it, the more I hear the voice of God telling me that, that's what I need to do."

"So why come to me? Why not go to the church you seldom go to?"

"I usually go to Living Waters Baptist Church."

The Bishop erupted in laughter, "No wonder you came here! I know that church! The pastor there use to go to the same college as I, and well, we were always in competition. Sometimes people don't want to hear the truth. Do you understand what I'm saying?"

"I think I do. I don't want to make assumptions."

"Well, I always tried to help him out. The way he was beginning his church ministry was all wrong. He wasn't going to make anything by preaching what he was preaching about. When we were in seminary school, his practice sermon was dry and, well, old school. He just wasn't reaching them. I tried to help, but he waved me off saying that I didn't agree with his spirit."

"I bet he wished he didn't listen to his spirit," Daniel snickered, "Well, I'm listening to mine, that's why I'm here. You're reaching people all over the place, worldwide, and I want to spread the Gospel like that too. I just don't know where to start. Pastor Bradford Smalls is a nice guy, but he's thinking small and I'm thinking big."

"So tell me, why do you *really* want to go into this ministry?"

"It's just like I said, I believed I'm called to preach."

Bishop Wilkens leaned further back into his extra-large leather office chair. He placed his hands together in front of him as if he was praying. Bishop kept his eyes on Daniel. He was trying to figure him out. He seen his type all the time and every time he threw them out the office, but Daniel was different. He knew Daniel could be the person he can actually help with a little coaching.

"Going into the ministry is a lot of work and it takes times and a lot of patience. I didn't start off like this, in an eight and a half million-dollar church paid in full. Did you notice my new car?"

"No, I didn't see it."

"You must have come in the front parking lot. I parked in my assigned space in the back. Come here let me show you."

Daniel got up to follow him to the large window that overlook the back parking lot. There was his sixty-five-thousand-dollar car Marshal was telling him about.

"She's a beauty, isn't she," Bishop said looking at his car with pride.

"Yes she is," Daniel smirked.

"You should see the car my wife drives. You know you have to keep the wife happy."

"Oh I know! I've been married for four years."

"You're young and you've been married for four years!"

"I married my high school sweetheart. We have a five-year-old daughter too. Those two ladies are my whole world."

"You had your daughter when you were in high school," he asked looking at him.

"Yeah, but that isn't why I married her though."

Daniel loves to show off his wife. He took out his cell phone to show off a picture of Nicole.

"She's beautiful," Bishop said, "Is she a model or something?"

"No, she's a secretary at a Christian school."

"Oh, she's a good girl," he joked, reeling Daniel in.

"She is; she is a good woman. She's supporting me going into ministry. I'll be able to support her and our daughter."

"Yeah and then you can get your wife a car like mines."

"That would be great," Daniel said still looking at the car with envy.

"So tell me the truth, you want into the ministry because of the money? You see my expensive car, my three thousand dollar shoes, big church, pictures of me with celebrities, and I know you know about my mansion. That's all you want."

Daniel was speechless. He didn't want the Bishop to know his hidden motives. So he lied.

"No, no, not at all. I just want to do what God told me to do. I think you got the wrong impression. Sorry, if I wasted your time and mine."

Daniel turned around to leave until Bishop Wilkens called out to him.

"And you give up so easily! You're not as hungry as I thought," Bishop Wilkens said.

Daniel turned back around to face him, "I don't give up and I'm hungrier than you think."

"The problem is," the Bishop said walking up to face him a little closer, "You talk too much. All you keep saying is how you want to get into the ministry because you are called by God, but your facial expressions told the whole story when you saw my car, the mention of my wife's car, A-list celebrities I hang with, and my large bank account. The words didn't come out of your mouth, but you said a mouth full. If you really want in, then you need to be ready. You will have so many pastors, ministers, and other bishops who will see right through you."

At this point Daniel didn't know what to do. He stood there facing the Bishop, only this time his thoughts were quiet. But he will find a way to prove to Bishop Wilkens that he could be just like him, but better. "Like I said, I'm hungrier than you think."

Daniel wasn't going to back down. At this point there was no turning back. Al had agreed to sell him the dealership when he retires at the end of the year. Daniel is still going to sell it and flip it to make a larger profit. One way or the other he wanted that easy money that the church has.

"Follow me," Bishop Wilkens said.

He turned around, with Daniel behind him walking out another side door in his office, only the side door was an entrance to another elevator.

Daniel walked inside and leaned back on the wall with his hands in his pocket, feeling pretty cocky. No matter how much the Bishop would try to convinced him to rethink his motives, he was going full speed ahead.

Bishop pushed the down button. The elevator doors closed leaving the two men in silence, listening to their own thoughts. No one said a word. Bishop Wilkens knew exactly what he was going to do. If this doesn't break him, he knew he found the right person. Daniel was just ready to go and get things moving with his future church and lucrative income.

The elevator doors opened to a large hallway. The sparling marble floors greeted Daniel once again. Daniel can see the coffee shop that the security had told him about. It was closed at the time but he can imagine the perfect aroma of fresh coffee every Sunday morning at church. He made a mental note. He will have a coffee shop too in his church. The Bishop opened a glass door which entered them into a very dark room. But Daniel can tell that the space they were in wasn't just any room.

"Wait here," Bishop said as he disappeared into the darkness.

At any other time, Daniel would have left in a hurry in fear of getting jumped in a set up, but he didn't fear the Bishop. But he wanted to know what he was in store for.

Suddenly the lights came on. Daniel's mouth dropped open. He couldn't believe what he was seeing. He finally got a chance to see what the sanctuary looked like behind those four double doors, but only he was in the front looking in the other direction. "Come here," Bishop motioned Daniel with his hand.

Daniel's heart began to pound as he moved forward. That wasn't a sanctuary. That was more like a performing arts center. There appeared to be thousands of seats and hundreds of rows that engulfed him. It was like four IMAX theaters put together to make one room. To his right, the band had their own section. There were two sets of drums, three different types of pianos, guitars, bass', chimes, trumpets, everything. When he approached the pulpit with Bishop Wilkens, he was over powered by the sight. Daniel couldn't believe that one man stands behind this pulpit at every church service preaching to thousands of people surrounding him. Daniel looked up at the ceiling as if he was shining bright without an unlit bulb. Bishop Wilkens looked at Daniel's expression. People get the same expression every time they walked into the sanctuary. Sometimes they would stand in their spot for a couple of minutes before proceeding forward. Daniels' eyes roamed around the sanctuary in amazement.

"Can you guess how many people can sit in this place," Bishop Wilkens asked.

Daniel couldn't speak. His mouth was dry because he had it opened in amazement the entire time. He swallowed very hard and said, "Eight thousand."

Bishop Wilkens laughed, "Try Eleven thousand."

Daniel believed it. He knew he had a lot of work to do.

"Every service, at all services almost nine thousand people fill those seats. But on Sundays, these seats are almost filled to capacity with maybe ten or the eleven thousand. Almost every person in this state has flocked here to hear the Word. We have two services on Sundays. We have an eight A.M. service for those who work in the afternoon or evening and then we have the noon service. The eight A.M. service isn't quite full but the noon service, *everybody* is here. Some people stay after the eight A.M. service for the noon service."

Daniel just stood there and listened, taking in the sights. "*Eleven thousand people,*" Daniel thought to himself, "*no wonder this man is rich. He must collect near a million dollars a month for preaching in this capacity.*"

"We have a lot of politicians and celebrities who attend here. One Sunday, the President and his family came….. So, what do you think," he said looking at Daniel.

"What do you mean, what do I think," Daniel finally spoke, "This place is amazing. I don't know how you do it every Sunday."

"Well, you'll find out on Sunday."

"Of course, my family and I would be here on Sunday. My wife, Nicole, would love to be here and see this marvelous church."

"I know she would, especially when she sees you preaching at the noon service."

Daniel shot him a surprised and scared look. "I'm sorry Bishop Wilkens but did you say I will be preaching at the noon service?"

"Yes I did. Is there a problem?"

"Uhm, I just wasn't expecting this. I didn't know I would be preaching here. I never spoke in front of twenty people before, let alone eleven thousand."

Daniel began to sweat just knowing what Bishop want him to do.

"I thought you was hungry," Bishop Wilkens mocked him.

Daniel just looked at him in unbelief. He couldn't believe Bishop was using his words against him.

"Listen, if you want this, then you would jump right in."

"I do but I was going to start small, not at *this* capacity. I mean, let me be honest, I have my quiet time and I read the Bible and pray, but I never quoted Scriptures and talked about God to this magnitude."

"But you do read the Bible! There's your experience! Just do some studying and you'll do just fine. I'll train you…. *only* if you do well on Sunday. Then I promise you, you'll be making money just like me."

Daniel looked at Bishop Wilkens curiously. He was in it for the perks too. He had him fooled. Daniel began to laugh, "I don't get it, you come off as an angel, a real Man of God, but you're just like the rest of us, you want to make a quick buck. Is what you preach Scriptural?"

"Of course, the Bible speaks about prosperity! God doesn't want us to be broke down and disgusted, right? So, use His Word to get what you want. You're still preaching His Word and living right."

"But how will preaching at the noon service help me," Daniel asked.

"I'm building another church in the next state over and I need someone to be the pastor there. I can't have two mega churches in this state. The church that I'm building will seat about eight thousand people. It'll have the same amenities as this one but at a much lower scale. I'll get a cut of the offerings of course, but I need someone who is *hungry* as you say, willing to pastor the people. It's a full-time gig. The salary will be around eighty thousand. The congregation will take care of the pastor."

"But how will the new pastor get the members? How will people join the church?" At that point Daniel was very interested. He wanted the eighty-thousand-dollar salary. That's more than what him and Nicole make combined.

"My name under the church will bring them in. I will be the Overseer of the church. People will join. People prefer to go to large churches anyways. There are tricks to this business that I will teach you, *if* I decide to train you. So," Bishop Wilkens said taking a deep breath, "Are you going to preach on Sunday at the noon service?"

Daniel thought about it, feeling more nervous about preaching in front of eleven thousand people but he wanted to better himself and his family. And definitely wanted to go for that nice salary. He was tired of living from paycheck to paycheck. He wanted the prosperity that God promised.

"And what if I do well on Sunday," Daniel asked.

"If you do well, then I will train you so you will be ready in a year to pastor the new church."

"Are you serious," Daniel asked. Daniel wasn't expecting all of this. This was sudden.

"I'm very serious. So, what do you say? I do have other appointments. I am a very busy man."

Daniel looked around again taking in the sanctuary. This was his shot at success.

I'm in," he said, shaking Bishop Wilkens hand firmly.

That Sunday came faster than any other day. Daniel spent three endless nights reading the Bible, writing, studying and did a little praying. He was having mixed feelings. He was excited, nervous, thrilled yet scared all at the same time. When he told Nicole the news she didn't believe him at first, but when he told her about the meeting in full detail, she was excited and just as nervous as he was. Right away he gave her his credit card and told her to go to the mall to get her and Simone something beautiful to wear. He wanted everyone to take a good look at his family, a soon-to-be-first family of a church.

When Daniel and his family took a seat in the front of the church, he felt thousands of stares gazing at them. Bishop Wilkens and his wife First Lady Monica greeted them with warm embraces, as if they were old friends. They had met in the Bishop's office before coming into the sanctuary. Bishop told them that they would be escorted into the sanctuary when the Praise and Worship team was in the middle of their last song. He and First Lady Monica are always in the sanctuary during that time. Nicole and Monica was busy talking about how beautiful each other looked. Monica was mesmerized by Nicole's beauty just like everybody else who be in her presence. What made matters even better was when Nicole told the Bishop and his wife the name of the Christian school she worked at, they were all were too familiar with the school.

"I heard the school hardly paid their workers," First Lady Monica said.

"Well, I can't deny that. The principal is always saying how God will provide. I've learned how to live by faith," Nicole replied.

Daniel had given her a heads up about the Bishop, but Nicole knew the right things to say to any kind of church folk. She perfected it when she worked at the school. She knew when to say, "Amen," "God is good", and how "Great God is."

"It takes more than faith to live," First Lady Monica responded.

"It sounds as though First Lady Monica know what my sermon will be about," Daniel said interrupting the ladies.

Daniel knew he had no other choice but to be ready. So when Bishop Wilkens walked onto the pulpit with his security team nearby in position, he knew his moment was about to come. Thousands of people applauded when the Bishop stood in front of them in the pulpit. Simone clinched her dad's hand because she was frightened with the numerous of people around them. Daniel bent down to hug her tight and whispered in her ear, "Don't be afraid. Stay close to mommy. Daddy is going to talk to the people, okay?"

Simone nodded in agreement but still clinching to her dad. Daniel stood back up to look at Nicole. Nicole knew he was nervous. She silently told him to relax. Daniel's mother and father and Nicole's parents sat behind them. Daniel's mother was praising God so hard and giving God so much praise. Her heart was filled with joy because her son was about to preach. She prayed for her son to come to church and to give his life to Christ but she never imagined him preaching.

"Amen church," Bishop Wilkens shouted.

"Amen, Amen," the congregation shouted back.

"Everybody look so beautiful this morning," he continued, "This is the day that the Lord has made and we will rejoice and be glad in this day always!"

The congregation began to shout and clap even louder.

Daniel stood there looking at the Bishop. He didn't want to turn around to look at the thousands of people behind him. He already has a full view of the numerous hundreds that are sitting on both sides of him.

"Today we have a guest with us. I have a friend who is visiting today and will bring forth the Word this morning. Every now and again your Bishop like to sit back and be minister to."

A couple more amen can be heard throughout the church.

"You can listen and watch the eight A.M. service online if you want to hear me preach but I'm excited to hear from a friend of mine. Everyone here knows Sister Evelyn Sanders who works with us in the Administrative Office. Sister Sanders makes sure everything and everyone is on top of their duties. Ah, Sister Sanders," he now says looking at her, "You're going to have to leave your other job to work here full time because you keep things going smoothly in the office. I don't know about those other people," he said joking and laughing waving his hand, "No, no, I'm playing around. We have some hard workers here at Abundant Love Church. But her son, Daniel, is here and I had the opportunity to talk to him this week at church; he is a powerful Man of God. He's here with his beautiful wife, Nicole, and their five-year-old daughter Simone. They are such a beautiful family. So, I'm going to introduce this young man of the hour, my friend, Pastor Daniel Sanders."

The congregation roared with applauses and shouts. His mother was jumping up and down in excitement. Daniel was surprised that he referred to him as a pastor. Before walking onto the pulpit, he kissed Simone and

Nicole. "You'll do great and if you get nervous just look at me," she whispered in his ear.

He turned around and began walking up to the pulpit. Once on the pulpit, he got a view of the entire congregation. He saw himself on the big screens as he hugged and shook Bishop's hand.

"Just take your time and you'll be fine," he said to Daniel, "Just breathe and let God do the rest."

As Bishop walked off the pulpit, Daniel was left with eleven thousand people to minister to. He didn't want to show his nervousness. He watched a lot of TV ministries and some of Bishop's sermons. He knew he had to capture the congregation. At that very moment he opened his mouth and shouted, "Isn't God great church!"

And with that one simple line, that key phrase that get every Christian up and jumping, the congregation went wild.

That was five years ago. Daniel and Nicole have been married for nine years now and Simone is now ten years old. At that first moment, Daniel's first time preaching he got an offering of fifteen thousand dollars. Usually Bishop Wilkens would get a twenty percent cut but he wanted Daniel to see what he would be getting. That motivated Daniel to take Bishop's offer.

Daniel squeezes Nicole, kissing her gently. He was living the life that he wanted to have for him and his family. They live in a two story Victorian mansion that isn't too far from the church that Bishop Wilkens had placed them in. He has a guest house that is behind the mansion. That's where Marshal and Darryl live. He had to bring his friends. He gave them jobs as his personal security. They were too eager to accept.

Nicole turns over to kiss Daniel good morning. She smiles at her husband glad to see him. Daniel got home in the middle of the night from preaching at a church across the country.

"I wasn't expecting you until this afternoon," she said.

"I was going to stay another night but I wanted to get home to my beautiful wife. You're lucky I didn't wake you up when I got in I wanted some cuddy," he says squeezing her.

"Nothing didn't stop you," she says kissing him, "So, how did it go?"

"I preached the house down. The three-night revival was a big success. Many people gave their lives to Christ but I made a lot of money."

"How much did you make this time," Nicole asked. She enjoyed the benefits of being the First Lady. The more money he makes, the more of a lavish lifestyle they can have. Simone goes to one of the top private schools in the state. Without the money, Daniel makes from preaching, they wouldn't be able to enjoy all of this,

"Without the three thousand dollars for me to be there, I raised about six thousand dollars in three-nights."

"Nine thousand dollars, that's not bad," Nicole smiled.

"No it isn't, which is why I'm not going anywhere for the next five days. I'll be here, giving you my undivided attention."

"You're all mine," she asked with excitement. Nicole has been missing Daniel when he has to leave and preach. The more popular he is becoming, the less he is at home but she knows he does all of this for them.

"Yes, I'm all yours. Tomorrow at church, I'm just going to preach one of my sermons I preached at the revivals and be done. Why don't you come with me on my next trip?"

"You know I just can't up and leave like that. Simone has school. I have to be here to watch her. And what about the women's ministry that I'm in charge of; we're supposed to meet next week."

"Simple, my mother can fly out here to watch Simone and I can announce at church tomorrow before my sermon that you want to have a brief meeting with the ladies in the women's ministry, problem solved. Besides, I don't think you would want to miss a trip to Paris."

"Paris," she exclaims sitting up, "You're going to Paris!"

"Yeah, I just got the news."

This is what Daniel has been waiting for. He finally made his name known overseas. Bishop Wilkens knew Daniel was ready for this step. Daniel worked hard for that moment to go overseas. An international ministry.... things are picking up full speed ahead.

"I got the call yesterday that they want me to preach at this church in Paris. Bishop told me that this church is massive. It holds close to thirty thousand. I'm also scheduled to be on a radio show."

"I would love to go. I need to go shopping and call your mother. Is Darryl and Marshal ready to go? Do they have their passports?"

"Yeah, I told them to get it when the Bishop and I spoke about me going overseas to minister one day."

"I've been meaning to ask you, when are you going to open a church under your name, so you can be an Overseer. Bishop Wilkens is over you. I think it's time for you to branch out. I know he takes his usual twenty percent every Sunday. It's time for you to find someone to train so you can be an Overseer too and get your thirty percent. You always want to stay a step ahead of the Bishop."

"I know; I'm meeting someone after church tomorrow. His name is Thomas Butler. He graduated from our ministry school last month. I saw a couple of his sermonettes and he's quite good. He's a little rough around the edges though. You can tell that he was from the streets."

"Oh, yes, I heard him preach a couple of times in their Bible class. He's beginning to create a name for himself in the new Ministers class. He's definitely hood. But I think he will be good."

"Yeah, he got saved about a year ago. He's new to all of this but I think he could be ready and up for a challenge."

"Did you pray about it," Nicole jokes.

"I'll pray about it later. Right now I want to prey on my wife."

Chapter 4

2 Peter 2:2 (MSG)
> "They've put themselves on a fast downhill slide to destruction, but not before they recruit a crowd of mixed-up followers who can't tell right from wrong."

"Pastor Daniel, are you ready to go downstairs," Marshal asked. Whenever Marshal and Darryl are on duty they address Daniel professionally, especially when there are church folks around.

"Yeah, I'm ready to do this sermon. I may end the service a little early. I'm still a little jet lag, but you know you can't put time on God," he said joking in his preaching voice.

Daniel and Marshal began to head downstairs, taking the elevator to the sanctuary. Daniel doesn't have an elevator in his office like Bishop Wilkens, but he does have pictures he's taken with celebrities, a couple of awards and a degree in Theology, thanks to the help of Bishop. Since Daniel was going to make this preaching thing his new career, he figured he mind as well get a degree and become officially certified. But anyone can become a certified pastor. Daniel heard about some pastors taking online classes and some just filled out paperwork and got their credentials within a few weeks. And then there were others like himself who got the proper training with a bishop of a church. Daniel did grow to love preaching and develop a relationship with God but he was still in it for the money, just like every other church leader he knows. When Daniel and Marshal got off the elevator, they heard the praise and worship team ending their song. "Is Darryl on his post", Daniel asked.

"Yeah he's there. I radioed him before we headed to the elevator."

What Daniel didn't know was, what comes with the job of being a well-known pastor. He received a couple of death threats and people trying to blackmail him. One Sunday, a man walked to the front of the church and began to yell at Daniel while he was preaching. The man was calling him a charlatan and said that he was going to burn in hell. Before the man was able to get to Daniel, Darryl and Marshal had already tackled him down. That scared Daniel; he never had that happened to him. Daniel didn't like the fact that the church was so open for just anybody to walk in, but he knows he can't deny people access. So he made sure Darryl and Marshal was alert to everything and everyone. Some deacons and members was urging Daniel to hire more security, but Daniel trusted only Darryl and Marshal with his life.

As they walked in the sanctuary, Marshal was in front of Daniel and motioned to Darryl to letting him know that they were heading to the front. Darryl took his place in the front of the pulpit. People isn't paying attention. Most of them is caught up in the Spirit. Daniel's church, Abundant Overflow Ministries, has one of the best Praise and Worship Team and church choir. They have about seventy-five faithful choir members who sing every Sunday.

As Daniel walks up to the front of the church, he shakes some people's hands. As Bishop Wilkens said, the church is to hold eight thousand people but the church's membership seems to double over the last two years. The church now holds a little over seven thousand members.

Daniel is standing next to Nicole as she is still applauding the praise and worship team.

"Where's Simone," he whispers to Nicole.

"She wanted to go to children's church today with her friends."

Daniel looks at Marshal signaling him to check on Simone.

"We worship you God, we worship you God," the praise leader said softly, "There's nobody greater. Just love on him church."

The live church band continue to play softly in the background. Daniel raises his hands to praise God with his congregation. He always gives reverence to God. Sometimes he feels that small conviction tugging at his heart about what he's doing, but he tries to ignore it because he feels that there is nothing wrong about providing for his family.

"Hallelujah," Daniel shouted.

This brought the congregation emotions back up back, Daniel couldn't wait; he feels he needs to speak at that moment. He walks onto the pulpit, still with his hands raised. The cameramen zoomed in on him for a close-up. Daniel has gotten use to the cameras and seeing himself on the television and the big screen at church. He also has a few billboards of himself and his church around the state. The praise leader hands him the microphone.

"Hallelujah," he shouts in his preacher's voice. Bishop told him that every church leader should have a preaching voice.

"I can't wait church! I can't wait until you or my neighbor to praise Him! I have to praise him now," he shouts.

The congregation begins to shout praises right along with him. This isn't out of character for Daniel. These are times when he seems to really feel the Spirit of God, but then his flesh would quickly take over. The last thing he wants to do is honestly transform.

"How do you expect to be blessed but you can't open your mouth and praise God! That's why you're still stuck in your situation! That's why you feel as though you can't make it! Do you know that if you don't praise God he will make the rocks, the trees and other non-living things cry out!"

The congregation went wild. People are throwing their hands up, waving it about, crying and speaking in tongues. Even Nicole with her pretty-self has both of her hands up and has her eyes closed. Some people began to run up to the alter to put money at Daniel's feet.

"People of God," he says calmly, "I know how it feels to live paycheck to paycheck. I've been there. There were times when I just wanted to give up and throw in the towel, but…but…," he says as he began to pace back and forth, "But when I took a step back and saw how God was blessing my family despite of our circumstances, I couldn't help but to give Him praise! I gave him praise when I found out my hours was cut from my job!" Daniel has full blown lied. He knows that praising God was the last thing on his mind when Al told him that he was cutting his hours.

"I gave Him praise when I didn't know how I was going to provide for my family! Because I knew my breakthrough was coming! Do you know when your breakthrough will come through? If you knew, you wouldn't care who see you praising God! You wouldn't care how you look! You got to have faith, beloveds! Have faith in God! That's all you need. Sometimes you don't feel like praising Him, sometimes you want to scream, sometimes you feel like a nut," he joked. The congregation laughed with him. "And sometimes you do feel like a nut, but you know that even a nut knows their day is coming! They know there will be a day when that nut will crack out open and all of the praise and goodness will come pouring out. You got to hold on saints. Hold on to God, hold on to Jesus! All the praises that has gone up, blessings are about to be released, lives are about to restored! But you have to believe! If you feel your break through is near, I need you to run up to this alter right now, without thinking about what you look like."

People began to run down the stairs believing that their breakthrough is coming. Darryl and Marshal take their positions in the front and motions for the other brothers to form a line in front of the alter. About five hundred people are standing at the altar and thousands of others are standing behind them wanting to reach the altar. Daniel is about to do something that will shock everyone.

"I need everyone who is standing and know that they're breakthrough is coming to raise your hand. That includes the people who are in the balcony." People began to raise their hands still praising God. "Ushers, I want you to take your place and give everyone whose hand is up an offering envelope."

Some people began to have confused looks which caused them to put their hand down. They weren't too happy about their pastor's forwardness about collecting money. Nicole is even wondering what he is doing. You can hear some people in the congregation snicker and make sly remarks. It took about thirty minutes for the ushers to give everyone whose hand was still up an envelope. But people kept on praising God as tears are sliding down their faces.

"Now I want those of you who have the envelope to write your name, address, everything. Fill out the envelope. Then give it to the ushers. Ushers, I want you to put all the envelopes in the baskets and bring it to me."

People began filling out their envelopes and giving it to the ushers. Others who refused to partake in the offering either went back to their seats to sit down or continued to stand trying to figure out why did Pastor Daniel break the atmosphere in the church.

"Don't stop praising Him church," Daniel yells out, "Choir, I want you to sing us a selection as people fill out their envelopes."

The choir is already standing, some filling out their envelopes. The music director walks onto the stage and led the choir in a fast tempo song.

Daniel leans over and tells Marshal to bring Nicole onto the stage with him. Marshal moves through the crowd toward Nicole, taking her by the hand. Marshal's towering figure towered over almost everyone. Nicole's hand is engulfed in Marshal's hand. The people created a small path for her and Marshal to walk through. Nicole looks great in her green wrap dress and matching pumps. She knows how to make sure she's looking good, especially on Sundays for times like this when she's standing next to Daniel in front of the whole church. Daniel takes Nicole's hand helping her walk up the stairs onto the stage. She wants to ask Daniel about why is he being so forward about getting money. Nicole is bothered by what he is doing things today. She was really feeling what he said until he told the ushers to hand out envelops. Daniel knows Nicole isn't thrilled by the look on her face. He leans over to whisper to her, "People are about to be blessed."

Nicole tries not to show her even more confused look and decided to just follow her husband's lead.

"Pastor Daniel, we collected all of the envelopes," one of the male ushers said.

Daniel turns around to tell the music director to quiet the choir. As the choir began to lower their voice, Daniel began speaking, "In the beginning almost all of you believed that your breakthrough was coming! I told you that your breakthrough is in your praise. Sometimes in your praise, God will have you do something you've never done. That is your sign of faith. Some continued to praise God when you were told to fill out your envelopes. Some put their hands down because they thought it was unusual." Daniel began to laugh, "Do you know that God will sometimes have you do the unusual when your breakthrough is right there? These empty envelopes that are in the basket," he says spreading his arm over them, "Is filled with your breakthrough. By the end of the week, each one of you who filled out the envelope will get it back with one hundred dollars inside."

The congregation went crazy. People who put their hands down, is now putting their hands on their face, covering their disappointed looks. People had the itch to run, but could hardly move because of the huge congregation.

"Wait, wait, I'm not done. Those of you who have sown a seed in the envelope, either it's your tithes or offering, you will receive double." People began to cry out, thanking God, and waving their hands. The service wasn't supposed to go like this, but Daniel wanted to do something different. He's not sure if he was led to do it but he knows, he is going to expect a big return out of this. Bishop Wilkens told him before that when a pastor does great things, he'll get something greater in return.

After Sunday service, Daniel was in his office sitting at his desk joking around with Marshal and Darryl. Daniel is waiting for Thomas Butler to meet with him. Daniel needs an armor bearer and feels as though Thomas will be good at it. He would become Daniel's shadow and Daniel in return will train Thomas how to be a successful pastor in the ministry just like him. He has no intentions of telling Thomas about eventually placing him in a new church to pastor. Daniel doesn't want to scare him away. What Daniel did this morning, got the ball rolling faster. Daniel is ready to take off and he knows Thomas will be perfect for the ride. Everything that Daniel's does, he does it for a reason. He is now trending in social media platforms and have the blogs talking about the major move he just did this morning.

"You should have given us a heads up Daniel. Me and Marshal could have filled out an envelope too," Darryl says.

"For real, I could have put two hundred dollars in the envelope just to get four hundred by the end of the week. You have everyone on social media calling you Pastor Oprah now," Marshal added.

"I wasn't going to do that. Honestly, I didn't have any intentions on doing that. But the idea came to mind. Just like a business, you have to invest in your investments. And by doing so, you'll get double maybe even triple in return. Watch the membership increase and more money start coming in."

"That's a smart move but you know you're going to hear it from some of the elders of the church," Marshal continued, "You know how they are. I'm telling you Daniel, they are the eyes and ears for Bishop Wilkens. I don't trust them. I told you before that I think Bishop Wilkens purposely set them here to spy on you. He can't allow you to get too carried away."

"I assume that they are spies too. I don't need to inform the Bishop about everything I decide to do. This is *my* church and within two years, I'm going to have to get a larger one. Mark my words, Abundant Overflow Ministries will have close to fifty thousand members."

"This church can't hold fifty thousand people. What's the plan," Darryl asked?

But before Daniel can answer the question there is a knock at the door. Darryl began to stand to answer it but Daniel waved him down, "Let me get it. Some people are already intimidated by the both of you. Image is everything." Daniel got up to open the door. There was two Elders of the church at the door.

"Hey Pastor Daniel, do you have a moment," Elder Williams asked. The other person with him is Sister Barnes. Both Williams and Barnes have been with Daniel since the opening of the church.

"You know that I always have time for the both of you," Daniel smiles as he steps aside to let them into the office. "Marshal and Darryl, I'll see you later. Tell Nicole I'm going to be busy for a little bit."

"We'll take her and Simone home," Marshal suggested.

"That's okay with me. Tell Nicole not to cook dinner. We will go out for dinner tonight."

As Marshal and Darryl walk out the office, Daniel closes the door behind them.

"So, you know why we need to speak to you, Pastor Daniel," Elder Williams asked.

"Take a seat", he motions to the leather sofas that is set against the wall. They took a seat on the sofa as Daniel took a seat in nearby reclining leather chair. "I think I know why you are here. It's about what happened in the service this morning."

"Yes, Pastor Daniel, why didn't you tell us what you were going to do," Sister Barnes asked.

"I didn't know I was going to do something like that. And besides, I didn't know that I had to inform you about my every move. I've learned in my five years of pastoring to never question God or the person in charged."

"But Pastor, what if every person in the building filled out an envelope. That's two point five million dollars that you gave away, not including if those people tithe! You're about to bankrupt the church," Elder Williams shot back. He is known to be a bulldog, very pushy.

"I know what I am doing. How many people turned in an envelope," he asked trying to keep cool. He didn't want Elder Williams to get to him.

"We counted five thousand and three hundred envelopes. And about two thousand people tithe and gave an offering. Altogether, you're going to put out nine hundred and twenty-two thousand dollars," Sister Barnes said.

"Fine, each person will get their money. We have more than enough to cover that and so much more. We have 2.5 million dollars in the church account." Daniel also know that, that will look good when they have to fill out tax forms concerning donations.

"After you give that out, we'll have about 1.3 million dollars left in the account! We still have to pay for the maintenance, lights, employees," Elder Williams blurts out.

"I know all of this Elder Williams! I was a salesman years ago. I know how to make a profit," Daniel shot back.

"You can't buy people Pastor Daniel. You can't make a profit off the members of the church," Elder Williams exclaims.

Sister Barnes taps the elder on the knee telling him to calm down. Daniel is beginning to lose his cool with Elder Williams.

"Let me ask you a question Elder Williams, did you put an envelope into the basket?"

When Daniel asked that question, the room became very silent. He is waiting to hear what the Elder had to say now. "I figure you didn't. Could it be that you're jealous or mad at yourself for not having faith like those who gave? Would you be saying the same thing if you put money into the basket? It's you who doubted God, not me."

Elder Williams is now sitting tight-lipped. He knows he is jealous. After he heard Pastor Daniel say what he was going to do, he was upset at himself just like so many others.

"I have plans for Abundant Overflow Ministries and if I feel as though you can't work with me then you can step down… the both of you as well as Sister May, and anyone else who works for me. This church is growing. Our membership has doubled within the last two years. I just finished writing my first book and am working on a second one. People all over the world have been tuning in to our church services and buying my Sunday sermons. I know I have a lot of haters because I've been pastoring for only five years and have grown so much and done so many things in a short period of time. I'm bound to have people who will speak against me. I've opened doors to the church for gays, trangenders and same sex married couples because other churches refuse to accept their lifestyle. Doesn't the Word say to love our neighbor and to treat others the way we want to be treated? I wouldn't want a church or any other religious sect to slam the doors in me and my families face because they don't accept us. I'm restoring people's faith. And today about five thousand people's faith have been restored. Do you know what people will do now that they're faith is restored, refreshed and anew? They are going to increase their faith. Word is already spreading about what took place this morning, now watch what happens."

Daniel is reeling them in. He wants only certain people around him that can respect the vision that he has.

"Pastor Daniel, I apologize for my outburst," Elder Williams said, "I respect your vision, but I wouldn't say that I am jealous of those who are getting their blessing. I was just concerned about how the church finances are being thrown about."

"And I can respect that, just know that I know what I am doing and all you need to do is to just follow my lead."

"Did you speak to Brother Thomas yet," Sister Barnes asked.

"No, he should be on his way to my office. I told him that I want to speak to him after service. Service ended about a half an hour ago. I would like to go home and spend time with my family. Which reminds me, Nicole is going to come with me to Paris."

"That's great! Do you and Nicole have plans for your tenth wedding anniversary," Sister Barnes asked.

"I haven't given it much thought. Is the church planning anything," he asks? Daniel always respected Sister Barnes calm nature. He was glad that she came to speak to him with Elder Williams. The situation could have gone another way.

"We do have something in the planning process."

"Whatever it is, just let me know."

There is another knock at the door. Daniel know it has to be Thomas, "Come in," he calls out.

Thomas opens the door a little nervous walking into the office. Thomas is taking in the awesome sight of Pastor Daniel's office. Daniel know that look all too familiar. He had the same expression on his face when he first entered Bishop's office.

"Hi Pastor Sanders, you wanted to speak with me," Thomas asked boldly. Some of the church members calls him by his last name while others call him Pastor Daniel or as the teens of the church call him Pastor D.

"Yes, Thomas, you can come in and have a seat. We'll continue this conversation later," he addressed Elder Williams and Sister Barnes.

They excused themselves as they left Daniel and Thomas alone to talk. Thomas took a seat on the leather sofa still looking around the office.

"Do you want anything to drink," Daniel asked as he got up to get himself a bottle of water out the mini fridge.

"No, I'm fine." Thomas is still wondering why Pastor Daniel want to speak to him. Out of nearly eight thousand members who attend the church, he chose to speak to him, why? Thomas admired the office. He sees a sixty-inch 3D flat screen on the beige wall, his certificate in Theology, which is hanging next to his BA and newly received Master's degree in Theology. He also sees a couple of awards for his Pastoral Service and Excellence. His office resembles a quaint manly living room, but he sees the flowers on the table that is giving it the First Lady's touch. He also notices pictures of the First family. That's something he always admired about Pastor Daniel. He always put his family first. Every time he saw Pastor Daniel outside of church during his leisure time, he is always with his family. He envied that because Thomas didn't grow up in a family. The only family he knew of and lived with was his grandmother who raised him and the street life. She was the only family that he knew of. He developed a church family and hung out with them whenever he went to church which was all the time. His grandmother kept him in church praying that he wouldn't get caught up in the street life like his father. Thomas was always into making that fast cash. That was the only way to survive when life puts you on a dead end street. Thomas is just getting back into church but still make drops to make extra cash. He stopped going after his grandmother died about five years ago. He only began to attend Abundant Overflow because he heard everyone talking about how great the church and pastor is. When he went inside the enormous brick and mortar church, it literally took his breath away. Everything in Abundant Overflow is state-of-the-art. He never saw or been to a church like it before. He'd seen Pastor Daniel on television preaching and saw a few billboards throughout the state. Pastor Daniel always seem larger than life to him. So when he decided to join Abundant Overflow he was shocked to see that Pastor Daniel stayed to shake people's hands. He looked up to Pastor Daniel from afar. He looked up to him so much that he took classes at their ministry school hoping that will keep him away from the streets as much as possible and it was an open door for him to make some money just like other preachers he sees. Thomas isn't sure if he wants to be minister one day or search for something else to do. Sometimes that street life calls him back. Since Thomas doesn't have a college education, it's hard for him to find jobs that he's qualified for. So, he felt that by going to the church's ministry school, he would feel like he accomplished something, especially since its free to members who qualify for free tuition. It was something that Thomas felt he was over qualified for. He didn't have a job, no income, he lives on governmental assistance, he's over qualified. He only graduated from the ministry school just last month as a certified minister and here he is sitting in Pastor's Daniel's office. He has no plans of being a full-time minister. He thought it would be cool to marry people and can get paid for doing it. Besides he doesn't look like a minister or pastor. Thomas has that street swag.

Pastor Daniel took a seat once again on the reclining leather sofa, drinking his bottle of water.

"Well Brother Thomas, it's good to finally meet you personally," Pastor Daniel says smiling.

"It's an honor to meet you Pastor Sanders. Although, I'm not sure why you want to meet with me."

"I'm looking for an armor bearer and I heard about you through Minister Perry who runs the ministry school. And he told me that you would be perfect for the position."

"What exactly is an armor bearer. I've heard the term used before in other churches." Thomas only know than an armor bearer is like someone's slave. And that's something he will never be; someone's slave.

"An armor bearer assists the pastor in church duties. Basically, the person is like a pastor in training."

"A pastor in training, huh? I've never thought about becoming a pastor of a church."

"You don't have to be pastor of a church, but only if you want to," Daniel laughs, "You would only work closely with me. You would be my ears and eyes. My covering as you say." Daniel tries to justify the meaning for him.

"But why me? Why not someone else you know personally," Thomas asked curiously.

"I already have my two best friends from childhood as my bodyguards, I don't want to enlist more of my friends. Let me ask you a question, did you put an envelope into the basket today?"

"Yes I did. Pastor Daniel, that was an awesome word today about faith. And I'm not just saying that because I'm getting a hundred dollars by the end of the week," he reassured him, "But all I've been doing now is living by faith."

Pastor Daniel leans back in the chair and chuckle silently. He placed his hands in front of his face as if he is praying. Thomas is in the same position he was in when he first met Bishop Wilkens. Only Thomas isn't as hungry as Daniel was when he had a meeting with the Bishop.

"Thomas, do you know that I was in the same position as you are about five years ago."

"I'm not understanding."

"Come walk with me." Daniel got up to get his wallet and keys. He is leaving the church with Thomas walking behind him. Daniel and Thomas heads for the elevator that's on the Administrative floor.

Thomas always wanted to take the elevator but you need an elevator key to go onto the second floor. When they step inside the elevator, Daniel began making small talk with Thomas.

"So, are you married," he asked.

"No, I'm not. I have a girlfriend though."

"Is she a member here at Abundant Overflow?"

"No, she has her reasons she doesn't go to church. I'm trying to get her to come but she feels as though we would be talked about because what we are doing isn't biblical."

"And what are you doing that isn't biblical," Daniel inquired.

"We live together. We've been living together for two years now. You mind as well know, since you want me as your armor bearer. That's only if you still want me after knowing that piece of information."

"Well, what you're doing isn't biblical. There's nowhere in the Bible that says that you can't live together before you're married."

Thomas shot him a surprised look and began to laugh, "Are you serious?"

"I'm serious," Daniel said looking at him. The elevator door opens for them. Daniel and Thomas walked out the elevator heading toward the front of the church, exiting the building.

"I've read the Bible about four times straight through; I study it every day. And there is nowhere in the Bible that says you have to be married to live together. It only mentions about sex before marriage."

"Well Pastor Sanders, we broke that law years ago."

"So have a lot of other people but that doesn't make them a bad person. Just a sinner like everyone else. Besides, are you planning to marry her one day?"

"Yeah, I'm just not ready to make that move. I'm still looking for work. I need money before I make that step with her."

"Don't let that stop you. You never want to lose a good thing. Where's your car parked?"

"It's parked in the back parking lot,"

"Your car will be fine where it is. I want to take you for a ride. Are you in a rush to go anywhere?"

"No, I have nowhere to go but home."

Daniel pushed the button on the remote to unlock the doors to his seventy-five-thousand-dollar car he purchased a couple of months ago. Thomas mouth drops open in astonishment at the sleek beauty that is in front of him. He always eyes Daniel's car imagining himself driving one, but he never thought he would get a chance to even sit in it.

"I'm trying to keep cool Pastor Sanders but I'm loving your car," he says with excitement.

"I had to have it when this new model came out."

They opened the car doors to get inside the majestic ride. After closing the doors, Daniel starts the car. The smoothness of the engine made Thomas love the car even more. Thomas is doing a good job fighting off the temptation of closing his eyes and taking a deep breath of what richness smells like. Rich people have a certain fresh and alluring smell. You can just imagine the floating trails of money behind them as they pass you by.

Daniel began to drive off, away from the church, heading to his Victorian mansion.

"Thomas, about five years ago I was in your position. I know you, heard the story before but you never heard the full story."

Thomas sat back ready to learn from Daniel.

"As you know I was a car salesman and I followed God's calling into ministry and was lead and trained by Bishop Wilkens from Abundant Love Ministries. Let me tell you, before then, First Lady Nicole and I were high school sweethearts. I remembered when I saw her during our freshmen year, I knew I had to lock her down before someone else made a move. Nicole was beyond gorgeous. A lot of guys were intimidated by her and there were some who thought that because she was a pretty girl, she was easy. Nicole was far from easy. But I made my move. I assumed she would turn me down because I'm your average looking guy, but she surprised me when she agreed to go out with me. To make a long story short, we ended up getting pregnant at the end of our junior year in high school. Thank God for our parents, they helped us with our daughter Simone so we can graduate high school. They wanted us to go to college so we wouldn't have to struggle but I wasn't trying to have to owe the government thousands of dollars for a college education. So, Nicole and I eloped, got our own apartment, and tried to make things work. It was hard. Nicole had a job that barely paid her, and the money I was making as a used car salesman, wasn't enough for my family to survive on. But I refused to think that I had to have a college degree to live comfortable. A lot of our friends who went to high school with us, went off to college, only to graduate not able to find jobs and is left with a large debt. So, I know how it is to live by faith, paycheck to paycheck."

Daniel is very sensitive to people in that position because he remembers how it was for him.

"But you have a college degree now. I saw the degrees on the wall in your office," Thomas said.

"I got that degree when I was in training to be a pastor. I was taking the required classes at Abundant Love so I continued to get my degree. Only because it was something to do and it was free."

"That makes sense." Thomas never dismissed the idea of having a college degree though.

"Living by faith and patiently waiting got me all of this," Daniel says. As if it was scripted, Daniel pulls into the long driveway that leads to his Victorian mansion.

Thomas mouth drops open even further when he got a perfect view of the two story mansion in front of him. The perfect two tone tan Spanish mansion is sitting perfectly on an extra large well-manicured grass with a broad cobblestone walkway in between leading up to the driveway and the magnificent house. Thomas didn't have to wait for Daniel to tell him to get out the car. As soon as Daniel turned the car off, Thomas was out the car. He only seen these houses on television and magazines that advertise celebrity living. He never thought he would be standing in full frontal view of one.

Daniel just laughs to himself at Thomas' eagerness. He got out the car, standing next to Thomas and said, "This is what God bless me with. Come on, let me show you the inside."

As they walked, Thomas took noticed of the arched openings. When Daniel opened the door, Thomas couldn't keep his excitement in any longer.

"Oh my God! Pastor Sanders your place is awesome! I've never seen something like this before!"

Nicole heard the excited tone in the front foyer. She got up from the sofa to see what was going on. She notices Daniel walking toward her with an unfamiliar person.

"Hey Danny, I thought we were going out I didn't know we were having company," Nicole smiled curiously.

"We still are but I wanted to bring Brother Thomas Butler to the house. I would like to train him *but I thought he needs a little bit more convincing*," he says softly to her making sure Thomas doesn't hear him. Thomas is already in the living room looking around in amazement. He couldn't believe that the fireplace in the living room was a large see through glass that shows the back of the house. That's where he was stuck. There is an Olympic size swimming pool in the back with sparkling blue water shining from the sun.

"I know, I get stuck in this room all the time," Nicole says now standing next to him. "This room made me agree to buy the house. I didn't have to see any other room."

"How long did you guys live here," he says now looking at Daniel and Nicole. This is his first time face to face with Nicole. He sees what Daniel is talking about. Nicole is extremely beautiful. He tries to keep his eyes on Daniel and the extravagant house to keep from having impure thoughts about Nicole. He hears a lot of men talk at the church, saying how they visualize Nicole when they pleasure themselves or with their girlfriends. He doesn't want to get sucked into that kind of thinking, especially if he decides to take Pastor Daniel's offer.

"We moved here about three years ago," Daniel answered, "Before we were here, we lived in an apartment about thirty minutes away. I would show you the whole house but it's too much to cover. Nicole, Thomas and I will be right back," he says as he proceeds to go outside to the pool.

"It was nice meeting you Thomas," Nicole said.

"Nice meeting you too," he said, already two steps behind Daniel. He didn't want to even shake her hand. Daniel closes the glass door behind them as they stood looking at the calming view.

"Is that a guest house in the far back," Thomas pointed to the left.

"Yes, my friends Marshal and Darryl live there. So, what's on your mind?"

"A lot of things Pastor Sanders."

"Call me Daniel when we're not in church and off duty."

"Cool… I just don't know why you're showing me all of this."

"Thomas, not only do I want you as an armor bearer but I want to train you too. I see so much purpose in you and I know God wants to use you to do great things. What I have here, is what you can have too."

Thomas can see himself living in a great house like this with Jessica by his side. Daniel didn't have to convince him any further. Thomas wanted his prosperity too.

"I'm in, let's do this. Just tell me what do I have to do." He had to contain his excitement because he doesn't want Daniel to get the right impression. Thomas wants the money but he doesn't want Daniel to know that. Whatever he has to do to survive, he will do it.

"Well, first, we'll begin small. I'll put you on the church's payroll. Wherever I go, you go and Jessica can come too if Nicole is coming. Do you have a passport?"

"Actually I do. Jessica and I went to Jamaica last year."

"Good, be ready to leave for Paris next week. Don't worry about the expense. The church will cover you. Since this will be your first time traveling with me, come by yourself. Jessica has to miss this trip. This is my first time ministering overseas."

"Okay, wow! I didn't know this was going to happen so fast," Thomas said. He is beyond words. He is ready to do whatever it takes to be as large as Pastor Daniel.

"Well, hold on, because it gets faster," Daniel smirks.

Chapter 5

Ephesians 6:11 (MSG)

> "So take everything the Master has set out for you, well-made weapons of the materials. And put them to use so you will be able to stand up to everything the devil throws your way."

When Thomas left to go back to his tiny apartment in the hood, he wanted more of the luxury life that Pastor Daniel has. After leaving his mansion, Thomas feels like he is so close to having that life. He didn't know that his day would turn out like this. Sure, he believed he was going to get that miracle when he put the envelope in the basket, but he didn't expect to get a hundred dollars by the end of the week and a position with Pastor Daniel by the end of the day. He's been unemployed for a year and a half and he knows that his unemployment is about to run out. The money that he gets under the table from various hustles and street drops can't sustain him and Jessica. He's tired of relying on Jessica for money. He's the man; she should be relying on him. Jessica graduated from a HBCU with a degree in social work. Jessica makes enough to support the both of them but he can tell that her patience is wearing thin on supporting a grown man. Thomas knows that she's getting pressure from her friends and family. He hears the conversations and he sees the intolerable stares. He stopped hanging out with his friends because he was always the center of the jokes. Thomas wants an honest job. He doesn't want to hustle on the streets anymore. It would just make things worse if he gets arrested or worse, killed. Being incarcerated is worse to have to put on a job application than to have no experience. Before he left Pastor Daniel, Daniel gave Thomas about eight hundred dollars in cash. He didn't want to take it, but Pastor Daniel told him to never dismiss a blessing. Daniel told Thomas to consider it as an advance.

Thomas pulls up to his tiny apartment building praying that one day soon he will be pulling up to a better place, in a better environment. The same crew of guys are hanging out in front of the building as usual. He's tired of walking through Chris and his boys. Every time Thomas wants to shy away from the street life, he gets sucked back in when Chris ask him to make a drop for him. A simple drop can put three hundred dollars easily in his pockets. Chris and his crew always have something to say when Thomas comes home from church every Sunday. Thomas lean his head back on the back of his chair hoping that his prayers are finally heard. "God, I really hope you hear me," he says out loud, "I'm ready to make this move by any means necessary because I'm getting tired of waiting. I want what Pastor Daniel and his family has and I will get it."

He takes a deep breath, finally getting out the car.

"Yo, here come Thomas," Chris calls out, "What's good T?"

"Nothing much, I'm just coming back from church," Thomas said.

"Did you get your blessing at church today? Did the Lord come down and give you a job or do you want to make it official and be down with the crew? I can use you. Those little drops that you do for me can help you bring in serious bank."

Thomas just laughs it off. He knows the job offer he just received is better and safer than running around with Chris, and when they see him and Jessica moving out of the projects and into the suburbs with him driving the fancy car, he'll know why he turned down his offer.

"No, I'm good Chris but if I need to roll with you I'll call you," he answered as he gave Chris a quick hand shake.

"Jessica's girl is here too. You need to hook that up for me. She's always stunting when she comes over here," Chris said.

Thomas told him that he'll see what he can do as he heads inside the apartment building. The hallway walls are a dull, dirty tarnish color with little pieces of paint chipping off. It has the usual stale dry odor of bug spray, moth balls and dried urine in the air. The hallway reeks to those who doesn't live in the building. Those who do live here has grown accustomed to the tainted polluted smell. Thomas began walking up the stairs to the third floor. Every day he is thankful that he doesn't live on the seventh floor, the last floor. The one elevator they have in the building break down so much, that those who live on the seventh floor rather walk up the seven flights than to take the elevator with the high chances of getting stuck for hours. Thomas' heart is thumping with excitement of the news he has to share with Jessica. In the next couple of days, he will be flying out of the country to Paris. Who would have known he would be flying out the country so soon? Thomas' faith in God is beginning to burst wide open. *Finally*, God has heard his prayers. Never did he imagine he would receive all of this. He quickly put the key in the door as his hands shake with nervousness and pushes open the door with pure excitement.

"Jessica! Jessica," Thomas shouts.

He closes the door, looking around the tiny apartment waiting to see Jessica appear from the kitchen. He can hear the television on in the bedroom. He races to the bedroom door, "Jessica you would not believe what happened," he says as he pushes the door open, "To me today," he says as his voice trails off.

"Thomas," she panicky screams, "Thomas let me explain."

Thomas is standing in the doorway to their bedroom watching a confusing scene before his eyes. Jessica is in the bed with her friend, Diane.

"Thomas let me explain," Jessica says again trying to put on her t-shirt. Diane is saying sorry over and over again. Thomas turns around to leave. How could he not have known this?

"Thomas please let me explain," Jessica says touching his arm.

"How can you possibly explain this to me Jessica?" Thomas yells, "I caught you kissing Diane! How can you explain that?" As much as Thomas wants to be angry, he couldn't. He is more hurt than anything else.

"This just sort of happened between Diane and I."

"And that is supposed to explain why you decided to cheat on me with your best friend, who is a chick!"

"Fine! Would it have been better if it was a guy," Jessica yells.

"No! It would have been better if you didn't cheat on me!"

"Thomas, you are never here! This was bound to happen with her or someone else. You are hardly here!"

"I was never here because I was out looking for a job and doing what I do to keep money in the house!"

"And what job interview have you been to lately besides doing drops for Chris and running with some of his goons?"

Thomas is standing there just looking at her. If she only knew the good news, he was about to share with her.

She continues, "None! I support you and am tired of supporting a grown ass man. I pay for all of this. I paid for the clothes you wear! I work all day and come home to cook your dinner! You should be cooking me dinner!"

Diane came creeping out the bedroom with her clothes now covering her thick body. Thomas can see the embarrassment in Diane's eyes.

"Does it matter if I was sleeping with Diane? Tell me Thomas, when was the last time you made love to me?"

Thomas look back at Jessica holding in his anger. "You can't honestly stand here and blame what you did on me! You're not going to turn this on me."

"It's always been on you. I can't support a grown man who can't support himself and his woman."

"Jessica that's enough," Diane blurts out approaching her. "Jessica, we both were wrong and you know it."

"Diane, don't stand here and try to feel guilty now. We both knew what we were doing and what we wanted."

"So are you telling me that you want to be with women now," Thomas ask firmly.

"I'm telling you that I don't know what I want but I do know that I can't be with you if you can't support me."

"Wow, ok," Thomas says nodding his head, "If that's what you want, then it's over. I'll get my stuff and will be out of here in fifteen minutes."

Thomas storms past Jessica and Diane heading back to the bedroom to gather his stuff. As he is gathering his stuff he can hear footsteps coming toward the bedroom. He then hears Diane yell at Jessica, "Why are you being so heartless? This is exactly what you wanted to do. But now you are taking it too far."

"Thomas!" Jessica yells as she is now standing in the bedroom doorway, "You're a grown man. You need to figure out how to support yourself. Leave all the clothes that I bought you."

"Are you serious! Jessica, what have I done to you for you to be so mean?"

"Thomas, you need to go," she says softly.

"Jessica, you are wrong and you know it," Diane said standing behind her.

"Why are you taking up for me." Thomas shouts, "I just caught you with my girl! I don't need your help."

"Thomas, I'm sorry. I really am. But this isn't what," Diane reply before getting interrupted by Jessica, "Diane, you don't need to explain yourself to him," she says looking at her. Her eyes are telling her not to say anymore. Nothing was going to happen between the both of them, but it was Jessica's only idea to make Thomas break-up with her. Turning back around to face Thomas she continues her rant, "Like I said, I've had enough. I need someone who will support and care for me. I'm tired of doing everything by myself."

"You've said enough," Thomas said as he continues to throw clothes in his old faded black duffle bag.

"Thomas, I told you….."

"What exactly are you going to do with men's clothing? You know what, don't tell me. I wouldn't be surprised if you're screwing another guy brains out."

Thomas reach in his back pocket to take out his wallet. Pastor Daniel gave Thomas eight hundred dollars before leaving his alluring mansion. Pastor Daniel said that he didn't want Thomas to have an empty wallet and should prepare for his unexpected trip to Paris and to take his girlfriend out for dinner. Thomas thought about what he was about to do. He snickers, shakes his head and put his wallet back into his pocket.

"You know what Jessica, at church today the message was about faith. With all the faith that I have left, I trusted God. And with that I wanted to share some great news with you today. I was going to take you out for dinner and tell you that I have a job at the church."

Jessica's facial expression turns from condescending to comical. "A job at the church," she laughs.

"That's right. I'll be working with Pastor Daniel himself."

Jessica stops laughing.

"Oh no, please keep laughing. Cause I was just laughing and having a good time at his massive crib. Not only is the pay great and he gave me a little advance, which I'm not going to tell you the amount, but I will be leaving with him and a couple of others next week to go to Paris."

Jessica's now and non-existent comical facial expression turns into amazement. Her jaw drops open surprised to hear what Thomas just told her.

"I was ready to give you everything and more but you did me a favor."

He takes the duffel bag off the bed, finally smiling and said, "You showed me what kind of person you really are. You don't deserve a guy like me. Enjoy the rest of your day with your girlfriend."

Thomas was once angry but took his anger back and walk out the tiny poignant apartment with pride. He walks down the stairs with anticipation to begin his new life God has placed him in with the snap of a finger. But as he approaches the first floor, he began to slow down. Thomas began to think about where was he going to stay. He has nowhere to go.

"What the heck am I'm doing," he said out loud, "Where am I'm going to go?"

He turns around to look back at the ascending stairs. *Maybe we can work this out. I just need some time to get myself together, she'll understand,* he thought to himself. He turns back around to go back to Jessica's apartment with his packed duffel bag in hand. His pace began slow but picks up speed as he knew what he was about to do was a good idea. He takes his keys out his pocket, as he's standing in front of the door. He fumbles with the key in his hand. Unlocking the door, he walks back into the tiny apartment and see Jessica sitting, crying with her head down on the kitchen table. Diane is sitting next to her rubbing her back. Thomas stands there watching her cry. Jessica picks up her head and looks at him with red, teary eyes. At that moment, Thomas began to remember when they first met and when he realized that he loved her.

It was about three years ago. Thomas was working as a manager at a retail store at the mall. It was during the holiday season and his store was busy as usual. His store had the top sales in the region. Thomas knew how to hustle, giving people what they really want, a bargain. Because of that, people kept coming back. So it's to no surprise that the holiday season was extra busy. While he was walking the floor, he noticed a beautiful woman looking confused at some suits. Her skin was glistening. He approached her, admiring her. She had her hair pulled back into a tight high bun. She had very little make-up on and had high cheek bones and well arched eyebrows. She was a beauty.

"Excuse me Miss, do you need any help," Thomas asked with a smile.

"Yes," she says smiling.

They were both caught off guard with each other. Not only was she gorgeous but she had the perfect whitest teeth he's ever seen. Jessica was captured by his hazel eyes. She saw him when she first walked into the store. He was busy assisting customers and playfully playing with a little girl. Jessica admired men who love kids. Being a social worker, she experienced her heartbreaking moments with deadbeat dads and abusive fathers. So seeing men, love kids and make them smile and laugh was always a turn on for her.

"I'm looking for a suit for my cousin who is in town for the holiday. He doesn't own a suit at all," she laughed.

"I can help you with that. How tall is your cousin?"

"He's about five-ten, a little on the hefty side. He's a truck driver, so all he does it eat, sleep and drive," she said looking into his eyes. All she wanted to do was stare at him.

"Okay, I would suggest you get a size forty in the pants. Do you have a price in mind?"

"I don't want to go over a hundred and fifty dollars?"

"Well, what if I told you that you won't come near one hundred and twenty dollars and I can throw in free tailoring?"

"I would say that you got yourself a sell. You must really want that commission," she said following him to another rack of suits.

"No, I'm the manager of the store. Commission doesn't mean a thing to me. What's your name?"

"Do you ask all of your customers their names?"

"No, not at all. But I would like to know yours, if you don't mind me asking."

"My name is Jessica, Thomas," she says pointing at his name tag.

Thomas just smiled, showed her a couple of suits and they exchanged numbers before Jessica left. They began dating a couple of weeks later.

Everything was going well. Thomas was about to propose to Jessica but he found out that his store was closing. He tried everything, he tried to buy the store or possibly get transferred to another store but to no avail. There was a dead end to every turn. Jessica suggested that he moved in with her. Thomas was against the idea at first but changed his mind after giving it some thought. He was a grown man. He never saw himself relying on his woman to support him. But he had no other choice since Thomas didn't have anywhere else to go and nobody else to rely on. His unemployment check wasn't enough to cover his rent and the utilities. Jessica was right there by his side. Jessica always encouraged him and helped not feel like he was less than a man. She knew she could handle all the bills herself. Her mother taught her how to depend on herself and not look for handouts. She allowed Thomas to pay for some of the bills but she continued to double up on the bills and put extra money in her hidden savings account. Jessica was no fool. She knew Thomas' unemployment was going to run out before he was able to find another job. So, she was prepared to take care of everything. She had seventy-five thousand dollars saved because she had a good paying job working for the state. She wasn't worried or stressed about anything except the constant badgering comments from family and friends because she was supporting Thomas. She felt the pressure and the pressure was too intense for her. So, she knew she had to let him go. So, she planned the whole scene with her friend Diane.

"I just came back to return the key," Thomas says softly.
He took the key off the chain and places the cold metal key on the table.
"Thomas," Jessica cried softly.
He took a deep breath, looking at her, with tears forming in his eyes.
"I didn't mean to hurt you like this," she continued.
"But you did," he interrupts her.
Before he allowed her to say another word, he left quickly out the door. Closing the door behind him, all he can hear is her loud sobbing.

This feels very surreal to Thomas. Never did he imagine being in Paris ever in his life. After leaving Jessica, he stayed at a motel downtown. With money he'll be bringing in, he can afford to find an apartment to live in after a month or two saving up some cash. So, he spoke to the motel manager to work out something for the next two months. The manager agreed to let Thomas to stay for two months for twelve hundred dollars. Thomas gave him cash and was ready to begin his new life. He didn't bother to unpack his bags, since he was leaving soon for Paris. And here he is, standing in front of the Eiffel Tower. Daniel told Thomas to take the day to look around and to meet them at a restaurant called Epicure. Thomas knew Pastor Daniel just wanted some alone time with Nicole. Marshal and Darryl invited Thomas to a hostel club, but Thomas declined. Thomas heard about the raunchy clubs here in Paris. He also isn't too fond of Marshal and Darryl. The last thing Thomas wants is to mess things up with his new position with Pastor Daniel. No one knows that Thomas is in it for the money and he wants to keep it that way.

He takes out his phone and began to take pictures of the Eiffel Tower. After he took about four pictures and a couple of selfies, he walks over to a bench to have a seat to take in the site. There are numerous of people here taking pictures, smiling and laughing. There are more couples than the usual friend's getaway. He is feeling the emptiness in his heart that Jessica once occupied. *Why the heck did she had to do that*, he thought to himself. He never saw that coming. The more he thought about it, the further depressed he became.

"Ahhh," he screams out, "F***in' b****," he says out loud to himself.

A guy walking by looks at him, as if Thomas is crazy. The French man just shakes his head and proceeds to walk away.

"You never heard a man talk to himself before! Can't I have a moment!"

The Frenchman continue to walk further away ignoring Thomas and his emotions.

"Excuse me sir, is there a problem," an officer asked standing behind Thomas.

Thomas doesn't want to cause any trouble. Turning around, looking at the officer he says, "No sir, I'm just about to leave."

"No, you can't leave," the officer says in his French voice.

Thomas took in a deep breath. The racial tension has now spread to overseas. A black man can't get any peace. "Officer is there a problem," Thomas asked looking at the officer directly in his eyes. Thomas is always harassed by the police. But he knows he has to keep his cool because he's working for Pastor Daniel now.

The officer places his hands on his waist, holding his belt. The officer looks like a toy cop that Thomas used to play with when he was a little boy. He is dressed in a dark blue shirt, matching pants and hat. You can only can tell he is a police officer by seeing a large symbol on the shirt and hat. The officer has the same belt as the American cops, the flashlights, handcuffs, gun, etc. And to Thomas they appear to have the same attitude toward black men.

"Yes, you're sitting here in front of the greatest structures in the world, mad at the world, cursing and shouting at a man," he replies in his French voice.

Thomas laugh, breathing a sigh of relief. "I apologize for the commotion officer. I'm just a little stressed that's all."

"You Americans stress too much. What can possibly be stressing you?"

"A female," Thomas says looking at the French officer.

"Ah, a mademoiselle, they can make any man in love emotional, do you love her?" The French officer walks from behind the bench and stands in front of Thomas.

"Yeah, I love her. I thought she loved me."

"How do you know she doesn't love you?"

Thomas isn't about to tell a complete stranger that she cheated on him, especially with another girl. "I don't know. Maybe she still does."

"If you love her then fight for her. I don't think you should give up that easily. And if things don't work out, at least you tried."

Taking a deep breath, he thought about what the officer said and thought about if he should fight for her. The officer shakes Thomas hand and told him to have a good day and to cheer up before walking away. Thomas began to think about making things right with Jessica and being thankful for a lucrative job.

"Good morning France," the radio announcer said on the radio microphone. "We have a special guest with us this morning. This man of God is making waves all over the world, especially after what he did on church last Sunday."

Daniel chuckles a little at the opening. Daniel, Darryl, Marshal and Thomas arrived at the radio station about forty-five minutes ago. Nicole decided to sleep in while Daniel handle business. Getting up early for Darryl,

Marshal and Daniel maybe simple but it's a struggle for Thomas and Nicole. He's still jet lag from yesterday. Thomas wish he can sleep longer too like Nicole, but duty calls.

"Pastor Daniel Sanders is with us ladies and gentlemen."

The engineer plays applause and cheering sounds for the background effect. This isn't Daniel's first time at a radio station but every time he enters a studio it feels like the first time. It's those first time jitters. You never know what questions can be asked.

"Thank you for having me here. It's great to see the other side of the ocean in this capacity."

"I know you come to France leisurely with the First Lady, so this is new for you. As the number one gospel radio show here in the UK, we had to have to you here. We know how renown you're becoming in the US. I'm glad you decided to be here given such a short notice."

"Well you know I had to change my schedule," Daniel jokes, "But I didn't want to turn down this opportunity."

"So, besides doing this radio show, I hear that you will be ministering here in the UK?"

"Yes, I'll be ministering at Bishop Paul Myers church."

"Oh Yes! Yes! He is a powerful man of God. I'm a member at his church."

"Really, so I'll see you this evening?"

"Most definitely, especially since you're turning into Pastor Oprah. Can we expect some giveaways tonight?"

Ever since Daniel did the extraordinary reverse tithe and offering, people have been calling him Pastor Oprah. Thomas is sitting back with a smile on his face remembering the blessings first hand last Sunday.

Daniel laughs, "I can't say no or yes. We have to see where the Spirit of God leads me. I've heard about my new name, Pastor Oprah. Trust me, I'm not Oprah. I wish I had Oprah's money. I just followed the direction God gave me at that very moment. My wife had no idea I was going to do that, nor did the elders, my team or even myself. When I walked onto the pulpit, I just heard the voice of God… The Spirit was so high that day. To experience the move of God like that was so intimate." Daniel is now laying it on extra thick.

"I know you're glad you had the funds to back it up. Weren't you worried about not meeting the expectation?" The radio personality is beginning to reel him in.

"Sometimes God will ask you to do the unexpected. That was the message on Sunday."

"I'm all for the blessings that occurred last Sunday. As a believer, I know that God will require us to do the unimaginable but there are quite a few people who question your lifestyle and how you gave away money on Sunday. They are saying that you are pocketing money from the church to support your lifestyle and how it is, that a pastor of a church can just *give away* money so freely?"

"Well first," Daniel says pausing for a moment after getting caught off guard with the question, "Let me just say this. I'm doing this ministry full-time. My congregation tithe and give offering. The tithes belong to God, which goes to the house of God, the church. Whatever the church needs, it comes from the tithes. With the tithes, we take care of the house and the offerings is given to me. But I have people on payroll. So no, I don't get it all," he says.

"Your congregation must really take care of you then," the radio personality said, "You have quite a lifestyle and I see that you brought three full time bodyguards with you," he continued pointing at Darryl, Marshal and Thomas.

Thomas chuckles and shakes his head no.

"Oh, you're not a bodyguard," the radio personality asked.

"No, no, a little skinny guy like me can't be a bodyguard compared to these two guys," Thomas responds still laughing a little.

"No, his name is Thomas," Daniel interjects, "I was led to bless this brother and he's actually one of the ministers at Abundant Overflow. I'm training to lead one day. I recently just put him on my team. He has a testimony similar to my story. He's a great guy. And those two," he says pointing to Marshal and Darryl, "They're my bodyguards. I've known them all my life. I trust them with everything. They live with me and my family. In the city I grew up in, we would always say if I make it, then you make it."

"And you kept your word Pastor Daniel. I heard about the great things you've done in your community back home. I heard that after you bought a used dealership, you sold it to a small business owner under market value."

"The more you give, the more you get back. So, the people who are talking about my lavish lifestyle, must not give as much as they should. The Bible talks about prosperity, being prosperous is what God wants for his people. You know it's funny, you have celebrities living in mansions, owning private planes, driving three or four expensive luxury cars, traveling all over the world promoting their brand, and people never question that. But as soon as a pastor of a church buys a beautiful home, drive an expensive car, fly first class, dress in designer suits and everything else, people want to talk. I love what I do just like a celebrity. I love preaching and that's what I do. I'm not here to make people happy. Sorry, but that's not my job." Daniel had to stop himself because his emotions was getting the best of him and he needed to regress.

"Well, with that being said, we're going to take a break."

The on-air light went off and Daniel took a deep breath.

"Are you're good," the radio personality asked Daniel as he looks at him intently.

"I'm great. I hope I'm bringing in listeners."

"Oh I believe so. Simply off the record, how do you support your lifestyle? Honestly," he whispers, "I mean I know the game," he continued in a hush voice.

Daniel leans forward and whispers, "If you think that this is a game then this interview is done. Spreading God's Word isn't a game." He sat back in the chair not taking his eyes off him. Daniel is very cautious about people who try to catch him out there. He knows the radio host is trying to trap him. Just because the on-air light went off, doesn't mean they aren't still recording. Daniel also didn't trust or know this guy. The less people know what really goes on in the ministry, the better. The lifestyle him and his family grew accustomed to can easily disappear which is why they always save money and created a separate account for Simone. Simone has a nice couple hundred thousand dollars saved in her account. Daniel and Nicole wanted to make sure Simone will be set for life. She doesn't have to worry about college tuition, buying a home, car, or struggling to take care of herself... nothing. She'll be the only black doctor without loans. Her paycheck will go directly to her and she can do what she wants with her money. As for him and Nicole, they have money to sustain them for about three years, but that's not enough. Daniel wants to have enough money to sustain them through retirement.

Daniel finished the interview within the hour. When the radio host said to him, "Hope to see you again on the show," Daniel just chuckled, shook his hand and said, "We'll see."

"What was that all about at the radio station," Marshal asked Daniel while they were eating lunch.

"Nothing, he tried to catch me slipping but I flipped it on him," Daniel replied.

"What do you mean, you flipped it back on him? I thought the interview went well," Thomas said.

"It went as expected. One thing you will learn Thomas, is that people are always out to get us."

"We call them haters," Darryl blurts out. Daniel and Marshal began laughing.

"Preachers have to make money too. We have families to support, do you agree," Daniel asked Thomas.

"I most definitely agree. How else are you supposed to earn a living?" Thomas agree eating a piece of steak.

"Exactly…it's a living…a prosperous living that you are *now* enjoying. You reap the benefits. What people don't understand also, is that church is a business."

"A business," Thomas asked curiously.

"There's a business side to this ministry thing. But you'll learn about that some other time." Daniel doesn't want to tell Thomas too much so soon. In time, Daniel will find out if Thomas can handle the reality of the church.

"You have me curious."

"I like your curiosity."

Thomas continues to eat his steak excited to learn more about the business side of church. This is the lifestyle he can get used to. Daniel, Darryl and Marshall looks at each other and smile.

Chapter 6

Matthew 6:24 (MSG)

> "You can't worship two gods at once. Loving one god, you'll end up hating the other. Adoration of one feeds contempt for the other. You can't worship God and Money both."

TWO MONTHS LATER....

It's been two months since Daniel made Thomas part of his team. During that time, Thomas moved out of the motel and is now living in a nice three-bedroom Brownstone townhouse in the suburbs that he is renting. He was also able to lease a new car. Thomas made his move quietly. He hasn't seen Jessica and have been ignoring her calls. There were times he wanted to answer her calls, but every time he thought about doing so, he remembered how much she hurt him. He doesn't know what to say to Jessica or even know how to start the conversation. No matter how much he avoids her calls, he knows that they have to talk. It also helps that Daniel has been keeping Thomas quite busy. He has time for himself after Sunday's services, if Daniel isn't preaching somewhere, and all day on Monday. But all the other days are non-stop meetings, conventions, interviews, photo shoots for magazines, and services. Thomas didn't realize how busy he was going to be. It's a good thing that he's single because he wouldn't know how to divide his time. But when Daniel gave Thomas his first paycheck, Thomas was beyond ecstatic. He never had a paycheck as much as this. He couldn't help but stare at the $2535 check that he will be getting every two weeks. Daniel want to make sure Thomas stay put and not leave the church. He knew what can keep a blind person from the truth…money. Daniel has plans, big plans and he wants Thomas to be a part of it. Daniel knew Thomas can possibly be the one to help branch out from under Bishop Wilkens and start new ministries within the church. He knows that Thomas is familiar with the street life and sometimes a church can use a little edge to draw more people into the four walls.

Daniel is sitting in his office looking over some comments and articles that was written about some interviews he's done. A couple of articles are questioning the *behind the pulpit* role that many pastors has. Daniel's lifestyle has caused quite a few people to raise their eyebrows. Many people said that he made valid points when he compared celebrities to pastors. It made sense to them. Most people who commented on the articles are all for Pastor Daniel and what he's doing in the church. Daniel never thought he would be trending in the virtual world. Two days after the radio interview in France, he was once again trending on all social media, which caused his schedule to become very full and hectic. Everyone wanted to talk to Daniel, especially Bishop Wilkens which is the cause for an important meeting that Bishop requested. The Bishop never asked for a meeting with Daniel before. They've done dinners, they preached at each other churches, they go on double dates with their wives, but never had meetings. Whatever they had to talk about, they did it over dinners or a simple phone call. So, Daniel knew that this had to be serious. The Bishop never said anything to Daniel about the interviews he's been doing, but Daniel has a gut feeling that the meeting has *everything* to do with the that faithful Sunday that happened two months ago. Daniel played out all the interviews in his mind. He listened to the interviews online a couple of times and there's nothing that was said to alarm the Bishop.

Thomas walks into the office with the lunch Daniel asked him pick up for him.

"They didn't have the red wine vinaigrette dressing so I told them to put Italian dressing on the side."

Thomas saw Daniel intently looking at his computer screen. He's standing there waiting for Daniel to say something but no response. "Pastor Daniel," Thomas blurt out.

"Yes," Daniel jolts back into the reality, "Thanks, thanks Thomas. You can put the salad on the table," he continues as his voice drift off.

"Are you okay," Thomas asks putting the salad on the table.

"Oh yeah, I'm fine. I'm just working on Sunday's sermon that's all," he answered lying. His mind is racing about what the Bishop wants to discuss with Daniel. Daniel doesn't need anything that will block the major plans that he has brewing.

"What about tomorrow's Bible Study? Did Sister May contact the pastor from the city? I tried calling him but he never returned the call."

"Actually, I told her not to contact him," he says now looking up from his computer, "I have someone else in mind." Daniel stared at Thomas without blinking hoping he would get the idea.

"Who do you have in mind?"

"Who do you think I have in mind," Daniel respond, raising an eyebrow.

Thomas began laughing, "You can't be serious? You want *me* to do Bible Study tomorrow?"

"Yeah, why not? I heard your sermonette when you were in the ministry school. I think you can do it. You're a certified minister. It's been awhile since you did a sermon."

Thomas began to calm his laughter, "You're serious aren't you?"

"Yes, I'm very serious. It's time for you to get your feet wet. So go home, tell Jessica that you'll be doing your first mini sermon at Bible Study. I'm sure she'll want to be there and you can introduce her to us. It's been two months now; I'm surprise you haven't brought her at the church yet."

Thomas didn't tell Daniel about the break-up between him and Jessica. After returning from overseas, he's been too busy to give her much thought. And that's the way he likes it.

"Pastor Daniel, I don't think I'm ready. I mean, everything is going too fast for me. I haven't even read the Bible in its entirety yet."

"And you will…it takes time to read the Bible. Trust me, if I felt you wasn't equipped for this position I would have never hired you. Besides, we'll be taking up an offering for you."

"For real," Thomas says. He is now excited. Thomas is ready to make some extra cash. "Why?"

"Let's put it like this. You preach, you get paid. It's that simple. If you minister to people in any platform either preaching, singing, dancing, or whatever, you get paid."

"How much do I get paid," Thomas asks sounding intrigued.

"That depends on you. If you can get the people shouting and dancing, they will open their wallets."

Thomas is taken aback, *open their wallets*, he thought. Thomas is thinking that what Daniel had just said, sounds like a hustle.

"Did I catch you off guard by saying that," Daniel asked. Daniel knows what Thomas is thinking because he was in the same position and mind frame, when he came to his realization about the Bishop.

"Yeah," Thomas chuckles, "A little, but I feel where you are coming from."

"You do want this Thomas, don't you?"

"Most definitely."

"Then you need to make that step tomorrow."

Thomas is standing there smiling and nodding his head. The thought of making some extra cash tomorrow is helping him to comply to the sermon.

"Let's meet here in my office before Bible Study. I can go into a little more detail about what I see you doing. Until then, go get ready for tomorrow night."

It isn't an hour after Daniel has told Thomas that he wants him to minister at Bible Study. As Daniel finish his lunch, he is looking at the increase membership at his church, Abundant Overflow Ministries. After the giving away of money during offering, people has been flocking to the church for nightly services and attending every Sunday service. The church has been taking in over a hundred thousand dollars easily every Sunday. He's contemplating on a new move but wants to wait to see why the Bishop wants to meet with him first. Daniel has big plans for his ministry. There are different avenues of the church business that he can dip his hands into. Just the thought of what he has in mind will take being the Overseer of his own church to a whole new level.

"Pastor Daniel, Bishop Wilkens is here to see you," his secretary says on the intercom.

"You can send him in," he replies.

Daniel palms beginning to sweat a little. Any other time they meet he's relaxed, but this isn't the usual hangout, hi and bye. This is a sit down meeting that Bishop Wilkens *insisted* that they have.

"Hey Daniel, how are you," Bishop Wilkens belts out as he walks into the office.

"I'm well. I have nothing to complain too much about."

The two gentlemen firmly shake hands. Daniel closes and the lock the door, leaving them uninterrupted.

Bishop has on a black suit by a highly profile Italian designer. Daniel always admire his expensive taste in clothing. But that isn't Daniel's thing. He isn't into the flashy expensive clothes. That is always the Bishops territory. Bishop Wilkens is would wear six thousand dollar shoes, three hundred dollar belts, twenty thousand dollar suits with gold or titanium cufflinks.

Bishop sat on the sofa and crosses his legs, manly style. No matter who you are, whenever you are in the Bishop's presence, he doesn't make you feel insignificant, but makes you aware that he's the one in charge. Daniel wants to have that personality but it was never in him to take the lead in the manner Bishop does it. Sometimes the Bishop can be quite pushy. Daniel takes a seat in the single plush arm chair to the left of Bishop. He sat back ready to know why he called for this special meeting.

"How are things going with your family? I know you're still coming to my Bar B Q next week," Bishop asked breaking the awkward silence.

"Everything is well. You know we won't miss your annual Bar B Q. As long as your First Lady is making her potato salad, I'm there."

Bishop Wilkens has the largest Bar B Q every year at his mansion. His place sits on five acres of land. If you get the private invite you're considered most favorable amongst his friends. Nearly three hundred people show up to his annual Bar B Q.

"You know, I'm not here for small talk. We could have done that over food or on the phone," Bishop says, "I'm here because I want to know what were you thinking about two months ago when you decided to give out money in church? I've been busy traveling so I couldn't come see you sooner, and this is a conversation that must be had face to face."

"Bishop, I can't tell you what I was thinking because I had no intentions on doing that. I just followed the Holy Spirit."

Bishop Wilkens cuts his eyes at Daniel with raised eyebrows, "You're not on a radio show doing an interview or talking to one of the elders at the church. You're talking to me," he says pointing at his chest. Bishop leans forward, still looking at Daniel, "So what is it going to be, the truth or the cover story."

Daniel chuckles taking a deep sigh. He should know not to pull one over on Bishop.

"Okay," Daniel says raising his hands, giving in, "I wanted to invest in the church."

"Invest?"

"Yes, invest, let me explain, when a business wants to make a profit they have to invest in their product. If a church wants to bring in more money, the church must invest in the members."

"I'm not following you."

"Since I've done the *unthinkable*, membership has tripled. For the month alone the church has brought in near five hundred thousand dollars in just tithes and offering."

The Bishop jolt up in excitement, "Are you serious?"

"I'm very serious. Now that I increased the membership, I want to give money away again, only this time it'll be on a much lower scale, of course."

"Of course, you don't want to go bankrupt," the Bishop says agreeing with him.

"Exactly, so it'll be at a Bible Study or a workshop the church has or just randomly putting money in envelopes and mailing it to people. That will bring even more people into the church."

Daniel stands up and began walking as he continue to tell Bishop his plan, "More people, means more money, more money means more investing, the more I invest the more people will come and the cycle continues. Investing in people mean jobs. I am looking to build a strip mall on the busiest strip in the state. In the strip mall, there will be numerous of businesses, a beauty salon, barber shop, nail salon, a couple of clothing stores, a coffee shop, a pet store that has a daycare for dogs and cats, which was Nicole's idea, and maybe two or three restaurants. I'm talking big. I'm looking to expand. And the employees would be our members who are unemployed. After we hire them, then we can extend open positions to the public. Bishop this is going to be big."

Daniel has been thinking long and hard about expanding. Just like he used the car dealership, Al let him buy from him as a stepping block, he's using his ministry as a stepping block into investing in his and his family's secured future. He never seen himself continuing on in the ministry for the rest of his life. Daniel laughs at the seventy plus year old preachers who are still going around preaching and still looking broker than when they started. Then you have some who are financially secured but they are too comfortable to expand their horizon. Daniel wants more.

Bishop Wilkens is very intrigued by Daniel's ambition. He never thought on a scale as Daniel. Looking and listening to Daniel, makes him realize that Daniel was the perfect follower he had chosen years ago. He was always leery of those coming to him about starting their own ministry, but Daniel was different. Daniel wanted more and would be willing to do anything to get more. Daniel is in it for the money just like he is and with this new business venture that Daniel is looking to do, they are bound to make more money.

"I like it," Bishop said, "I love the idea. Have you found the land?"

"Yes, I'll be meeting someone in the next couple of days at the site." Before Bishop can ask the next question, Daniel bluntly ask, "Do you want in? Do you want to be partners?" This is Daniel's plan and he isn't trying to have the Bishop to take the lead on this one.

Bishop want to be in on this grand venture. Without hesitation he says, "Yes, I would love to be in the deal. So, this is simple. We split the profit fifty-fifty."

"Ah no," Daniel said as he chuckles, "My friends Darryl and Marshal are in on the investment too."

"You can't be serious," Bishop exclaims. He stands up to stand in front of Daniel. "Sure, hire them as your bodyguards and allow them to reap the benefits of being able to live lavishly like we do, but to have them invest in something of this magnitude is absurd. They are not equipped to do this kind of business. They don't know anything about investment. You need to X them out of the equation!"

Daniel takes a step closer to Bishop. One thing Daniel knows is that Bishop likes to be in control but he isn't intimidated by him. "They're my friends. Hell, they're family. If they want to invest, they can. I support them in any decision they make. I don't allow anyone to my punk my family. And I'm definitely not going to have you put your mouth on them. My lawyers already drew up two papers. One is with the four of us, me, Marshal, Darryl and you, splitting the profits twenty-five percent and there is another with just me, Marshal, and Darryl splitting the profits thirty-three percent. Now if I want, I can easily take sixty-five percent and split the rest with whomever invest with me but I'm not that greedy. It's about being smart.

"Are you forgetting who you're talking to? *I* made you. *I* put the first thousands of dollars in your pockets by allowing you to preach at *my* church when you were just a little run down used cars salesman. *I* placed you here in this church that *I* built. *I* got you to where you are today. So don't think you can sit up here and start commanding *me*."

"Bishop, no one is commanding you. But, I am giving you an option. Either you can take it or you can walk. No matter what you do, I'm moving on with or without you."

Bishop didn't budge. He can't believe what is coming out of Daniel's mouth. He knew he had it in him to become more than just the usual preacher which is why he can't be too mad at him. But at the same time, he must remember who put him in the position so he can do what he's about to do now. Bishop Wilkens continued to stand in silence. This is difficult for him. He's usually in charge. He usually has his hands in everything, but maybe this is his time to step back. Daniel is becoming very powerful and Bishop doesn't like it. In the five short years Daniel has been preaching, he is gaining more notoriety and fame faster than him. "I need some time to think about this. I think the business will require too much of my time."

"Listen Bishop," Daniel says calmly, "I really do appreciate everything that you've done for me. I really do. You taught me the hustle to this church business, which is why you have to trust the people I have close to me."

"Ump," Bishop grunt walking away, "What about this guy Thomas you have on payroll now? I hear he's your armor bearer in training."

"Yes, I'm training him. Actually, I'm going to allow him to minister at Bible Study tomorrow night. You should come check him out."

"I won't be able to be here tomorrow night but does he have it in him to be in the ministry? Did you check his credentials?"

"He's a good guy. He was timid, a little unsure but after getting a dip into what this life is like, I think I'll win him over by tomorrow night." The less Daniel tells the Bishop, the better. Daniel is beginning to feel a little uneasy about the Bishop now that he basically turned down the offer to the mini mall.

Bishop nod his head in agreement. "Just keep an eye on him. Remember, you can't trust everybody."

Thomas is a nervous wreck. He has nowhere to start. He doesn't know what to do his first large public sermon on in Bible Study. At Abundant Overflow, their Bible Study is like a normal Sunday service at a regular normal size church. There has been more people attending Bible Study services. Thomas knows it has everything to do with the random monetary blessing Daniel did about two months ago. He has no power or money to pull something like that. There's only one person that can help calm his nerves… Jessica. She is all he can think about. She was the one he spoke to whenever his mind was crowded. Which is why he texted her asking her to meet him at the Barcode Lounge around seven this evening. She never replied to the text, but Thomas still showed up at the lounge, sitting in the back at a table for two. The lounge is filled with the after work crowd, mingling, laughing and dancing their stress away. There's a live band playing a nice R&B jazz compilation. Thomas always wished he knew how to play an instrument, especially the saxophone. The saxophone player has a certain appeal to him. As the saxophonist is playing, there are about three women standing in front of him allowing his music to rapture them.

Thomas takes a sip of beer, laughing a little as he sees the women try to squeeze in front of the musician. To have that kind of attention would be nice, Thomas thought to himself.

He looks at his watch and see that it is fifteen minutes after seven. He doesn't have time to wait any longer. He has a service to prepare for. He chugs the rest of his beer, let out a low but strong belch and proceeds to get up. He was hoping to see Jessica. He misses her. He hasn't seen or spoken to her since he left her apartment. She would call him but either he would ignore her calls or she would have the phone ring twice or three times then hang up.

As Thomas began walking away from the table, he sees Jessica walking inside the lounge. It is taking all of him to not run to her and kiss her passionately. She is as beautiful as she was when he first met her. The only thing stopping him is the vivid image of her in bed with her friend. She walks slowly but with anticipation toward Thomas. Thomas doesn't know what to expect out of this conversation but seeing her is good enough.

"Hi Thomas," she spoke rushed, "I apologize for being late. I had a meeting that ran over time. I should have called you."

He smiles and says, "No problem, we had a table toward the back. It should still be available."

He turns around to walk back to the table as Jessica follows behind him. She can't help but notice a change in Thomas. He appears to be more in shape, his wardrobe is more fashionable, but there's something else that has changed. Jessica is nervous about talking to Thomas. She's been nervous since she received his text message asking to meet here. She has so much to say, but she's the one that screwed up because she decided to listen to others.

Thomas pulls out a seat for Jessica and took a seat in front of her at the table.

"How's your day," Thomas asked trying to get comfortable. He is nervous like Jessica.

"It was a crazy day. I'm just glad it's over…How is the new job coming along?"

"It's going great. As you know, I went with Pastor Daniel to Paris two months ago," Thomas says bragging. He wants Jessica to know that he is doing fine without her. Although, a smidge of his emotions feels like he will do better with her.

"It must have been quite a trip."

"It was nice. I took a couple of pictures of the sites." Thomas takes out his phone to show her the pictures. Jessica look at the pictures with a hint of envy as she swipes through the pictures. She wonders if he met someone there or if he is now talking to someone else late at night. It's been two months since they last spoke and seen each other. She wouldn't be surprised if he talking to someone else. She doesn't want her thoughts to get the best of her. She hands Thomas his phone. "Nice picture Thomas…So why did you want to meet with me?"

"I want to see how you're doing, you know. And I think it's time for us to talk."

Jessica takes a deep breath, closing her eyes. She knows no matter what she tells him, the relationship is over. She motions for the waitress so she can order something to ease her nerves.

"Can I have a Cosmo?"

"Sure, did you want anything," the waitress asked Thomas.

"No, I'm good." Thomas doesn't want to get a second beer. He has to focus tonight for tomorrow's Bible Study.

"Pastor Daniel wants me to preach at Bible Study tomorrow night."

"I didn't know you wanted to be a preacher. I mean, I know you took classes at the church but you've never came across as the preaching type."

"I never did. I mean, I never gave it a thought. Sure I'm certified minister because I went to the classes but it was just something for me to do. I'm nervous out of my mind."

"Why is he having you preach tomorrow? You just got hired about two months ago. You've just started, don't you think it's too soon?"

"He thinks I'm ready for it. I had little sermons here and there when I was in class but nothing to this magnitude."

"Well, are you ready for a platform like that?"

"I wouldn't know until tomorrow. Besides, I'm supposed to be getting paid to preach tomorrow night."

"Paid?"

"Yeah that's what Pastor Daniel told me. I have to meet with him before the service."

"What's your topic?"

Thomas shrugs his shoulders, "I don't know, hopefully something will come to me tonight."

Jessica touches his hand and said, "You'll do just fine. I know you will."

Thomas asked the question, "Why?"

Anyone's normal response would be, why what? But Jessica know Thomas want answers.

"Thomas, let me first tell you that I didn't mean to hurt you," she says moving her hand off his. "I really didn't mean to."

He leans back in his seat looking at her in disbelief. *She meant to hurt me*, he thought to himself. *Why else would she cheat on me in our bed?*

"I had no intentions of doing that." Jessica took a deep breath breathe before continuing, "I mind as well tell you….. It was actually it was planned."

"Planned," Thomas repeated the word.

"Yeah…My friends and family kept talking in my ear about me leaving you because they felt as though you were freeloading off me. Every day it was something. Every day someone had something to say. When you decided not to apply to some stores at the mall or other retail stores, just because they wouldn't hire you as a manager, I began to believe them."

"Jessica, you knew I didn't want to settle for just any job or be demoted to a lower position."

"I know that but it appeared that you just gave up. But, I didn't want to leave you. I couldn't leave you, no matter how hard I tried to walk away…So, I came up with a plan for you to leave me instead."

The waitress came back in time for Jessica to drink her alcohol.

"I'm sorry Miss, can you please bring me two shots of vodka," Thomas asked the waitress.

The waitress gave a look to Thomas and Jessica knowing that they must be having a heavy conversation with shots of vodka being brought to the table. She walks away to get the numbing shots.

"So, you decided to hurt me the worst way possible just so I can leave you? You decided to cheat on me."

"I'm not happy with the decision. I assume being with a woman would be easier.

"Are you serious! Why couldn't you just be woman enough to talk to me," Thomas says raising his voice.

People around them are too caught up in their own conversations, drinks and music to even care about a regular spat between a couple. But Jessica is still embarrassed, looking around, wondering if anyone is watching them.

"Can you keep your voice down?"

"You've just told me that you've planned cheating on me, and you want me to keep my voice down! How else do you think I'm supposed to react?"

She can't say a word. She knew she was wrong. She knows what she did is unforgivable.

"I can't blame you for reacting like this. You have every reason to be upset. All I can say is…I'm really sorry, I really am. If I can take back what I did, I would. I'm sorry Thomas."

Jessica quickly gets up to leave. "I hope all goes well for you tomorrow night." She quickly walks away with tears in her eyes.

Thomas is sitting there watching Jessica disappear in the crowd. He just sat back feeling more furious than ever. He can't believe Jessica would do something as low as to purposely cheat on him.

"Here are your vodkas," the waitress said setting the two shots on the table.

"Don't go," Thomas says to the waitress. He takes both shots to the head, letting the alcohol burn his chest. He reaches for his wallet to take out a fifty-dollar bill.

"Keep the change," he says as he stands up to walk out the lounge.

"Hey big guy, are you ready for this," Marshal said playfully punching Thomas on the shoulder.

His punch is very hard. Thomas can feel the sting, but doesn't want to show it.

"Yeah, I'm ready. Nervous but ready."

"You should be nervous. You're about to stand in front of hundreds of people to preach."

"Not to mention our online viewers," Darryl added.

Thomas is already sweating on the inside. He doesn't need to be reminded of the additional viewers.

"Leave Thomas alone," Daniel says, "Go outside for a moment. I need to talk to Thomas."

"Be ready in ten minutes. They already started Praise and Worship."

Marshal and Darryl walks out of Daniel's office still joking around.

"They love to joke around. Don't let them get to you."

"Pastor Daniel, I have to be honest with you. I don't know if I'm ready to do this. I had a rough night. I'm all over the place with my notes. I haven't even read the whole Bible like I said; I don't even know where to start."

"Relax, relax…Start here," Daniel says walking over to pour something in a glass. "Here, it'll help take the edge off," as he hands him a glass.

Thomas drank the dark brown liquor. He lost his breath. He never had anything strong like that before.

"What was that," Thomas asked out of breath.

"Just a little something to relax you."

Daniel sat down next to Thomas. "I want to talk to you before service because I want you to learn something about the church business."

Thomas nods his head indicating that he is listening but still suffering from the toxic drink.

"As you know, church is a business. Everything is tax-free dollars. Of course, we have to keep track of everything because we still have to answer to some people but to run a business, you have to make money. Everyone who gets behind the pulpit make money. That's our livelihood. That's what support us. Pastors make money, but Bishops make more than Pastors and Apostles and Prophets make more than Bishops. I assumed you wanted to preach after attending the ministry school. And I have to say I like your style of preaching. You can reach the people too."

"To be honest Pastor Daniel, I only went to the school to do something besides sit around. I got certified in the process but I didn't think about preaching to make money," Thomas lied.

"Okay, well, I guess I was wrong. I'll get someone else to take your place. I was looking to hire a pastor for a new church I will be building. I can still use you on my team, if you still want to be part of it."

"Of course, I would."

"That's good, that's good. Only thing is you can't participate in the overseas and across the country traveling. I would need to train someone else to prepare them for this kind of lifestyle. I hope you understand."

Daniel always has a back-up. But he is hoping that Thomas will take the assignment. Thomas is feeling a little frustrated because he wants to enjoy the luxury that he's enjoying now. "I guess you have to do what's best," Thomas said.

"But I hope you're still preaching tonight. We already have your name of the bulletin. People are expecting to hear from you."

"Yeah, I can still preach tonight, Pastor Daniel.

"Great, then I can give you this." Daniel reach for the white envelope on the table and hand it over to Thomas. Thomas opens the envelope to see a check with his name on it. His mouth drops open when he sees a check for three thousand dollars for him.

"Three grand just to preach," Thomas exclaimed.

"Yes," Daniel laughs, "Because we are a megachurch, we pay our guest speakers. You get paid to speak."

"Three thousand is a lot for a first timer. I'm not complaining though."

Daniel continue to laugh, "I know but can you imagine when we have those famous Bishops that come preach. We're talking fifteen or twenty thousand dollars."

"Are you serious?" Thomas is surprised. Now he knows why some preachers drive in expensive cars and live in the beautiful houses.

"It's all about business, that's all," Daniel said.

"So, winning souls is a business," Thomas says looking at the check,

"Exactly." Daniel has a sly smile on his face.

Thomas is beginning to have second thoughts now. If this is a way to make legit fast cash, then maybe he can keep up with the undetected lie.

"Let the church say amen," Daniel said as he walks onto the pulpit.

"Amen," his congregation shouts.

"As you know, I'm not preaching tonight but our very own Minister Thomas Butler will be preaching. Many of you have seen him working alongside with me in the last two months. He has graduated from our ministry school. He tells me that he went to the school because he wanted to do something. What he didn't know was that God was up to something through him."

"Amen Pastor." The congregation shouted.

"So, God placed it in my heart to pour into this young man. And tonight we are ready to hear a Word from the Lord. Please stand as we greet our very own Minister Thomas Butler."

Everyone began to stand up as Thomas took his place on the pulpit. He shakes Daniel's hand and gives him a hug. Thomas has no idea what to say but now isn't the time to panic. Daniel walks off the pulpit to stand next to Nicole. He held her hand and winks at her. Thomas is standing in front of hundreds of people. He sees so many people looking at him clapping and smiling. Some are standing just looking at him knowing he is a nervous wreck. He sees Darryl and Marshal holding up tablets reminding him that people are watching online too. He put his head down to giggle a little. They are helping him make light of the situation.

"Please be seated," he says in the microphone. As everyone sat down, he sees one person still standing waiting to make eye contact. Jessica is here. She is the last to sit. Thomas cannot take his eyes off her. After last night he thought he wouldn't speak nor see her again for a while. The congregation grew quiet as they are waiting for Thomas to begin. Daniel clears his throat to get Thomas attention. Daniel is praying that Thomas wouldn't renege on the preaching assignment.

"What's wrong with him," Nicole whispers in Daniel's ear.

Daniel is too tense to respond. His eyes never left Thomas. He is praying that Thomas say something and stand on the pulpit looking like a fool. Daniel is praying that he didn't push Thomas off the cliff too fast.

"I'm sorry everyone," Thomas finally spoke, "I was caught off guard by a simple phrase that I'm hearing." Thomas paused... "I was going to talk about being Christ-like but I am reminded of this simple phrase, unconditional love," he says looking at Jessica. "Unconditional love means to love without a condition or a boundary. It means no matter what you do, you will still be loved. That's how Christ loved us."

People begin to say amen and hallelujahs. Thomas continued, "We on the other hand love on conditions. I will love you only if you do this for me or for the rest of our lives. I will love you only if you don't hurt me."

Jessica lowers her teary eyes knowing that Thomas is referring to her hurting him. This is one of the many reasons why she doesn't like to attend church. The pastors can make you see yourself, the true person that you really are. But for Thomas to use his hurt as an example is really hitting home.

"But recently someone has shown me how to love unconditionally."

Jessica slowly lifts her head, smiling a little, hoping that they can give their relationship another shot. She's not too sure about this whole preaching game but she'll find out his motives.

"The first person or people to teach us unconditional love is our parents. And sometimes their love turns conditional. But to love unconditional like Christ means to love all of them, all of their faults and flaws. It's hard to do but it's something we have to aim for to be Christ-like."

At that moment, Thomas realize that his unconditional love speech was the introduction to his lesson being Christ-like and a response to Jessica from last night that he will always love her. He's not sure if things will work out between him and her but he is willing to work things out. But first he has to get through his first sermon.

Chapter 7

2 Timothy 4: 3 - 4 (MSG)

"You're going to find that there will be times when people will have no stomach for solid teaching, but will fill up on spiritual junk food- catchy opinions that tickle their fancy. They'll turn their backs on truth and chase mirages."

"The people are still talking about your Bible Study from Wednesday night, Thomas," Nicole said to him. Nicole, Daniel, Thomas, Darryl and Marshal are at a seafood restaurant in the city. It has been a couple of days since Bible Study and Thomas has been on a high ever since then. Especially when he saw Jessica there. He never expected for her to come to the church to hear him speak for the first time. It was an utter surprise to him. Seeing Jessica at Bible Study helped Thomas to relax. He began to loosen up and enjoy what he was doing. He was showing off for her, feeling extra confident in himself. It helped that the congregation loved it too. He had people standing on their feet and waving their hands like the way the old time church people did back in the day. Not only did Jessica surprised him, but he was caught off guard by the offering Daniel had the congregation take up for him. When Thomas was finished preaching, Daniel walked on the pulpit and told the congregation that he wanted to take an offering up for Thomas and he would lead by putting a hundred dollars in the basket. Thomas was jumping for joy on the inside. He was getting extra cash on top of the three thousand that he received to preach. In offering, Thomas collected close to fifteen hundred dollars. He went home with a little over four thousand dollars in his pocket. He never in his life had that much money. The next morning, he wasted no time depositing the money into his bank account. He put half of it into his savings and the other half into his checking account. Thomas is no dummy. He now knows that he has to save for a raining day. After being unemployed for almost two years, having saved emergency money is on the top of his list.

"You had me worried at first," Daniel said to Thomas, "For a moment, I thought you weren't going to preach. You were standing on the pulpit quiet for a long time."

"I was caught off guard for a moment."

"Yeah, we saw that black Barbie you were gazing at," Marshal added pointing at him and Darryl.

Thomas started laughing. He was caught staring at Jessica. He is ready for the jokes. He knows Marshal and Darryl loves to joke around. He isn't going to hear the end of this.

"Was that Jessica," Daniel asked.

"Yes, that was Jessica," Thomas answers still smiling.

"Why didn't you invite her out for dinner with us? I would have loved to have met her," Nicole said.

"Jessica is usually busy so I didn't ask her to come out tonight. She's been working overtime since she's up for a promotion at work. I was surprised that she had time to come to Bible Study. Maybe you can meet her next time."

"I'm curious though, how did you get a girl like that," Marshal asked, "She seems like she's out of your league. From what I saw, she is a black beauty and appears to be a good girl. You are rough around the edges. She seems like the type that would be with some rich dude. I'm still baffled at Nicole being with Daniel."

Everyone started laughing at the table. Thomas get that question all the time. He loved the attention.

"You will never stop wondering will you," Daniel continues to laugh, "Thomas, Marshal has been envious of me ever since I started dating Nicole. It's something that he will never get over."

"Hell yeah," Darryl interjects, "She turned him down a week before you approached her."

"Seriously," Nicole interjects, "I'm sitting right here you know. Marshal never stood a chance with me or any other girl in high school."

"Whatever, I was just too much for you, but back to you Thomas," Marshal says facing Thomas, "What's good with you and that shorty?"

"Yeah, why are you keep hiding her," Darryl asked.

"I'm not hiding her. I told you that she's busy. I'm busy; we're just two busy people. I barely have time for myself. Not that I'm complaining about that," Thomas says holding his hand up in Daniel's direction, "I love what I do."

"Daniel, have you met her," Darryl asked.

"No, I haven't. Thomas doesn't talk about her." Daniel is curious as to why Thomas hasn't introduce Jessica to him and everybody else. But he knows that it's none of his business and he also knows that Thomas is using his busy schedule as an excuse. Whenever he's ready to introduce Jessica to the crew, he will.

Everyone knows that Thomas is dating Jessica but has never seen her before. He doesn't want to talk about her or bring her around because he doesn't know what the two of them are going to do with the relationship. After Bible Study, he texted Jessica thanking her for coming to hear him and asked her if she want to go out for dinner after church on Sunday just the two of them. She obliged and he told her that he will pick her up after service. So, Thomas has two more days to think about if he wants to really take Jessica back.

"You'll meet her one day, don't worry. And I'll make sure to keep her away from Marshal. Being that you want women, that you can never get or have."

Everyone began laughing. "Women who are unavailable have no strings attached. I'm not looking for a relationship or anything," Marshal says still laughing.

"Not all women," Nicole chimes in, "You better be careful Marshal."

"So, Daniel when are you going to have Thomas preach again? I must say, he was really good," Darryl asked.

"That depends on Thomas," Daniel said looking at Thomas.

Thomas hasn't told Daniel if he wants to do the ministry gig full-time. He has had a change of mind ever since Wednesday night. Bringing home that kind of money that is legit, is every person's dream. He would be a fool to turn that down. That was the main reason why he wanted to get involved in the ministry in the first place.

"I think I can get use to preaching every now and again just to get my feet wet before going full-time, *maybe*."

"I knew once you saw what you were going home with, it would change your mind," Daniel said as he clicks glasses with Thomas. "Remember, the Bible talks more about being prosperous. It's about time that you live it."

"And you're right," Thomas agreed, "As pastors, we're supposed to be an example. I would rather attend a church that is thriving and have a thriving pastor instead of listening to a pastor who is constantly struggling."

"You are going to meet a couple of struggling pastors *real* soon. I'm having a new church being built in the west side and some store front pastors don't like it."

"Why not? The people in the hood need to see a thriving church and pastor too. That's the problem. All they see is a broke down mentality, that's why the hood stay broke down. I'm from the west side and trust me, that's all that we've seen. That's why everybody comes to your church."

"The pastors feel threatened that's all. And they should feel threatened," Marshal added, "If they aren't doing anything, then they need to feel threatened! People get tired of seeing those broke down preachers preaching. They need to see that the Word actually works."

"Who do you have in mind to be the pastor at the new church," Nicole asked. Nicole knows who Daniel has in mind. It was a set-up for Thomas. They are slowly reeling him in.

Daniel cuts his eyes at Thomas discreetly. Daniel's plan was to train Thomas and to place him in the new church that he is building within a year.

"Oh no! You can't be serious," Thomas exclaims.

"I'm very serious. The church isn't going to be ready until next year. You'll be ready by then."

Thomas had no idea that Daniel wants him to pastor the new church. He just did his first of many sermons to come. He just started working with him two months ago. Things are just going too fast for Thomas. All he wants is the money, he wasn't trying to make this a full time career anytime soon. But Daniel has a vision and he sees Thomas being a part of it, even if Thomas doesn't see it himself.

"Why me? What about the other ministers at the church? What about Minister Perry? He runs the ministry school at the church. I think he is more qualified than I am."

"You're the one I'm close with. Besides, we can talk figures if money is an issue. I'll be the Overseer of the church, so you don't have to worry about too much. And when you are ready to fly solo or if you want to fly solo, the church can be all yours. And it's in your old neighborhood, I'm sure people will come to hear you preach."

"Thomas, I think you should go for it," says Nicole, "Isn't this what you want? Don't you want to be financially secured for life and have the best? I'm sure Jessica would be thrilled about the idea. I know I was thrilled about Daniel going into ministry. It's scary at first but you have us." Nicole flashes her dreamy eyes and bright smile. Just like any man, he can't resist. If that makes her happy, he can only imagine what Jessica will feel.

"I tell you this, I would be stupid to turn this down," Thomas says, "Enough talking, I'm down for whatever," says Thomas finally submitting, "If I would have known making money by preaching would be this easy, I would have done it sooner."

"The sooner, the better," Darryl said, "Get some of your boys to have your back too because you'll come across some crazy people."

"When will you announce this new church," Thomas asked.

"Maybe in a couple of months. We'll be on Ebony TV and another local syndicated channel," Daniel announced.

"When did this happen," Marshal asked astonished.

"I signed the contract last week and I got the green light this morning."

"That's right; my baby is over here doing big things," Nicole says hugging his waist, "He's giving the people exactly what they need. I have to tell you, everybody here at this table came out the slumps. This is what the people want to see."

"Amen," everyone said.

Thomas is ready to swim fast. Going back to where he was, was never designed for him. Prosperity is his ticket and he's with the right team to continue on that path.

Daniel is standing on a dirt full, grainy ground looking at acres of empty land that he, Marshal, and Darryl now owns. They signed the contract yesterday. Bishop Wilkens decided not to sign the contract because he didn't want Darryl and Marshal in on the lucrative deal. The real reason is because not only he didn't want them to be a part of this deal, but he wanted to spearhead this plan. He is jealous that Daniel had thought of something genius. Daniel is becoming a danger to Bishop Wilkens and the Bishop doesn't like it one bit. Although Daniel's church, Abundant Overflow, is in another state, Daniel's popularity is soaring faster than Bishop Wilkens. The membership at his church has increased almost surpassing Bishop Wilkens members. Daniel is making more moves and doing so much more than Bishop Wilkens. After Daniel became "Pastor Oprah" that Sunday, Bishop Wilkens had to pay him a visit. Daniel knew the Bishop was envious of him which is why he offer him a cut on the deal. See, when Bishop Wilkens first took Daniel on as an apprentice, he thought he would be able to control him, like he controls other pastors who are under him. But Daniel had other plans. He wanted more out the deal. He wanted to provide for his family and make sure they are secured for generations to come. He is a husband and a father first and a business man second. Whatever Daniel does, it's based off business. With Daniel building a new church, he gets a fifteen percent cut from the offering. The boss has to be paid. Daniel know he has one year to train Thomas. He has to teach him about what people want to hear. They struggle every day. They don't want to hear about getting over. They want to get over and stay over. They not only want to hear about loving everyone no matter who they are, but actually seeing the church accepting everyone, no matter who they are. What Daniel is doing is causing a major shift in the church world. He hears the whispers and the loud talking about him. People are going to talk about you regardless of who you are. But people are quicker to say something about prosperous pastors. He doesn't flaunt his lifestyle in everyone's faces. He wouldn't go as far as to getting his own private jet or wearing outfits that would cost nearly ten thousand dollars like some he knows. Daniel feels that's where a lot of well-known, big name pastors, bishops, prophets and others mess up. The more money they make, they messier they get. Daniel isn't here to get messy. He's going to keep this hustle going for as long as he can.

The warm wind is blowing as Daniel continue to stand and look at the empty lot. This is where he wants the mini strip mall, in a perfect location. The mall will sit on a major roadway with busy flowing traffic with other stores and restaurants.

Nicole is standing beside him in her skinny jeans and Abundant Overflow t-shirt. She kept her word by not looking like a First Lady. She made sure she looks good before she walks out the house no matter where she goes. There's been a couple of times when some older members will give her a church hat as a gift. With class, she would politely decline and tell them that hats aren't her thing. She'll rock a baseball cap for an old school retro look, but will not be caught in a brittle, oversized, bold colored, net looking hat. There's been more times than she can count at the numerous hateful stares she will get at some of the young single and married women. Nicole is beautiful and no matter who you are, women despises other beautiful, sexy women. But there are others who hate her because they wish they were in her place. Nicole see the many women who have their hungry eyes set on Daniel. She doesn't view them as a threat. She trusts Daniel and knows that he will never do anything to defy her trust. Then there is the issue of not only her but both of them being so very young. Daniel is twenty-nine and she is twenty-eight. It was a struggle to get people to trust them because they were so young. But with her immaculate reputation at a private Christian school and with Bishop Wilkens stamp of approval, people began to warm up to them.

Nicole places her head of Daniel's shoulder as she looks at the empty lot with him. She will never tell him about the stress she feels about this move he's making with the mini mall. Nicole feels like that it's a little too much. She hears the whispers about her husband and it makes her furious to hear people talking about him. Daniel can ignore it but she can't. With this big business move, Nicole knows that it will just bring on more whispers, more stress, and a brighter spotlight on them. She doesn't want it. She doesn't like the attention but Daniel does. She goes along with everything Daniel wants to do, even if she is against some of it. Besides, that's what a good wife does. Not only that, but Daniel is providing for his family the way he always wanted to. Nicole loves it but the attention and the sideline talks she can do without. The idea of opening a church under him and bringing Thomas into the fold is a great move; she encouraged Daniel to do it. She knows that, that will ease the slack on Daniel, bring in more income and allow the church to branch out. Her only concern is Daniel's lust for more money which can make him blind and sloppy. She tells him all the time that they have enough, but he feels like their "enough" isn't good "enough".

Daniel gently kisses Nicole on the forehead, "A nickel for your deep thoughts," he says.

Nicole takes a deep sigh not wanting to tell him her honest feelings, but she knows he'll never stop asking. "Are you sure you know what you're doing," she asked, "Owning a mini mall is a lot of work."

"I know it is, but things will turn out fine. I'm not owning the stores on the lot, just the space. So, whoever put their store there, they will pay rent, like a property tax, that's all." Daniel put his arms around Nicole to give her the reassuring comfort that she needs.

"But, do you think people would want to put stores on the lot? Especially since Bishop Wilkens doesn't want anything to do with this? This will be the first major move without being under the Bishop. And since this has nothing to do with the church, people may not be receptive about putting stores on the lot."

"I already have three major stores that are looking to put their stores on the lot. I don't need the Bishop's approval or name. I made my own name when I started blessing people. Bishop Wilkens didn't sign the contract because he won't be in control of this. He didn't even want Darryl and Marshal to be a part of this."

"Well, Danny maybe he's right. Maybe Darryl and Marshal shouldn't have invested in this project."

Daniel takes his arm from around Nicole and looks at her in disbelief. "Nicole, you know they're like family. I can't leave them hanging like that. This will help them get on their feet. They're not going to be bodyguards forever, Nicole. They have to make a living in other areas too."

"Danny, I understand that," she says looking at him, "But they don't know anything about running a business. They never took a class in business. How would they learn how to run multiple businesses? It's more to it than collecting money from people, Daniel."

"I've never went to school and learned about business. Are you doubting me too? Bishop Wilkens taught me a lot…."

"Yes, a lot about church," Nicole interrupted.

"And church is a business! Businesses are all run the same way," he interrupts her, "Look at everything we have Nicole! I got everything for us! I learned from Bishop and I did the work! *I* did the work! All he did was place us in a church! *I* did the rest," Daniel raises his voice even louder. Daniel and Nicole never argued; he usually backs down and walk away to cool down, but this is one thing Daniel wasn't going to back down on. "*I* increased the church membership! *I* took the church to the level that it's on now!"

"Yes! But with the help of Bishop Wilkens too! You can't assume that you did everything by yourself Daniel because you didn't! You had help... You know what," Nicole says taking a step back, "We never argued. We never got into a yelling match like this. Do you see what this is doing to you? You are so consumed with getting more money, you are becoming so blinded by money."

"Nicole, you have to trust me," he says finally calming down.

"I do trust you, but you're not thinking clearly. You are doing too much, too soon. Just work on one thing at a time."

"If you trust me, then know that I got this. I know what I'm doing."

That is the last time Nicole will tell him her thoughts but she didn't want to let this go. "Do you have anyone that you can talk to about the business side of things, other than the church? I'm not saying running a church isn't like a business in the real world, but I'm sure there is more to it."

"I have our accountant Shawn on top of things, as well as my lawyers. I want to make sure that we are set for life and nothing will screw us over later. I told you that when I started doing this clergy hustle, that we will come across some preachers that think on a small level. We always have to stay a step ahead. I want to be part of that two percent that will enhance the church in different areas too. One Bishop got the movie industry on lock, you have another that is trying to lock in on the music industry and there's me clamping down on the corporate industry beginning with this mini mall and I think you should set your sight on the fashion industry."

Nicole burst out laughing. That was the funniest thing she heard all day. "You can't be serious," she continues to laugh.

"I'm very serious. You said that you want to do something besides being a full-time mom and wife. I think you should look into the fashion industry, maybe start your own line. I have connections and can set something up."

"Whoa, whoa, slow your roll. You can probably pull a fast one on Thomas, but I'm not falling for it. I don't know anything about fashion."

"No…But you do look good in it," Daniel says as he pulls Nicole close to him. He looks into his wife's bright gray eyes. No one can turn him on instantly like she can. He began to kiss her gently on the lips. Nicole easily takes him in. She can't resist Daniel. She gently sucks his lower lip.

"Let me think about it," she says in between kisses.

"My persuasion isn't enough," he says back softly.

"I need more convincing."

Nicole and Daniel has always been an intimate couple. Many of their disagreements end with a sweet embrace or make-up sex. Nicole isn't thrilled about getting involved in the fashion world. That has never been her thing but whatever makes her husband happy, she's all for it.

Pulling back from kissing, Nicole has one more question, "One last thing, when will you have time to train Thomas? The new church will be ready in a year."

"I'll make time. It doesn't take much to tickle the fancy of people's ears. All he has to do is say what people want to hear. That's what they want today anyway. When he continues to realize that, that is all he has to do for people to open their wallets, he'll be a fast learner."

"I have to admit Danny; this is one way to make fast legit cash. I couldn't believe it when we first started this church thing but as time moved on, I became a believer and I think Thomas will too."

…Thomas can't wait until Sunday to see Jessica. After having dinner with the team and talking about Jessica he had to see her. It's already getting dark and he's been sitting in his car for a half an hour debating if he should go inside her apartment, or if he should just call her or if he should just wait until Sunday to see her. He doesn't know what to expect. He doesn't know if there is another man or woman that is occupying her time. He sees the usual crew hanging out in the front of the building. Nothing has changed. It's been two months since Thomas been here. He was expecting something different, anything different, but everything looks the same. The only thing that is standing out is his new 2017 SUV Hybrid. Thomas purposely parked a few houses away not drawing attention to himself. "What do I want? Do I really want her back," he says to himself? That's a question he hasn't answered yet. Thomas got out of his vehicle ready to talk to Jessica.

"Is that Thomas old ass," Chris calls out.

Thomas is ready for the jokes and Chris questioning him about being down with the crew. This is one thing he doesn't miss from the old neighborhood.

"Yeah that's Thomas. Where has this nigga been," one of the guys said.

Thomas is finally face to face with them smiling. "Hey, Chris what's good?"

"Oh s***, so the rumors are true," Chris says, "You're working at that church Abundant Overflow. I heard you're working with the Pastor himself."

Thomas smiles even harder feeling proud to be a part of Pastor Daniel's team, "Yeah, I'm working with him."

"You make me want to go to church," another guy said looking at Thomas new clothes.

"A, how much are you making? Are they still hiring," someone asked?

"There's some things in the works that will need some people. But I don't think there are any open positions now. If I hear anything, I'll let you know," Thomas lied. Thomas wasn't about to have straight up thugs work for Pastor Daniel. "But until then, why don't you come to the church on Sunday?"

"Man, I don't know. People be looking at you all funny in church when you're new or come in not all dressed up. Besides, they know who I am," Chris says, looking at his boys snickering. Chris knows he has a bad reputation on the streets, especially in the church.

The other men agree with him.

"Let me tell you something. People at church are just like you and me. They are no better. They are there to get help just like everyone else. Don't let them push you away and stop you from coming. If you take a good look at the people at Abundant Overflow, most of them don't have their stuff together, so they fake the funk like the rest of us. I'm telling you Abundant Overflow is the place to be. What church around here do you see giving out money and jobs? We got you. We accept anybody. The other Sunday, we had two wives join the church."

"Word! That's what's up!"

"They're no different. They want love just like the rest of us. Isn't nothing wrong with two women," Thomas said.

"Hell no, I would love to be the mattress on their bed," a guy said.

Everyone started laughing.

"The Bible says to love and accept everyone."

"Yeah, but it doesn't say anything about accepting just *anybody*."

"And that's where Abundant Overflow comes in. Pastor Daniel is turning the game. He is doing big things that is going to change a lot of what we know about church. We love and accept everyone; no matter who you are."

"Does Pastor Daniel still give out money," Chris asked, "I wish I was at your church that Sunday a while back."

"You have to come to church to find out," Thomas says. He knows Daniel is planning to surprise people on Wednesday at Bible Study. Thomas is watching Pastor Daniel's every move so he can learn how to be successful like him.

"So, what's good with you and Jessica? We heard she kicked your ass out. That's why you left with your bags. Your ass was lying when you said that you were going on a trip," Chris asked.

"No, it wasn't like that." Thomas knows better. He doesn't tell people his business. The less people know what goes on in his life, the simpler his life is. "I had to take care of some stuff."

"Yeah ok," Chris responds not believing a word, "Well, if you were wondering, she had some dude over here last week. We've been looking out for you."

"True, true, you know Jamal that lives on the second floor," a guy said.

"Yeah, I know him," Thomas says as he is feeling the anger on the inside.

"He said he saw a guy walking with Jessica in the building and that he stayed with her for like a couple of days. I haven't seen the dude," the guy said pointing to himself, "But we figure you should know what your girl has been doing since you left."

"Thanks man, I appreciate that."

Thomas gave them manly handshakes before heading into the building. Thomas is now boiling on the inside. Who is this guy that stayed with Jessica? *No wonder she was trying to get me out the house so bad*, Thomas is thinking to himself. He's not about to fight over a woman that doesn't want to be kept. The hope of them getting back together no longer exist in his mind. Seeing Jessica now is to end things, not to make amends.

Thomas looks at the faded brass numbers forty-three on the door. He can't fathom anyone touching Jessica sexually, especially a guy. Jessica planned the moment to cheat on him with her friend Diane, and now a guy is in the picture. Thomas feels like Jessica wanted him out the picture for a while.

He quickly knocks on the door before he changes his mind and decide to leave. For all he knows the guy can be lying in the bed him and Jessica once shared.

Jessica opens the door in amazement to see Thomas standing in front of her. "Hi, hey Thomas," the words flutter out her mouth. She is trying to contain her emotions. He is the last person she expects to see at her door.

"Hi Jessica, I was in the area and decided to come by to see you," he says lying.

"That's nice of you. Come in."

Thomas walks into the tiny apartment. Compare to his new townhouse, this apartment he once lived in with Jessica, he sees that he is living the life of luxury. He can fit the kitchen and the living room inside his bedroom and still have more space. He's just thankful to have a place he can call his own.

Jessica can smell the crisp newness of his black leather jacket he has on. Thomas is standing a little taller and has a wider chest than he had the last time he was there. He looks different from a couple of days ago.

"We can sit here on the sofa," Jessica said directing him to the tiny living room. Thomas walks over to the sofa, walking behind Jessica admiring her shapely figure in her leggings and small t-shirt. He can't help but have his eyes gaze at her perfectly rounded onion bottom. It's been months, but Thomas knows he has to control himself. He can picture his hands all over Jessica. He misses touching her and squeezing her body. Jessica takes a seat on the sofa and pat her hand in the empty spot next to her, offering Thomas a seat.

"So, how are things," Jessica asked.

"Things are going very well. I can't complain. How is everything with you?"

"Good, things are good. I really enjoyed your service on Wednesday night. I never knew you was so good with preaching."

"Yeah neither did I. I was nervous. I must admit," he nervously laughed.

"Well, I couldn't tell. It was an honor that Pastor Daniel allowed you to preach at his church. And you were scared for what? I see how he saw something in you."

"Yeah, well I guess he sees a lot," Thomas said. He isn't going to tell her about the new church, not yet at least. "I was surprised to see you there though. I wasn't expecting you, especially after the night prior."

"You know I'll always support you."

"Do you really? I mean, you planned to cheat on me because you couldn't ignore your family and friends. I wouldn't call that support."

Jessica takes in a deep breath, "I know what I did Thomas. But, you can never say that I've never supported you…So, tell me why exactly are you here? I think we've said what we had to say to each other the other night. There's nothing else to discuss."

"We still need to talk Jessica. We can't act like we weren't dating for almost three years and just stop talking without some kind of closure."

"Closure," Jessica repeated. Her heart began to race. She doesn't want closure. She wants to be with Thomas. He's the one that she wants.

"Yes, we need closure. I think will be the best for the both of us,"

Jessica knows he's a man of the cloth now, but he's still a man. But she can't resist. She pulls him over to her and began kissing him. Her hands are all over him, massaging his head. Thomas is caught off guard by her forwardness, but he wants her just as bad as she wants him. He pulls her on top of him so she is sitting facing him. He kisses her, holding the sides of her face. The sensations of their bodies began to take over. Continuing to kiss him, she helps him take off his jacket and pull his shirt off. His hands glide up and down her back, pushing her t-shirt off over her head. He buries his face in between her breasts. Tears are beginning to form in her eyes. Thomas began to gently suck on her dark chocolate skin. It's been a while since he felt Jessica's smooth skin against his. The heat from her body is arousing him even more. This is the longest Thomas and Jessica has gone without having some kind of sexual contact. They want each other badly. He is thinking about all the things he did with her and what he wants to do with her right now. But images of her being with someone else enters his mind. Before Thomas take it too far, he stops.

"Wait, wait, we can't do this. This isn't right," he pants. He wants her badly, "I'm sorry," he says silently.

His heart is crush and torn. As much as he wants to be with her, he can't because she had some other guy here. His anger began to bottle up again. He moves her off him and stands up, picking up his shirt.

"What's wrong," Jessica ask sitting on the sofa in disbelief. She thinks his reason is because of his new lifestyle, but what comes out his mouth shocks her.

"I can't sit up here and act like you didn't have some other guy staying here last week!"

Thomas is holding his shirt in his tightly closed hand. Jessica can't be turned on by his bare muscular chest because of his assumption. She can't believe that Thomas would accuse her of sleeping with someone else. At the same time, he has every reason to believe it. After all, he did catch her kissing Diane.

"So you think just because I has some guy staying with me last week, I was sleeping with him?"

"You were ready to sleep with Diane, why not..."

"Why not Austin," she interrupts him. She stands up facing him with pure hatred, "Because that's my cousin! He needed a place to rest his head for a couple of days!"

Thomas now feels like a fool. Her cousin Austin is a truck driver, who drives across the country. Every now and again, he would come by to stay over for a night or a couple of days. Thomas smooths his face with his hands. "I'm sorry Jess."

She snatches her shirt off the sofa to put back on.

"I think you need to leave. Clearly we can never get pass what I did, without you thinking I would cheat on you again. Or believe Chris and his nosey ass boys!"

Thomas doesn't want this to end. He wants to make things work with Jessica. Taking things slow is his only option. Slow as in, he wouldn't tell her too much about his real reasons for going into the ministry. The less she knows the better.

Thomas is standing there looking at her with her hands on her hip with an attitude. He loves when she gets mad at him. It turns him on even more. "I'm not going anywhere," he says. He pulls her toward him, lifting her and throwing her over his shoulder, as he proceeds to the bedroom. Jessica didn't resist.

Chapter 8

2 Peter 2: 2b-3 (MSG)

"They give the way of truth a bad name. They're only out for themselves. They'll say anything, anything that sounds good to exploit you. They'll come to a bad end for God never just stood by and let that kind of thing go on."

THREE MONTHS LATER......

Thomas was very excited. He wasted no time asking Jessica to move in with him. After their passionate love making, about three months ago, he wanted her. He wanted to be with her and start their lives over again. She was hesitant at first but she wanted to make things work and she missed him terribly. She was hesitant because she didn't want to jeopardize his new job or character within the church because he was living with his girlfriend. She also wasn't so sure about being part of the church world. She doesn't go to church and knew moving in with Thomas, he would expect her to come to every service with him.

"Don't worry about the people in the church. I'm not fazed by them. You're my lady. They don't need to know our business," he said to her,

"I understand that but your business becomes everybody's when you're in the pulpit. What about Pastor Daniel? I don't think he would accept the person that he is mentoring playing house with someone you are not married to."

"I'll talk to Pastor Daniel. Besides, he knows all about you. I'm sure he wouldn't mind. And Pastor Daniel is a cool guy, as well as his boys Darryl and Marshal. He isn't like those religious pastors that you see or hear about every day. When you meet him, you'll see what I'm talking about. I never thought I would be preaching and talking in front of people but he convinced me. He showed me that you don't have to lose yourself in the ministry. You can still keep it one hundred. That's what people want."

"Tell me," Jessica asked curiously, "How much does preachers make? How much do you make? I'm sure it's a lot because of your new ride and your nice townhouse you live in. I heard you live in the new developments on the other side of town. Those Brownstones aren't cheap."

Thomas repositioned himself in the bed to face Jessica. "Do you want me for my money," he asked playfully.

"No silly, I want to know what I'm getting myself into and also it's a question I think everybody wants to know." She wanted to know more about how he can keep up with his lifestyle. She's seen pictures of Daniel's exquisite house and other material things. And since Thomas began working for him, he's able to live in the expensive townhomes. They are almost three thousand a month.

"Well, it all depends on the pastor. It depends on how he preaches. The pastor can talk about the fiery pit of hell and scare people to death, or always condemning homosexuality making people feel unwanted, or how being envious of someone who has everything they've always dream of having, making them feel like they shouldn't want to strive to get those things, or how making love to their significant other is the most ungodly sin, and those are the pastors who don't make the money. Those are the ones who still rent store front churches or have Sunday services in their living room. Now pastors like Daniel, Bishop Wilkens, and I, which I can now include myself on the roster now, preach the opposite. We preach the truth but with love and acceptance. We accept everybody. We don't condemn them."

"But how much do they get paid? I've seen Pastor Daniel's car and pictures of his mansion online and in magazines," she asks persistently.

"I can't tell you how much he gets paid because I don't know but he is a business man too. So, I'm sure he has other funds coming in from other sources. Now me, I'm salary. I signed the contract and filled out paperwork telling me I make about sixty thousand a year," he says lying to her. His antennas had gone up because she is being very persistent about knowing about how much money he and Pastor Daniel makes. It's none of her business or anyone else. Pastor Daniel told him to never tell his salary. "But that doesn't include incentives."

"Incentives," Jessica asked curiously.

"Yeah preaching incentives," Thomas responded as-a-matter-of-factly.

Jessica got very quiet. She was raised in the church and she knew about corrupt pastors. She knew what was right and what was wrong. "Thomas, have you read the Bible for yourself about some of the things you've said like sex before marriage and homosexuality?"

"Of course I did, but that only applies to sleeping with multiple people not the one you intend to marry. And we all know what the Bible says about homosexuality but it never said to not to accept them."

"Hmm, I guess I can't argue with that."

Jessica didn't move in with Thomas. She felt it was too soon to be moving in with him after being broken up with him, and not speaking to each other for two months before they rekindled their relationship three months ago. A lot has gone down in the last five months. Thomas began working with Pastor Daniel, them breaking up for two months, Thomas traveling all over the country with Pastor Daniel and now he's preaching at quite a few Bible Studies. They still need time to work things out and figure out their relationship. She also doesn't know if she wants to be a part of Abundant Overflow. What he was telling her about how pastors get money has raised an eyebrow. Never once during the three years they've dated has he ever shown interest in being a pastor. He hardly went to church until he was unemployed. She knew he was going to their ministry school, but he only did it so he wouldn't be laying around the house, or running drops for Chris after he went searching for work. It also gave him something to do on his down time. Jessica also knew how nervous Thomas was when Pastor Daniel told him to be the speaker for Bible Study three months ago. She saw the anxiety on his face when she met him at the lounge the other night. But all of a sudden, he's interested in preaching. Thomas never told her how much he got paid with incentives. Starting someone with no experience with sixty thousand a year should be given a side eye. But getting paid like that with bonuses should be seen as suspicious. Jessica knew better. She's aware of the crooked pastors and if Thomas wants to dabble in it, she doesn't want any part of it.

As you can imagine Thomas wasn't thrilled about Jessica turning down his offer to move in with him. He was sure she would move in with him, especially after he put the big "D" on her. That was the most intense mind blowing loving making they've done. He answered her questions about how him and Pastor Daniel get paid. He was careful not to tell her everything because that's one thing Pastor Daniel taught him. He told Thomas that only a select few in the church game knows how and where to get their money. And those few are the ones who are millionaires. Thomas know not to say too much. Daniel told Thomas that he can't let everyone in the circle. Thomas only can think of having Jessica there but he isn't so sure anymore. Jessica has always been his ride and die girl. She should have been happy that Thomas wants her back. Most men would not take her back. They'll keep walking. "I need some time," Thomas remember Jessica saying.

Thomas feels like a fool. He should have known it was too soon for him and Jessica to get back together. It's been about three months since they started talking again. And within those three months, Daniel had Thomas preach at Bible Study every other Wednesday. Jessica never shows up for the support that he needs the most. When she showed up at the first Bible Study he spoke at, it made him feel at ease and could tackle the church world head on. But right now all he wants to do is focus on getting paid. Thomas knows Daniel is one of those ministry millionaires and he wants to learn as much as Daniel. He doesn't see anything wrong with what Daniel is doing. There's nothing illegal. Whatever Thomas needs to do, he'll do it. He doesn't have the gift of gab that you need to get people hyped in church but he feels that, that shouldn't stop him.

Thomas is getting ready for a three-day conference that he and Daniel and some other ministers from the church are attending. Going to conferences is something Thomas still has to get used to. He has passed up on four conferences within the five months he began working with Daniel. Thomas knows that he has to put forth the effort if this is something that he really wants to do full-time. That's the downside of the church game. It requires so much of your time. He doesn't see how Daniel have time to spend with Nicole and their daughter. Spending time with family and friends is something everyone needs, which is why he wanted Jessica to move in with him. At least he can see her every day and night. Coming home to an empty place is dreadful. And she could come out to dinner with them too, whenever they go out. Thomas feels like he is forcing himself to be friends with them, which he doesn't mind. They're cool people but to have your own people outside of church would be better. The only people he hung with outside of church was Chris and his crew. And that definitely wouldn't be a good look for him. But at the end of the day, the incentives that come along with the church hustle outweighs everything. Now a day, money talks and this is becoming easy money for him. He stopped packing for a moment to take a good look at where he is now. Thomas began walking around in his Master Suite. Never in his life did he ever own or slept in a king size bed. A beautiful fireplace sits opposite from the bed with a sixty-inch flat curve Ultra-HD flat screen mounted on the wall above it. He's enjoying the sinking sensation he feels as he is walking across the plush carpet to the marble bathroom. He flicks the light switch up to turn on the light so he can admire the double sink bathroom. The shower sits in the far right corner surrounded by double ply glass. The only bathroom he's ever showered in was the typical box shaped bathroom with a small toilet, skinny sink and a shower curtain that never keeps the water inside the shower shared tub. Now he has a separate shower and tub. He turns around to walk out the bedroom, passing by two large guest bedrooms that are thirteen by fourteen. The guest bedrooms also have a shared bathroom. He stops to look over the balcony. Admiring the living room and dining room below. The skylight above allows the light from the sunset cast a soft light on the soft grayish colors in the great room below. Another fireplace is in the living room implanted into a stone wall. Thomas began to walk down the stairs taking in the place that he now owns. He still has a lot to do with decorating but all of this is his. If someone would have told him five months ago that he will be living in a Brownstone and making a nice salary with the church, he would never believe them. Jessica told him that what he has is too much for one person to live in. Thomas doesn't care. He knows he can afford it and the way he sees it, he's just preparing for his future. One day, he will be married and have a kids. This is just preparation.

He made a bee line straight to the kitchen. He has a huge kitchen that he has yet to cook in. Thomas isn't much of a cooker. Jessica always did the cooking. He misses her cooking but he knows it's time to do for himself. So, like a typical bachelor, he took out the bread and cold cuts to make himself a sandwich. He grabbed a cold beer from the fridge and heads back upstairs to finish packing.

Daniel usually can't stand going to some conferences. In the beginning of his ministry career, Bishop Wilkens had him go to small conferences so he can get his face and name out there. Many of the pastors were small time, always struggling, with a fifty or ten-member congregation. Some of those pastors were beginners like Daniel but was under the wrong guidance because they still have the same members and most of their members are family. Bishop Wilkens never went with Daniel to the pastoral conferences. He wanted to be behind the scenes to Daniel, since Daniel was a rookie. Daniel would sit back and listen and take notes on what not to do. Daniel has learned that the easiest way to know what not to do is to watch what the majority does. And majority of the pastors aren't prospering and being the fulfilling example that they preach. Daniel was tired of scratching to survive. The conferences are boring. The panel consist of pastors that are well known in the community. They talk about issues that the churches face and solutions that can help other pastors. Then there are talks about spiritual growth and questions or concerns that others raise. The conferences Daniel love to attend are the ones with the pastors who have megachurches that are pouring into the pastors who are hungry and are striving to be like them. Some of them take what they learned and apply it to their ministry and some pastors are there to be entertained or just to brag about how they were at a major conference with all of these big name pastors. But this time it's different. This time Daniel is going to be on the panel. He was asked months ago if he could sit on the panel at the Building Up Pastors Conference. He was hesitant at first, but he changed his mind after thinking about giving guidance to other pastors who want to be like him and the nice pay he was getting just to be there helped too. They offered him ten thousand dollars to speak. This was big for Daniel. This was also a good opportunity for Thomas to get his face seen and name known. Daniel was told that a lot of pastors weren't registering for the conference but as soon as his name was added to the roster, they had to close registration because it was too full to take any more. The registration fee was set to five hundred dollars. Some pastors pleaded to be there and was willing to pay double, triple the amount of the registration fee. Daniel was happy and especially the ones who put the conference together.

Daniel places his bag on the floor in the foyer.

"Daddy, when will you be back," Simone asked as she is leaning on the sofa watching her dad leave again.

"I'll be back in two days' sweetheart. I'm not going to be gone for too long."

He walks over to kiss his now ten-year-old daughter on the head. "Why, do you miss me already?"

"Yes, which is why I decided not to have kids or get married."

"Whoa, where is this coming from," Daniel asked. Simone has Daniel confused.

"Nothing, forget about it," she says as she proceeds to walk away.

"Wait, let's talk about this."

"I don't want to talk about it." She continues to walk away.

"Simone! Come here," Daniel yells.

She stops walking and slowly turns around to face her dad and rolling her eyes. She wants to go back to her room to listen to her music and Facetime some of her friends.

"Get over here!"

She folds her arms and walk to her dad with a little attitude. It is taking everything in him not put his hands on her.

"First," he says with a raise voice, "You will never walk away from me again when I'm talking to you! Is that clear!"

Simone slowly unfolds her arms holding back tears. She has always been sensitive. Daniel has never yelled or put his hands on Simone.

"What's the problem? Talk to me."

It is taking everything for Simone not to cry, "You're hardly here! You're always busy! I don't want to have a family that will miss me because I'm always busy."

"Simone, you understand that I'm busy so I can make sure you have everything. Do you remember the small apartment we use to live in?"

"I remember it. My bedroom was so small I couldn't get a desk in the room."

"But we made awesome forts in your bedroom."

A little smile appears on her face. There are times when Simone missed her tiny room. When her dad would come home from work on Fridays, he would always come in her room to help her build a fort. Then he would stay the night in the fort while they eat popcorn and watch horror movies. Daniel can never be upset with Simone. She looks just like Nicole. Every time she smiles, her gray eyes sparkles too.

"But do you have to go? Why do you always have to go preach somewhere? Doesn't it get boring?"

"Don't you get bored reading about the human body and watching the medical channel?"

"Absolutely not! I love it! As a future doctor I need to be ready for those things."

"Well, just like you love it, I love it too. I love preaching. And you know I always spend time with you and your mom. You two are my favorite girls. I do all of this for the both of you. I have to make sure you and your mom are taken care of. That's what a husband does for his family."

"Well, what does a daddy do for his kids," she asks with a smirk.

Daniel laughs, "Well, a father takes care of his kids, be there for them anytime they need him. A father sets an example...And fathers are more fun and...," he pauses to consider his thoughts.

"And what dad", Simone asked.

"And unpredictable," he adds.

"Unpredictable?"

"Yes, which means. I need you to go upstairs and pack a bag. You're going to come with me."

Simone didn't seem too thrilled. "Dad, I've been to a conference before and they're boring."

"I know, but its where we're going to go after the conference."

Simone gave him a confused look.

"We can take a trip to Disney World."

"Really," she yells, "Are you serious?"

"Yeah, why not. I can book a flight after the conference and we can fly to Disney. We can stay for three days."

"Dad, I love you," she squeezes him really hard and takes off running and screaming.

Daniel feels very proud of himself. This is the first time him and Simone are going away by themselves. This can be the first of many father and daughter trips. Daniel grabs his phone to call his travel agent. This is the most-craziest, spontaneous thing that he has ever done since him and Nicole eloped after their high school graduation.

"Daniel, what the heck is going on," Nicole came walking briskly into the living room. Daniel raises his hand before talking on the phone.

"Hi, Lisa this Daniel."

"Hi, Daniel, how are you?"

"I'm good. Can you hold on for one moment but while you're holding on can you check flights to Orlando and tickets to Disney World, for one adult and one child."

"I sure can."

Daniel put the phone on mute so he can talk to Nicole.

"Daniel what is going on? Simone comes running upstairs screaming about going to Disney World."

"Yeah, I'm going to take her to the conference with me and then we're going to fly to Orlando from there. It will give us some time together and you can have some time to yourself."

"And when were you going to tell me this. Simone has school. You can't just take her out of school to fly to Florida."

"Nicole, she's only going to miss a couple of days. What's the big deal? Simone is a straight A student who never miss days. I mean, we pay her private school tuition. I don't see why she can't enjoy being with me."

"Daniel, you know I don't care but you can't just take her out of school spontaneously like this that's all. Did you know she's in the middle of testing? She's going to miss the last day of testing."

"And I'm sure she can make it up when she comes back...Nicole, you've been a little edgy lately. What's going on?"

"There's nothing wrong Daniel," taking a deep breath she repeated herself, "There's nothing wrong. Have fun. I'm glad you're spending time with Simone. Honest I am. I'll go help her pack for her trip."

Daniel knows there's something more to what she's saying. Nicole has never been the snappy type. She always went along with everything he does.

Nicole turns around to go upstairs to help Simone pack for her spontaneous trip.

"Nicole, don't leave. We need to talk."

Daniel unmuted the phone to talk to his travel agent.

"Hi Lisa, did you see anything," Daniel asked.

Nicole is standing there with concerned yet agitated eyes. Nicole doesn't care if they go to Florida or anywhere else in the world. She thinks it's a great idea, but eventually her and Daniel need to have a serious talk.

"Yes, I have a package deal for you with round-trip, two nights, three days at your usual suite with Park admissions for $3,270, which includes a three-day hopper."

"That sounds good. Go ahead and book that flight for me."

"Okay, do you want me to add any special activities?"

"Uhm, no, I don't think so. That will be all."

"Okay, you'll get a confirmation soon. Is there anything else?"

"No, that will be all."

Daniel ended the call now looking at Nicole. "I'm not going anywhere until I find out what's wrong Nicole."

"You're going to be late for your conference. Thomas should be here soon to pick you up."

"I don't care! My family comes first. What's going on?"

Nicole takes a deep breath, "There's rumors going around the church about how you are mishandling the church funds."

"Nicole, they are just rumors. No one is mishandling funds. I can assure you of that. Where did you hear this?"

"I overheard a couple of the board members talking last week about expenses that you are dipping into. They're not on board with the mini mall you are building either. They said that they are concerned about your over spending."

"I think it's time to get some new board members. I'm not dipping into the funds for the church. I can assure you of that. Everything that I do is from our savings. Don't worry your pretty self over those matters," says Daniel rubbing the side of her face, "They don't know what they're talking about. You should know by now that we will have numerous of people that doesn't like us because we are well off. It'll get worse as we prosper even more."

Nicole takes a deep breath. She knew the meaning of more money means more problems but she never thought she will experience the other side effects that comes along with the territory.

The turn-out for the Building Up Pastors Conference is a huge success. Thomas has never been to a place with so many pastors. Majority of them are men. Thomas came across a handful of women pastors. He was surprised Daniel brought his daughter with him. Daniel had told Thomas that after the conference he wanted him to take him and Simone to the airport. He had planned a last minute father and daughter trip. He also told him that he wanted him to preach on Sunday since he wasn't going to be in town. Thomas is beyond excited about the invitation to preach on Sunday at both services. He wonders how much he can take up in offerings. There are about two thousand people in the first service alone. The noon service is almost four times the size. At the same time, Thomas is extremely nervous. Preaching at Bible Study is one thing, but at a Sunday service is a different platform. He knows he has to switch up his approach. But how? But Thomas has confidence in himself that he can do it.

"Is anyone sitting here," a man asked Thomas, standing next to him.

"No, you can sit here. Luckily, you've found a seat. This place is packed. They should be starting soon."

"Yeah, I was looking for a closer seat," the man said as he sat down, "I guess this is as close as I'm going to get. I should have gotten here sooner. I'm Pastor Donald Knight." Pastor Knight offers his hand to Thomas.

"I'm Minister Thomas Butler," he greets himself, shaking Pastor Knight's hand.

"Your name sound familiar. What's the name of your church?"

"I'm a member at Abundant Overflow. I work alongside with Pastor Daniel."

"Really? Wow! Why aren't you in the front?"

"I like the background," Thomas laughs.

Pastor Knight can't stop talking to Thomas and was telling everyone around them who Thomas is. Thomas is enjoying being in the spotlight. He knows that this is something he can get used to. But preaching? He discreetly shrugs his shoulders, it's all about the money. As long as Pastor Daniel doesn't know his hidden motive, he can keep up this masked face.

The conference began in prayer. Simone is sitting in the front row next to Darryl, who decided to tag along at the last minute. Daniel was glad that he did because he didn't want Simone to sit by herself. Although Thomas is there, he didn't want to put that responsibility on him. It has been an hour since the conference began and all is going well. Many pastors seem to be focused on Daniel. Thomas notices the jealous glares on the pastors faces on the platform. Pastor Daniel is good at what he does. You can't be mad at him for that.

"Pastor Daniel, would you like to say something about expansion? Your church has grown extremely large since it began five years ago."

Daniel leans forward to speak in the microphone. "I can tell you that it's not easy. Many sacrifices must be made and many sleepless nights. What pastors need is a vision.

The crowd began to clap loudly.

Daniel continues, "Without a vision your church, your ministry is dead. Everyone's vision is different. My vision for my church may not work for you."

"I can definitely agree," Pastor Bradford Smalls interjects. He is sitting on the panel two seats away from Daniel. Thomas knows Pastor Smalls wasn't thrilled about Daniel being here. Every time Daniel spoke, he would shift his body with annoyance. Only this time he is bold enough to speak up.

"Not everyone can give millions of dollars to people in the church."

The crowd began to clap. Some sat there in silence watching what was going to unfold. They knew Pastor Branford Smalls didn't like Daniel because before he started, Daniel left Pastor Smalls to study under Bishop Wilkens. And Bishop Wilkens and Pastor Smalls had an already rocky relationship.

Daniel chuckles, "It wasn't millions, brother. But let me ask you a question. What have you done for your people in the church?"

Before Pastor Smalls can responds Daniel cut him off, "That was a rhetorical question."

Thomas is taken aback by Daniel's approach. Daniel nods to Darryl. That is the signal to take Simone out the room. Daniel can't shield his wife from the haters of the church but he can protect his daughter.

"Minister Thomas Butler, can you come up here please," Daniel asked.

Thomas is caught off guard. He wasn't expecting to be put in the spotlight. By the time Darryl and Simone left, Thomas is already walking on to the panel.

"This young man right here," Daniel says putting his hand on Thomas shoulder, "Is a living testimony just like everyone in this room. We all started out poor, struggling, searching for answers, trying to hear from God and wanting the sense of belonging. We were here!" Turning around pointing to Pastor Smalls, "You were here. Sadly," he says facing everyone else, "Some of you are still here."

The crowd began to moan and grunt a little.

"It all depends on one word, that is guidance. Who *was* guiding you? Who *is* guiding you? Who was guiding you when you *first* began your ministry? Was it the store front preacher? Was it the living room preacher? Was it a pastor with the church and hundreds of members? Was it a Bishop with thousands of members? Your guide helps you with your vision. If you are content where you are, then why are you here? This is a conference about building up pastors. Thomas was in the midst of those being blessed that faithful Sunday. That was the day that changed his life. I took him under my wing and began molding him into the person he is destined to be."

Thomas began nodding his head in agreement.

"When you build yourself, you build your church. I'm sure many of you have heard about the mini mall I'm building. That is for the community, the church, those who are unemployed. Why can't I have and my members have? Here's my goal. My goal is to make sure my members are taken care of, financially by getting jobs. So, I create jobs. But it takes money to do it. Invest in yourself so then you can invest in your church."

The crowd roared in praises as Daniel put the microphone back on the table. He motions to Thomas to sit in his chair. Thomas is engrossed by what Daniel said. Thomas is sitting on the panel now facing the applauding pastors.

He's thinking about his vision now. He doesn't have a vision like Daniel. The only vision he has is that fast cash, but maybe that can change. Pastor Smalls just is just sitting there tight lipped.

During the break, Thomas was in the lounge relaxing his eyes after the three-hour panel. This is the longest, boring day of his life. He is ready to go home and get in his bed. He has another day of this before he is free.

"Tired," he heard a familiar voice say.

He opens his eyes to see Pastor Smalls sitting next to his left.

"Yeah, a little."

"You should go to your *suite* and relax."

Thomas cuts his eyes at him. There's still a rough part of Thomas that he keeps inside for moments like this, but he knows it wouldn't be a good look for him or Pastor Daniel. This isn't the time nor place for him to make a scene. "No, but I'm sure your standard room is waiting for you."

Pastor Smalls chuckles. "I'm just making small talk. No need to become defensive…So, how do you enjoy going into the ministry? It's a lot of work."

"Tell me about it. I don't know how Pastor Daniel does it but I'll get used to it. What's your issue with Pastor Daniel?"

Caught off guard Pastor Smalls nearly lost his breath, "What do you mean issue?"

"What's your issue? Everyone sees it. You two use to squabble back in the day?"

"Squabble?" He laughs, "No, not at all. Pastor Daniel is a good man. He really is, but sometimes being good isn't enough. Have you ever heard him preach about salvation?"

Thomas is sitting thinking long and hard about Daniel's sermons. None has come to mind about him preaching about salvation.

"No, I don't think so. But that's not a problem, he does altar calls for those who want to be saved."

"There's a difference to preach about salvation and making altar calls to be saved. Pastor Daniel is what we call, a prosperity preacher. He only preaches about being prosperous."

"And what's wrong with that? People need to hear about being prosperous. The Bible even talks more about money than anything."

"But what's more important, the money or being saved?"

"Being saved of course but people hear about that all the time. They come to church to have their spirits lifted after a long tiring week of work, or finding work, dealing with the stress of life. That's why I joined Abundant Overflow years ago, Pastor Daniel's sermons is what got me through the week. That's what people need. That's what there needs to be more of. That's why I'm following in his footsteps. And I'm already seeing the blessings."

"Blessings huh? Blessings from other people's money. It's easy to preach about wealth when the congregation is the one supporting you."

"Does your members support you?"

"Of course they do. I'm full-time in the ministry."

"Then you have no place to talk either. To be honest Pastor Smalls, I think you are just envious of Pastor Daniel of what he has to offer the people and what the people offer him. I may get into trouble for saying this but you wish you was him with the big house, the fancy rides, the trip overseas, preaching at megachurches, being treated like a celebrity and the hot wife. That's why all you low budget preachers talk down about those preachers that are making major waves."

Thomas gets up to leave Pastor Smalls simmering in his own jealousy. He has enough entertaining Pastor Smalls. Thomas has just encountered one of the many pastors Daniel had told him about. He told Thomas that he will come across pastors that will speak negative about the him and the ministry that he is doing. Thomas has a lot to learn. He knows it is best to leave now because he can feel himself boiling on the inside. There will always be a man trying to bring another man down, especially a black man. No one mentions and condemns the white prosperity preacher on television with the fifty thousand members. But as soon as a man of color preaches the same thing, there's something or there's a catch.

"Maybe you should take note on how to build yourself," scoffs Thomas.

As Thomas walks away Pastor Smalls calls out, "Maybe you should take note on how Pastor Daniel is getting his blessings."

But Thomas is the one to get the last word, "Maybe you should just respect another man's game," he says as he headed to the elevator to go to his suite.

Chapter 9

1 Timothy 6:10 (MSG)

"Going down that path, some lose their footing in the
faith completely and live to regret it bitterly ever after."

"Your boy Thomas had a couple of words for Pastor Smalls at the conference,"
Darryl said. Darryl, Marshal and Daniel are playing pool in the game room,
in Daniel's mansion. Whenever the guys get a chance, they always play pool,
hangout, shoot some ball and chill. Mondays are the days Daniel always look
forward to because Mondays are considered the day off for all church leaders.
The people in the administrative office love it too. They only work Tuesday
through Friday and sometimes Saturdays, but are required to stay late until
eight if they need to. Although, the three friends are always together, they
don't have time to catch up on things. Darryl knew this is the perfect time to
fill Daniel in on some things within the church.

"What did he say", Daniel asked as he is watching Marshal studying his
next move.

"He called him a jealous, low budget preacher."

Daniel and Marshal burst out laughing.

"Do you know what happened," Daniel asked still laughing.

"I have no idea. But I'm sure he had it coming to him. He tried to put
you on the spot during the conference."

"That old man always had a problem with Daniel," Marshal adds, "He never wanted anything to do with you. You preached at so many churches except for his because he never invited you."

"That's because he can't afford me," Daniel jokes, "But seriously, its only because Bishop Wilkens was my mentor. He had an issue with Bishop Wilkens before I even got involved in this whole church thing. He and the Bishop use to go to theology school together and, well, Bishop tried to help him but he always turned him down. And to make matters more interesting, I use to attend Pastor Smalls church. I never joined the church even though he tried with all his might to get me to join. But I stopped going when I decided to get into the ministry game and study under Bishop."

"I didn't know you went to his church. When did you go," asked Darryl?

"I went from time to time." Daniel walks over to the mini fridge to take out three beers. "Pastor Smalls is always trying to start or find trouble. Darryl, you saw how he tried to call me out at the conference. He was trying to start there."

Darryl nods, "Yeah that's what I was saying, he had it coming to him. I'm surprised Thomas didn't punch him in the mouth because he seems like the type that will handle a person."

"Who *Thomas*? Our *Thomas*," Marshal asked shocked.

"Yeah, that guy is straight up hood. I've seen him around a couple of times."

Daniel is opening the bottles of beer as he listens intently to Darryl talk about Thomas. What Daniel is hearing isn't too surprising. Thomas always had that demeanor, which is why he wanted him on his team. He's different.

"I'm telling you, don't let that meekness, I'm a good church boy, fool you," Darryl continues, "I know Thomas has it in him."

"I see what you're saying now," Marshal chimes in, "The two times you had him minister at the church you can hear it in his voice, especially on Sunday."

"How was he on Sunday? What did he preach about," Daniel asked handing them their beers?

"He preached about salvation," Marshal said before taking a swig on the cold brew, "He had the church on fire."

"Really," Daniel said surprisingly. He never knew Thomas to be the aggressive passionate preacher.

"When you get a chance, check it out online in the church archives. He had people crying, shouting, and acting up."

"Yeah, what they call it," Darryl said snapping his fingers trying to remember, "Catching the Holy Ghost."

Daniel is shocked that Thomas took it to that level. "What made him preach about salvation though?"

"I don't know but he had people running up to the altar throwing extra cash at his feet." Darryl and Marshal can see the wheels tuning in Daniel's head. He appears to be in deep thought.

"Yo, D," Marshal calls out, "Are you sure about keeping him on the team?"

"Yeah...Yeah...he's cool," Daniel hesitantly replied before drinking his beer. But now Daniel isn't so sure.

"Are you up for the competition? Because that's what it's going to come down too. Think about it, you're about to give *this man* your church. Do you think some of the members will leave Abundant Overflow to become a member at his church? Why do you think Bishop Wilkens sent you here, the next state away? He knew it was a possibility of you becoming a threat to him."

Daniel knows Marshal is right. Bishop Wilkens said the same thing to Daniel when he placed him here. But Daniel wants another church here in the state. He wants to have the church in the west side. It's about a half an hour away. Some people in the hood want to come to church but have a hard time getting to Abundant Overflow because they don't have transportation and the bus schedules on Sundays are almost non-existent. At that moment, an idea came into his head.

"Listen," he says as he sits on the edge of the pool table, "What if the church becomes another connection to Abundant Overflow?"

Darryl and Marshal stopped drinking their beers looking at Daniel confusingly.

"What if it's just another Abundant Overflow, but in another location? We can have services, but at different times. For instance, we can still have our usual Wednesday night Bible Study at 7:30, but the other church can have one at 6. Those who get off work at 5 can go there for the 6pm service instead of waiting until 7:30. The other church can have a Friday night explosion. We don't have services here on Fridays all the time and if we do, Friday night explosion can be cancelled for that evening."

"That sounds good but how would you create the Sunday schedule? That's where most of the income comes from," Darryl asked, "It doesn't make since to use the church just for those services and closed on Sunday."

"You're right, not unless we use the Friday night explosions as their Sunday service. I don't know, but I'm sure we'll come up with something. We have to find something. As long as Thomas stays in his lane and not dabble in the preaching about prosperity and the good life, we're good. That's my job. I'm the northern prosperity preacher."

"But Daniel, you can't tell someone what they can or can't preach. Just move the church a couple of states away."

"We've already broken ground! I can't just stop building the church!"

"But it doesn't have to be a church. Sell the land to someone. You have too much going on anyway," says Darryl. He is waiting for a reaction from Daniel. Darryl knows that's the last thing he wants to hear.

"Now you're beginning to sound like Nicole." Daniel picks up the pool stick ready to get back into the game. He doesn't want to hear about how busy he is.

Marshal had to say something too, because Daniel is going over his head with the new church. He feels like it's too soon for him to do something like that. When Daniel and Darryl was at the conference, Nicole was talking to him about her concerns about Daniel and asked if he and Darryl can talk some sense into him. Nicole knew that Marshal and Darryl are the ones that can possibly get through to Daniel. So, Marshal gave Darryl a heads up about the talk him and Nicole had about Daniel's hectic schedule. "Daniel, Nicole and Darryl are right."

Daniel hits the red ball aggressively with the stick sending it straight to the side of the pool table, knocking the blue ball into the corner pocket. This is not how he want to spend his relaxing Monday. They need to appreciate the hard work that he is doing for the family, he is thinking to himself. If he never made this move, they will still be living in the hood, scratching to survive. They know that Daniel is always looking to make moves.

"You are doing too much. We have the mini mall that we are building, then you are booked at conferences that you are speaking at for the next two years, you have a meeting with the book publisher next month and let's not forget about the speaking engagements at other churches. Ever since you've handed out money, you've been an instant celebrity. We can't even keep track of the radio and TV interviews you've done. You're doing too much."

"Which reminds me, I'm scheduled to be on a talk show next week."

"See, that's what we're talking about! You're doing too much," Marshal says.

"But we're getting paid doing it! So what's the problem? I've set all of us up for life. I got us out the ghetto. The both of you talked about the luxuries of preaching before I even started this. So why change up now? Hell, I'm about to make the both of you millionaires with our business with the mini mall. I even crossed out Bishop Wilkens from the equation because he wanted the both of you out of the deal. The both of you and Nicole knew what I had to do to succeed."

"And you've succeeded! How much more do you want," Darryl asked.

"I want everything! Either you can continue to ride with me or get off the train! I want to make sure my family is set up for life, Nicole, Simone, her kids, *if she has any*, my parents, Nicole's parents and the both of you. I know I have a lot going on right now, but it's worth it. It'll be worth it."

"All we're saying is that you need to take some time for yourself. Stop taking on so many projects. We can tell Nicole isn't happy. You need to chill. We're your boys Daniel. Hell, we're brothers and we're just telling you to slow down because people are beginning to talk and take notice to what you're doing."

"Good!!! Let them take notice. I'm not doing anything but making sure my family survive for life and help a couple along the way. People are always going to talk. The both of you should know that. We're going to have people that will hate what we are doing."

"We know this but the board members want answers about how the finances are being spent. We heard that they didn't approve the mini mall. Sister May was on the administrative floor all day when you went to Orlando, watching and asking questions."

"Sister May is always nosey. That's how she is," Darryl says to Marshal, "You know how she's Bishop Wilkens spy just like the rest of them. She never liked Daniel from the moment Bishop took him in. Look," Darryl now looking at Daniel, "You know we stand behind you no matter what because that's what family does, but you need to chill on the projects…just for right now. You don't want the waves to overthrow the boat. I think we should hold off on the new church just for a couple of years. Focus on one thing at a time."

Daniel is thinking hard about what his friends are suggesting. Maybe they are right. It would give him some free time. He doesn't want to see his church go down the drain or worse be terminated as the pastor. "Ok, ok, alright, maybe getting another church is becoming too much. But what should I do about Thomas?"

"Oh we need him… The people at the church are warming up to him! Keep him around and when the time is right that's when you can release him to the new church. Put him somewhere else."

"Yeah picking Thomas was a good decision. He's cool, he helps bring in more money but he can become very powerful," added Marshal.

"But what should we do with him now because I'm not about to share the stage." Daniel knows it will not be a good business move if Thomas preach every other Sunday. He has to find something to do with him. He can't have him sit back. It wouldn't seem right. Plus, he knows that Thomas is getting use to his lifestyle. Then it occurred to Daniel what he can do. "We haven't found a new teen pastor for our teen church. Why don't we put him there?"

"That's not a bad idea. He can handle it," Darryl said. Marshal agrees with him.

"Then that settles it. I'll talk to Thomas about becoming the new teen pastor."

Daniel doesn't want to admit, it but he feels some pressure release from him. He's very thankful that he has best friends like Darryl and Marshal. Now there's one thing he has to do. He has to get back on track with Nicole. He places his beer down on the table. "I'm going to leave you two. I need to go see Nicole."

"Go make me another baby," Marshal jokes.

Daniel turns around to walk upstairs to talk to Nicole.

As Daniel walk upstairs, he began to think about where he is now. He has a magnificent home, an excellent and reliable car, an awesome family, an incredible after life. He doesn't want to go back to the old life. That life is so far behind him, it's a distant memory. He never wants to go back to it. He feels very proud of himself taking that step to meet with Bishop Wilkens. He feels even prouder that the Bishop decided to take him in and mold him into the person he is now. Daniel knows that he is powerful and is ready to take the church to another level. Another level, means more money, more money means more power. And people aren't quite ready for that yet. Daniel is the talk of the nation right now. His name is on the lips of every gospel artist, pastor, actors and hip hop artists. His voicemails and emails are flooded with secular celebrities that want to meet with him for counseling. He never thought in his lifetime he would ever talk to those people, let alone, them calling him on his personal phone. Ever since he became the Oprah of the church world, everyone from everywhere is running to his church. Just two Sundays ago, a couple came to him and told him that they moved to the area just to attend his church. And with their leap of faith, Daniel cut them a check for two thousand dollars just to say, "Welcome to the family." The excitement and joy on their face said it all. Daniel doesn't go around giving away money like that. What many pastors don't understand is that all of that money is not only tax-free, but you use that as a write off when tax season does come around. And the church brings in *a lot* of money during tax season. What you put out, you get back.

Daniel sees Nicole in the back lying back on the lounge by the pool wearing her sunglasses and skimpy bikini. He silently walks up to the back and is watching her quietly as she is enjoying the heat from the sun. She always enjoys the warm and hot weather. Her violet bikini fits perfectly on her sun-glowed skin. She gets beautiful every day, he thought to himself. He never seen a First Lady as good looking as Nicole. You can read the insecurities on the other ladies faces. Nicole is just beautiful, better yet breath-taking. They tried to conform her over the years. But she refused to lose her sex appeal. She still wears her skinny jeans, stilettos, bikinis on the beach, shorts and tank tops. She doesn't have to try to be sexy, she just is sexy in her own way.

Daniel clears his throat to get her attention, "Can I join you," he asked.

Nicole turns her head slightly to see Daniel standing in the doorway. "I guess I can have some company," she smirks.

Daniel walks to the empty lounge chaise next to her to stretch out.

"You must have really had a blast at Disney. Simone can't stop talking about it. She's been talking about it for a couple of days now," Nicole said.

"Yeah, it was fun. I think that's something I am going to do with Simone. Every year, we'll take a father and daughter trip somewhere for a couple of days."

"I think that would be an awesome idea. Just plan the trips during her vacation," she jokes.

"I can do that," he laughs, "So, I was talking to Darryl and Marshal downstairs and I wanted to talk to you about something."

Nicole takes in a deep breath. She isn't in the mood to hear about another idea of his that will keep him away from the family even more. Everything was fine when he was just preaching and making money from the church, but now he wants to dip into the business world. That's where it gets tricky. That money isn't tax-free and he can get into serious trouble if he gets caught doing something illegal.

"Nicole, are you listening," Daniel asked as he is trying to see if her hidden eyes are open.

"I'm listening Danny," she replies holding in her frustration.

"Darryl and Marshal had convinced me to stop building the new church."

Nicole jolts up a little, looking at Daniel. *Are you serious?*

"You don't sound too happy about that."

"No, I am happy actually. But what made you change your mind?"

"They feel as though. I'm taking on too many projects and its beginning to cause some problems. They told me that Sister May was on the administrative floor all day on Tuesday being very nosey. I'm not trying to raise any suspicions.

"That's what I've been telling you."

"I know you have and I'm sorry. I just want to make sure my family is okay. So, I'm just going to focus on the mini mall site. I'm going to let go of the new church. It'll give me some more time to spend with my family."

"Oh wow, I'm so glad you can squeeze us into your schedule," she says sarcastically.

"Nicole, you know we spend time together."

"Going to speaking engagements at our church and other functions isn't spending time together, Danny."

Daniel knows Nicole is right. The fancy hotels they stay in and shopping sprees Nicole goes on while he's at functions can become boring.

"Nicole, I'm really sorry. With my focus now just on the mini mall, I promise to give you my undivided attention. You're my world. And if you're not okay, then I'm not okay."

"I just don't want you to get so caught up on making money that you lose focus on things that truly matters the most."

"I understand but you have been on edge lately. And I have a feeling it has more to do with something that you aren't telling me."

She is sitting silently trying to hold back her tears. But to no avail, Daniel see a tear slide down her face. He didn't ask any questions, he quickly got up to hold her, rubbing her hair and kissing the top of her head. He gently takes off her sunglasses. She cries even more unable to hold back her tears. Daniel is hurting on the inside. He hates to see Nicole cry or even upset. He continues to hold her, "What's wrong Nicole? What has been bothering you lately?"

Nicole shakes her head slowly, "I didn't want to tell you," she cries.

"Tell me what?" Daniel continue to rub her head.

"I went to Dr. Cowl weeks ago and she told me that there is something wrong with my ovaries and I may not be able to have kids."

"What!"

"Daniel, I didn't want to tell. We've been trying for a while to have another baby and I knew something had to be wrong. I just didn't want to stress you out anymore. You have enough going on. Then with some of the people in the church talking about how the finances are being mishandled. It's just too much. I can't..." her voice drifts off, "I didn't want you to have any more issues to deal with."

Daniel picks her up and lays her next to him on the lounge chaise. He embraces her as she silently sobs in his chest. He is becoming very frustrated with himself to allow himself to get so busy he failed to recognize that something was wrong, and he is extremely mad about the board members. Their nosiness is now affecting his wife. Daniel clenches his teeth together.

"Nicole, you should have told me. You shouldn't have to hold that inside or keep that to yourself. I'm your husband…Is there anything we can do? There has to be something we can do."

"She mention in vitro but that's too much money, especially if the sperm doesn't take."

"Well, how much is too much?"

"It cost about $15,000 for two cycles."

"I'm sure our insurance can cover it."

"It doesn't. I checked. I know we have the money but with all the issues…"

"Don't you worry yourself about that," he says cutting her off, "Call Dr. Cowl to set up an appointment right away so we can get started."

"But Daniel what about the church?"

"Don't worry about them, I know what I have to do."

Daniel called an emergency board meeting to sit down with the three board members. He had enough about the rumors they are spreading. After speaking to Darryl and Marshal a couple of days ago, he wants to get to the bottom of it. Enough is enough. He's also going to speak to Thomas after the meeting to discuss with him about becoming the teen pastor. All of this is happening only because of the jealousy of others and how its effecting Nicole. And now since she is having an issue conceiving, she doesn't need the added stress. Bishop had told Daniel before about these kind of problems. He can handle it. He can handle the sly remarks by others, but leave his family out of it. Daniel told Marshal and Darryl to stay behind because he knows how hot headed they can get and he doesn't need them to start any trouble at the meeting.

Deacon Williams, Sister Barnes and Sister May and Brother Shawn, the accountant, should be arriving any minute. Daniel places a pitcher of water in the middle of the medium round oak table that is located in his office by the bookcase. He doesn't know how long the meeting will last. Which is why he asked them to be there by three. He doesn't want to stay long into the night defending himself. He doesn't understand what the problem can be. Everything he does is legit. Bishop taught him everything and how to keep things undercover. People are quick to put him in that category with the other preachers. And here he is ready to silence them.

Before he sat down on the sofa, he hears a knock at the door. Taking a deep breath, he looks around his office to make sure everything is in place. He opens the door and is shock to see everyone. It is as though they all rode together to attend the meeting. They always have to wait for Sister Barnes because she always runs late.

"Wow! Everybody is here," he says holding in his anticipation, "Come on in."

"Well, Pastor Daniel when you called this short notice emergency board meeting we knew it had to be serious," Deacon Williams said.

"Yes, well, we need to discuss a few things," Daniel responds after closing the office door. Everyone took their usual seats only this time everyone is quiet. Sister May and Sister Barnes is usually full of chatter.

Daniel took a seat next to Brother Shawn. He told him to bring the church expenses with him. Daniel is no fool. He knows the three board members already spoke amongst each other. If there are rumors that are being spread amongst the church about him, he wants to know every detail.

"Let's open up with a prayer," Daniel said.

He watched as the three board members close their eyes. Without closing his eyes, he began to pray, keeping an eye on them.

"Dear Heavenly Father, I thank you for bringing us together safely. We ask that you be here in this meeting to rectify any issues that we might have, in Jesus name, Amen."

"Amen," everyone chimes in as they open their eyes.

"Alright, I called this emergency meeting because there is an issue that was brought to my attention." Daniel didn't waste any time getting to the topic at hand. He leans back in his leather executive chair, relaxing his body posture. "I was told that there is an issue with how I handle the church's money."

Everybody's body language, except for Shawn's, began to get tense as Daniel continue to sit relaxed watching their body squirm. "Brother Shawn, can you pull up the account to the church please?"

"No problem," Shawn says. Shawn keeps track of everything just in case a time like this would arise, he can easily shut them down. Daniel hired Shawn as his accountant after the first year preaching at the church. He fired the accountant the Bishop placed at the church. The Bishop wasn't too happy about that but they moved passed that. Daniel didn't trust him and Daniel didn't like the fact that Bishop had too much control and eyes within the church.

"Sister May and Sister Barnes, you are awfully quiet. You usually have so much to say."

"Pastor Daniel, I don't know where these rumors are coming from," Sister Barnes replied, "This is all new to me."

"Yeah," Deacon Williams chimes in, "I haven't heard anything. You know I would have said something to you if I heard the church members talking."

Daniel just nods his head. "So why is it that I am hearing that its coming from the board members? Why is it, Sister May, you want to be nosey on the administrative floor, asking my church employees questions about me, the church's finances and my itinerary?"

"I wasn't being nosey Pastor Daniel," she snaps, "I was simply monitoring the staff while you were away."

"They're adults. I'm quite sure they can monitor themselves."

"I'll tell you this," Sister Barnes jumps in, "You're driving around in a $85,000 car, going on shopping sprees in Paris when you're supposed to be on duty for the church, handing out money to the people at the church as if we are a bank. You're opening a mini mall, and building another church. You're getting the money from somewhere. We, the board only approved the church, we didn't approve anything else."

"She is right Pastor Daniel," Deacon Williams finally agrees, "We approved to having another church to be built and the trip to Paris because of their request to have you minister there. But everything else is a no. Why do you need an $85,000 car anyways? People see you driving in your expensive car while they are still driving their cars that can barely get them to work. Some even take the bus here. It's a show-off! Now, I haven't said anything about this, but that's how I feel. And the house that you and your family live in, the church bought you and your family that house because that's what you wanted but it's too much!"

"Deacon Williams, it isn't a house. It's more like an oversized exclusive hotel," Sister May says laughing. "Why do you need an indoor and outdoor pool? Why do you need a house that has eight bedrooms and a full size guest house on the property that has four bedrooms in it? That house costed the church about 2.5 million dollars. But here we are living in apartments."

"I agree," Sister Barnes said, "You have people who live in the worst neighborhoods and you in a 2.5-million-dollar home in an exclusive suburb section on the north side. You should downsize to something smaller and reasonable."

"And let's not forget about his protégé he is bringing up," Deacon Williams adds, "He just bought a Brownstone townhouse and a new car."

"Yes, but that wasn't from the church. He bought that with his own money," Sister Barnes corrected him, "We only agreed to pay for his travel expenses whenever he goes with Pastor Daniel out of town."

Daniel just sat back and listened to them tell him how envious they are about him. Anger is swelling in the inside of him. He wants to lash out at them but he knows it will only make matters worse, which is why he told Darryl and Marshal not to come.

"Pastor Daniel, we have nothing against you but if you can settle down your spending and not throw money away, that would be great. Your spending is becoming frivolous. We know how much your salary is but we have concerns of where you are getting all of this money from. We know how much you admire the Bishop and want to have the things like him and other prominent pastors but you aren't them," Sister Barnes said.

"And you're right I'm not them. Brother Shawn, I know that we just paid the bills for the church and tithes was taken on Sunday, can you tell us what is the balance in the account," Daniel asked now facing Shawn.

With a stroke of a finger Shawn is able to access the church's online banking account.

"As of now we currently have 5.35 million dollars. We have more than enough to sustain the church. This is because of the increase in membership."

"People are only joining the church to see what they can get from the church," Sister May says.

"And because of that membership rose 25%. There is no other church that has an increase membership like this. We need to get a bigger church or expand on the property," Shawn said.

"Is the church paying for all of Pastor's expenses," Sister Barnes asked Shawn.

"You are asking him as if I'm not sitting right in front of you!!" Daniel has heard enough. He slams his fist on the table. "I don't need people like you on my team that don't share the same vision as I do. You've been a part of the board since the Bishop placed me here! If you had an issue concerning me, you should have come talk to me instead of talking behind my back as if I wouldn't hear it! I sign your checks that you get every two weeks! You chose to live in the ghetto, not me! You chose to drive the same run down car, not me! You act like you don't get paid to live comfortably! You're just like the other simple, no vision, low budget preachers. I don't waste my time and breath on them and I refuse to waste it on the three of you!"

Deacon Williams, Sister May and Sister Barnes is sitting motionless and speechless. They don't realize the nerve they have hit with Daniel.

"I chose to ignore the rumors, but when the rumors began to take a toll in my house, we have a problem! My wife is dealing with enough and doesn't need to hear your bullsh...," Daniel caught himself. He never resorted in cursing someone out and he isn't going to begin now.

Sister May clench her necklace in utter shock with Daniel's behavior. She has never seen this side of him before. Sister Barnes has watery eyes that are ready to explode. Deacon Williams had his arms tightly crossed against his chest as if he is trying to hold himself back.

Daniel always had a soft spot for the older people. He would want someone to treat his parents with the upmost respect and not the disdain he is showing toward them. But when his family is hurting, he doesn't care about age and being reasonable. "As of now, I release you as board members."

"You can't do that," Deacon Williams belts out, "Only Bishop Wilkens can call the shots here and you know that! We work for him!"

"Yes I can because I just did! So, since you work for the Bishop, get out my church and go work for him!"

Without saying a word, Deacon Williams got up from his seat and storms out the office.

"But Pastor, what are we going to do? We are on your payroll," Sister Barnes cries out now releasing her tears.

Taking a deep breath, Daniel sighs, "I'm not that heartless."

"But what will the church say? What should we tell the people?"

"Here's what I'll do, on Sunday I'll tell the church that you retired. But I tell you this, if I hear anything, anything else about how I run this church and its finances, I will cut you off so fast you'll be back on Medicare before you know it."

The ladies seem to be a little more relaxed.

"So ladies, is there anything else you need to say?"

"No, no," Sister May said silently, "We'll talk to Deacon Williams."

"There's no need to talk to him. He said what he needed to say. I don't want anything to do with him."

They slowly rose to their feet surprised at what just happened.

"Uhm, Pastor Daniel," Sister Barnes said, "We do apologize for everything. To bring closure to this matter, I didn't talk to any of the people at the church about this, nor did I talk to First Lady Nicole about these issues we had. What I said here, I only spoke to Sister May and Deacon Williams."

"Same here, Pastor Daniel," Sister May adds, "I didn't talk to anyone else about this. And I wasn't being nosey on the admin floor, I was honestly making sure everything was being done properly."

Daniel nods his head in agreement, "Ok…fine, expect a little increase in your paycheck. I can't say the same for Deacon Williams being that he is now no longer on payroll."

"Thank you Pastor Daniel."

The ladies left the office feeling much better than they did about fifteen minutes ago.

Daniel leans back in his chair to make sure they left.

"Daniel," Shawn began to speak.

Daniel held up his hand. He got up to make sure they are alone. He looks out his office door to make sure the floor is empty.

Turning around he looks at Shawn and they both started laughing.

"Daniel, you are brutal," Shawn says.

"I could have fired them if this was in the corporate world. This is a business and I'm the CEO," Daniel yells with his arms stretched high.

"I knew something was up when you told me to be here for an emergency meeting. I honestly don't think its Sister Barnes and Sister May that's talking. Deacon Williams has had an issue with you for a while now."

"Yeah, I don't trust him."

"We have enough money in the church to do anything you want. It's nothing wrong with the church taking care of you."

"My point exactly. You take care of me, I'll take care of you."

"I think you just came up with your sermon for Sunday."

"I think so too. Also, I'm going to stop the building on the new church for now."

"Okay, but we already dished out the money for the property."

"Sell it and we can use the money for something else. I don't know for what, but I'll figure it out."

"We need new board members too. Do you have anyone else in mind?"

"As of now, no, I don't. But we'll get some members. I have to use who I have here and who I can trust. Did you look into the beach house in Hawaii?"

"Yeah, the realtor told me it about 2.3 million. Do you want to go for it?"

"Heck yeah! But the price has to come down."

"Did you tell Nicole about it?"

"No, not yet. She's too stressed right now." Daniel doesn't have any intentions on telling Nicole. The less she knows, the better. Many pastors have a two or three homes. Nicole always loved going to Hawaii, so he wants to surprise her with a nice beach house in Maui.

"That will be the perfect stress reliever."

"Especially now... And before I forget I need about fifty thousand dollars from the personal account."

"Big spender," Shawn smiles.

"Yeah, I have to keep the wife happy."

Shawn never ask questions. He gets paid a hefty salary and will always be Daniel's yes man.

"I'll also transfer the usual amount into your personal savings," Shawn says, "I'm going to create a separate account so it won't be too noticeable in your regular personal savings."

"Alright, did you give the Bishop his portion?"

"Yeah, he's covered. When are you going to branch out from the Bishop? The extra hundred grands a month can go straight to you. Since you are going to stop the building of the other church, that is going to set you back."

"Yeah I know...But I rather take my time with this. This can go either way. I have to talk to Thomas about becoming the teen pastor."

Shawn began to laugh, "Thomas is going to be upset. He isn't going to be making that money like he thought he was."

"He'll be okay. We'll just increase his salary a little."

"What's the going rate for a teen pastor?"

"Well, at those run down churches, they don't get paid or barely do. They get maybe seven thousand. But at megachurches like this, a full-time teen pastor can make about seventy thousand and that doesn't include money from speaking engagements."

"Dang! I think I'm in the wrong line of business."

"I said the same thing five years ago and here I am," Daniel says as he leans back in the leather executive chair, with his hands folded behind his head.

Chapter 10

1 John 4:1 (MSG)

> "My dear friends, don't believe everything you hear. Carefully weigh and examine what people tell you. Not everyone who talks about God comes from God. There are a lot of lying preachers loose in the world."

Thomas is walking around the back of Daniel's Victorian style mansion. The last time Thomas was at Daniel's majestic house was when he was offered to be his under Shephard. That day changed everything for him. It's been about five months and he is finally at a place in his life that he's been aiming for and all it took was a step in the ministry. Jessica still isn't thrilled about his sudden interest in ministry because she feels that Daniel has always been blinded by the money in the church. She doesn't want to break-up with Thomas because she still loves him but, she refuses to get caught up in that lifestyle. Which is why she doesn't want to meet or hang out with Daniel and them. Surprisingly, that doesn't bother Thomas too much. The more Jessica pry about how he makes his money in the church, the more he wants to keep her away from Daniel. With her constant questioning, she is beginning to push him away.

Thomas stops to look at a flower garden that is adjacent to the guest house. There are multiple of red and white roses, lilies, periwinkles and a growing sunflower. Thomas isn't a flower type of guy. Instead of a flower garden, Thomas is thinking of a regular garden. His grandmother who lived in the deep south had a vegetable garden. He remembers her working in the garden every day weeding, watering and planting. She had numerous of vegetables you can think of and some you've never heard of. She would have Thomas in the garden every time she saw him laying around the house watching television. She would have him in the garden and in church. Thomas doesn't care so much about gardening, but thinks of his grandmother every time he gets a moment to look at a garden. As far as church, he has no other choice but to like it. It's his only source of income. An income he is quite happy about. And now since Daniel is going to place him in a church of his own next year, he knows he's really going to be banking more money. His grandmother would have been so proud of him. He's going to be a pastor of a church and living comfortably in the ministry. Maybe he'll have his own garden too one day when he gets his first home and family.

Thomas takes a glance at his watch. Daniel told him to wait in the back, after letting him inside the house, almost twenty minutes ago. Daniel appeared to be preoccupied when he answered the door. If it was a bad time, Daniel should have rescheduled, Thomas thought to himself. He doesn't have time to waste.

Thomas took a deep breath and put his hands in his jean pockets. He had made reservations at a restaurant that Jessica wanted to go to for a long time. They had opportunities to go, but Jessica would have had to pay for the dinner. And that was a big no-no for Thomas. He didn't mind her treating dinner at the kick back weekend type places, but certain restaurants should be an exclusion, and this was one of them. He feels like a man should pay for those high-end, five star restaurants.

"Thomas," Daniel calls out to him. Thomas turns around to see Daniel casually walking toward him. "I'm so sorry to keep you waiting. I was just taking care of some things."

"That's alright. I was enjoying your backyard, if this is what you call a yard," Thomas jokes. With a garden, a full size guest house, a gazebo, and an in-ground pool with a pool house, this isn't your usual backyard.

"Let's sit over here on the patio," Daniel laughs.

"How is First Lady Nicole? I heard you say that she was sick last Sunday."

"She's fine. She has to get some rest that's all."

The two pastors pull out a seat to sit down under the beige sun umbrella that's is attached to a glass table.

"This is some weather we're having huh," Thomas said.

"Yeah, I wouldn't trade this weather for the crap they have to deal with further north… So how's everything with you? I've been so busy lately, We'd never really get a chance to catch up on things because we've been extremely busy these past few months."

"Oh everything is fine. I can't complain. I'm just enjoying life."

"Now, I asked you before but, when am I'm going to meet this Jessica? Are you two still together, cause you're hiding her from us? It's been five months now and I still haven't seen her. Is she the not going to church type?"

Thomas laughs, "No, I'm not hiding her. Going to church has never been her thing, that's all. You'll meet her soon. Maybe after church tomorrow. She can come with us to Lafayette."

"That sounds like a plan. I would like to meet her. Did you want anything to drink?"

"No, I'm good." Thomas is becoming a little impatient. He hoped Daniel didn't bring him there for small talk.

"So as you know the board members had to retire last week."

"Yes, I remember you mentioning it at church last Sunday."

"Yes, it was soon to happen. You know when you get older, you want to settle down. It's just too bad Deacon Williams wasn't there to get honored too."

Thomas nods his head in agreement, "Deacon Williams is always in church. I was surprised he wasn't there." Thomas can tell that Daniel is a little troubled concerning Deacon Williams absence from church. He knows there has to be more to the story, but it isn't his problem that has him concerned.

"Well since we are short on board members, there has to be some changes."

"Does some of these changes have anything to do with me," Thomas asked pointing to himself.

"Yeeeahhh," Daniel replies hesitantly.

Thomas is now attempting to keep his temper under control. After a half a year of working alongside with one of the rising top pastor in the country, he is getting the boot. How is he going to pay for his new lifestyle now? He refuses to go back to the ghetto. Thomas remains quiet so he can hear Daniel tell him that he is no longer needed, and then explain to him why he is losing his position before he punches Daniel in the mouth.

"We are in need of a teen pastor for the teen church and I want you to lead it. You will have total control."

Thomas sat forward catching his breath.

"Are you okay," Daniel asked.

"Yeah, I thought I was about to be fired."

Daniel laughs, "Of course not! I need you; I wouldn't fire you."

"Man, you scared me for a moment," Thomas chuckles, "I was trying to think about how I was going to pay for my car, my Brownstone and other bills."

"No, I wouldn't do that. So, are you willing to take my offer?"

"Uh, I never worked with teenagers before. I wouldn't even know how to preach to them."

"That's the thing, you don't have to preach. Just teach them. Talk to them on their level. You can do so much with the teens. Do you know about the big event they host every year with the top gospel artists in NYC?"

"Most definitely! They have thousands and thousands of people at the two-day event."

"Well, what if I tell you that I can possibly get you to be one of the headliners to preach there at the one two years from now?"

"Wow," Thomas says, "That's too big of a platform. I'm not sure if I'll be ready for something that big. I'm hardly ready to teach at Bible Study on some Wednesdays and I really wasn't ready when I first walked in your office about five months ago."

"Listen Thomas, its either you're in or out. You have to trust yourself. I don't want to push you to do anything you don't want to do. If you feel like all of this is too much for you to handle, then you are free to go. Cause at this point, I can't have doubters on my team. It's either you're with me or not. Now if you need time to think about it, then I'll give you some time."

Daniel is beginning to fume on the inside because ever since he chose Thomas to be his trainee, Thomas always seemed hesitant about the whole preaching gig. He doesn't need anyone like this in his camp.

"Daniel, I didn't mean to make you feel a certain way. I appreciate all of this. I really do. I'm actually becoming comfortable preaching. But you have to understand that all of this is still new to me. I'm sure you remember the feeling you got when you had to preach in front of hundreds."

"I remember it quite well. After a couple of times, I was good but I think I know what the problem is."

The wheels in Thomas' head is beginning to turn. He hopes that Daniel doesn't cancel him out. He came too far to give up what he's doing.

"You weren't as hungry as I was. I wanted into the ministry. I wanted everything that the ministry had to offer. I can't say the same for you," Daniel says as he sat back in the chair, "I misjudged you. Tell me something, why did you really go into the ministry school? Why become a certified clergy if it's something you aren't sure about doing? Why did you accept my offer from the beginning? You could have just said no and I could have found someone else."

"Well," Thomas began.

"I want the truth," Daniel abruptly cuts him off.

"To be honest, I don't think you can handle the truth," Thomas snaps back intently. Thomas' laid back, good boy behavior disappears. Thomas knows that he is taking a chance but he can't continue to be someone that he's not. He is prepared for Daniel to kick him out and if so, there is always work with Chris.

"Try me," Daniel smirks. He already had a heads up about Thomas from Darryl and Marshal. Daniel knows all about Thomas running drops in the streets and hanging out with the wrong crowd. He hopes Thomas will stay on board and stay away from the wrong crowd. Daniel is always about helping others t. And if he has to pull someone off the streets to get a taste of this life behind the pulpit, he'll do it, depending on who the person is. And Thomas is that one person, he'll help.

"I only got into the ministry because of the money. I saw what you had and played along. There's your truth! So, if I have to bounce and make my money elsewhere then so be it."

Daniel leans back in the chair and chuckles lightly.

"What's so funny? Go ahead and give me the boot."

"Thomas, you can't fool me and you never did. I always knew you were here just for the money. Every person who goes into the ministry thinks about the fast cash."

"Why did you choose me? I know you said Minister Perry told you about me but why take the word from one man, especially since you knew that I am here for the perks from that life." Thomas has now flipped the script.

"Besides Minister Perry, I watched your sermonettes. You are different from those that I've heard preach."

"What do you mean you watched my sermonettes. You were never there. I would have remembered seeing you."

"We record everything in the ministry school. What appealed to me was your appearance."

"My appearance?" Thomas is confused.

"You looked out of place. You are rough around the edges. I can tell you're from the streets. I'm not from the streets but I grew up around it to know when I see someone from it. So besides the obvious, which is money, why get involve in the ministry?"

"Besides the money…it was something to do. It was either make runs for my boy and make that fast cash or do something that's legit. I was unemployed for two years before you took me on. I looked for work and no one would hire me. While I was unemployed, I began going to church. You know how we do, when things don't go right, turn to the church and God. When I heard about the ministry school, I had to get involved. I figure its free and maybe I can get a job as a preacher making money. I can make my own hours and its legit. Sure, I want to see people get saved, you know, I grew up in the church so I know all about that, but I have to live too."

Thomas finally came clean. He has to admit, the lifestyles that he sees many pastors living are ideal. One of his friends he grew up with was the biggest man whore. But somehow this friend ended up a politician and became a preacher. He sees him riding around in his Mercedes, with his wife and kids, living in a two story home and still manage to keep a mistress or two on the side. Thomas always felt that if God can bless that, then surely he can bless a legit guy like him.

"If that's your reason then you should have no problem doing the job," Daniel said.

Thomas was not too shock a Daniel's response. He knows Daniel is just like the rest of them. He wants the money too.

"Just be yourself Thomas. After hearing you, I think you would be perfect for teen church. So are you in?"

"Yeah, I'm in. Like you said this is what I wanted to do. So, since I'm being myself, I can ask you if the pay is still the same."

"You'll be getting a little more because more is expected from you."

"Let's hear it," Thomas replied, ready to take on more responsibilities.

"You are now in a place where you will have a lot of people and pastors testing your creditability. As you are well aware, we have a lot of pastors, bishops, prophets, apostles, who are quite upset with the lifestyle us successful pastors have. You have to know the Scriptures and what it says. So, you must read the Bible but focus on the main points, prosperity, love, wisdom and of course salvation. Those are the main key points every pastor will question and attack you on. Be ready. No one can sit you down from the church, but me. But no one, absolutely no one, can strip you from being a preacher, except for yourself. You play the deck that is handed to you correctly, you'll win at life. Like I said before, what you see here can be all yours."

"I can do that. I'm all in. I didn't know how you would respond to my intentions which is why I was always hesitant. You have no idea how hard it was to put on a mask."

"Well, you have to wear that mask when you are around church folks. And when you preach, use a preaching voice. Notice how my voice changes when I'm on the pulpit or when I talk to certain church people? As to what I'm hearing about you, you are doing an awesome job. So keep it up. And watch your surroundings. Which means you have to leave your boy Chris in the hood."

Thomas is shocked to hear Daniel mention Chris' name. He doesn't like the fact that he knows so much information about him. Thomas hates people in his business, but then again, Daniel isn't just a regular person. Daniel is really trying to look out for him and help him out.

"I had to check out your background before allowing you fully into the fold. That's why I wanted to know the truth. If you want to be taken seriously in the church world, you have to leave the street life fully behind because it will destroy you. And also, I don't need that around my family. I took my family out of the hood. I don't need the drama from the streets come knocking at my door. And lastly, understand that technology now will destroy you before you even know it too. Sometimes when you think no one is watching, they are watching closer than you think. There are people waiting for us to slip up. People are quick to record you or snap a picture of you as soon as they see you slipping."

Thomas is listening very closely and holding on to every word Daniel is telling him. If he wasn't ready before, he is definitely ready now.

Thomas is sitting across from Jessica admiring her and the city skyline behind her. This is the first time since they decided to work on their relationship, that they've gone out. They usually stay at Thomas' house to watch Netflix and chill or just watch Netflix and sleep. Thomas has been busy traveling and helping Daniel. But since he's to be the new full time pastor of teen church, his traveling should slow down a bit. Although, he finds it quite entertaining to travel and see the country, he just misses being home sometimes. But he sure does love what he is doing. Can't nothing change that. He now has his passport stamped for France, a hefty bank account, a new ride, a home and a full-time job. He should have gotten into this line of work years ago.

He takes Jessica's hand into his hand. He loves rubbing her hand and cuffing her fingers when his. He loves how she pampers herself. She gets a manicure and pedicure almost every three weeks, sometimes two. Jessica tries to get Thomas to get a couple's massage with her, but Thomas isn't down for that. Massages isn't his thing unless he's getting a physical massage from Jessica. But now since he's going to be the new full-time teen pastor, he has to trend lightly with getting his "*special*" public massages from her.

"How's work coming along? Did you apply for the new position," Thomas asked?

"Yes, so now you can stop hounding me," she laughs, "I should be hearing from them within two weeks."

"You'll hear from them before then. There's no way you can be turned down for the supervisor position. You've been at the company for almost eight years now."

"I hope you're right. The pay is pretty nice. Instead of my measly fifty-thousand, I will be making seventy-two thousand."

"That's great! So, will you be in the same office or will they relocate you to the new office in the city?"

"I'm not sure, I know the supervisor position is in the new building on the north side of town."

"So, I'm assuming you are going to be looking for a new place to live? I know that's an extra twenty-minute drive for you."

"I'll definitely be moving. I just started looking for a place. It's getting crazy over there. Chris and his crew hang-out in front of the building all the time and is beginning to attract unwanted people. And now I'm hearing that Chris is having someone do drops by Madison."

"Madison? That isn't his turf. What exactly is he trying to do beside get himself killed?"

Jessica shrugs her shoulders, "I don't know. I don't say much to them besides, 'hello', I'm doing fine', and 'goodbye'. I'm glad you're not doing drop-offs for him anymore."

"You make it sound as if that's all I did. I've done a couple of drops for him. And I only did that when things got rough. But since I have a full-time job, things are looking up for me." Thomas began to feel a little cocky. He's quite proud of himself.

"So, how long are you going to be doing this?"

"What, preaching," he replied looking at her. Her smile began to decrease, "Aww Jess, you know I'm in this for good. And, Daniel just made me the full-time pastor of teen church."

Thomas releases her hands and sat back as their waiter put their entrees in front of them.

"Since when Pastor Daniel became just Daniel to you? And why would he make you pastor of teen church? You don't be around kids like that, especially teenagers. They can very ruthless."

"Things are on hold with the building of the new church, and so because he already has me out in the forefront, he wants me to be pastor of the teen church. I can preach to the teens. I'll just talk to them on their level. It's not that difficult."

Thomas picks up his knife and fork and began cutting his sirloin steak. Thomas is just happy to be making enough money to dabble in this luxury. He put a piece of the succulent steak in his mouth. "Mm, this is good. Now, this is what real steak taste like. I tell you one thing. I've been eating and drinking the best there is. Tomorrow after service, I want to introduce you to Daniel and Nicole. It's been long enough. They've been wanting to meet you for a while. We're going to meet them at Lafayette."

"Lafayette is quite expensive; don't you think?"

"Can't settle for less anymore." Thomas notices that Jessica hasn't touched her chicken marsala. "What's wrong? Why aren't you eating?"

Jessica just stares at him before responding, "So is that it? You're in it for the money?"

"Here you go. Why can't you just be happy for me, damn."

"I don't think pastors are supposed to curse," mocks Jessica.

"I'm a man first. And as a man I would appreciate if my woman would support me. I mean, Damn, Jess, you were complaining before about me not having a job and plotted to cheat on me. And now that I have a full-time job, you have a problem with what I do."

"But I can't support this if you're preaching for money, Thomas. You won't be good to anyone in the congregation. You'll be just like everyone else. I'm just going to ask you a simple question and I want the truth, are you in it for the money?"

"Come on Jess, are you serious right now? I brought you to a nice upscale restaurant that we've been trying to come to for a minute, with a romantic view and s***, and plan to go for a walk along the lit up pathway with the rest of the couples, and you're ruining the experience because you can't support with I do. I don't have to do this. If I would have known you was going to ruin the night, you could have just stayed home."

"Thomas, all I said was that I can't support what you're doing if you're in it for the money, that's all. You're the one who is flying off the handle, ruining the evening."

Thomas is keeping quiet. He continues to eat his steak and suppress his anger. He can't be in a relationship with Jessica if she can't support what he is doing. Just like any job, you work for the money. Thomas has been fighting the urge to break-up with Jessica but after this, he knows what must be done. There is no way he can have her around and she's questioning everything and everybody. He would rather be happy alone.

Jessica picks up her fork, and slowly cut the chicken. She lost her appetite. She knew she shouldn't have said anything, but she just doesn't want Thomas to be in the mix of some shady church business. They're the ones that made her mother go broke. Her mother gave to the church all the time. Her life was the church. She even began to assist the pastor of the church. Her mother was hardly home because she was always at different church services with the pastor. Her mother would give most of her money to the church and always ordered things from the television ministries. Although, her mother struggled because she would give her money away to the church, she made sure the bills were paid with the little she had left. It got to the point that the members began to leave the church. Eventually, her mom was the only member left at the church and decided to move away to state, and leave the church after the numerous of talks from family and friends. Jessica's mom had to do what was best for her spiritually and financially. But her pastor never gave up, and continued to hound former members and her mom about sending donations to her folded church.

It was a scam. It's all a scam.

"When people tithe at the church, what do you do with the money," she proceeds to ask.

Thomas is already aggravated. He huffs loudly, "Why Jessica? What do you want to know?"

"With all the money that the church brings in what does the church do with the money besides pay the staff, you and Pastor Daniel?"

"There are bills that have to be paid, just like any other business."

"Business?"

"That's it," Thomas says dropping his fork in anger, "I can't do this, we can't do this."

Jessica looks at Thomas anticipating him to defend his church again.

"I brought you here to have a romantic date. We don't spend time together because we're both so busy. All we do is chill at my house, talk on the phone and text like we are some high school teenagers. I'm trying to work on this relationship and make it work. But all you seem to care about is the church funds and questioning me concerning preaching."

"I question you because you always said that you were uncomfortable and am just curious to why the sudden change."

"But the way you are questioning me is all wrong. You don't support me. The last time you didn't support me, you cheated on me. But yet I decided to give you another shot. I don't trust you. I can't trust you. And I can't be with someone who can't support me and question my every move."

"What are you saying Thomas," Jessica asks as her heart is pounding in her chest.

"I love you but I can't force this relationship. I can never make you happy like I use to. Even if you've never cheated on me, you will still question me. So, let's just enjoy what is left of this dinner, I'll take you home, and we'll part ways from there."

Jessica's eyes fill with tears. She wants to make the relationship work. She lost him before because of her stupidity and she doesn't want to lose him again.

"Thomas, I'm sorry," she says softly, as the tears slid down her face. "I don't want this to be over. I'll support you. I'll do whatever you need me to do. I'll go to church with you. I don't want to lose you again."

"Jessica it's over. We'll just coming back to the same issue. I'm done. I know that I can never make you happy. So, we need to part ways." Thomas didn't lift his head to look at Jessica because although he meant what he said, he can't stand to see her cry.

She wipes her tears with the black cloth and excuses herself from the table. As she walks away, Thomas looks in her direction, watching her walk toward the bathroom. Thomas continues to eat his steak trying to not have a care. He is through with Jessica questioning him and now she is becoming nosey concerning the church. He doesn't need her around him or anyone else constantly asking questions. He doesn't understand why she is being extremely nosey. If she was so concerned about his motives, she would have said something to him when he went to the ministry school and became certified. Why is she so interested now? Why does she want to know his motives now? Something doesn't add up and its troubling Thomas. So avoid any uprising drama with Jessica, it's best if they end their relationship.

Jessica had dried her eyes in the bathroom and knew that she did her part. It's out of her hands now. She freshens up her make-up and walks quickly back to the table. She is ready to go home. There is no need to finish this dinner.

He said his peace. Approaching Thomas with more confidence she says, "Take me home please. I'll be outside waiting."

Thomas is now confused with her sudden perkiness. She came back to the table with a little more bounce in her step. He doesn't know what she took in the bathroom but he is ready to go too. It is time to end the night. He motions for the waiter to send him the check. Their waiter was watching everything unfold between the both of them. He knew it was a matter of time for them to leave. When he gives Thomas the check, the waiter said, "You deserve to be with someone that is so much better, if you don't mind me saying."

At any other time, Thomas would have snapped, but he knows that the waiter is right. He nods his head smiling and gave the waiter two hundred dollars and told him to keep the rest for tip. Thomas didn't bother looking at the check. If he did, he would have realized that he just gave the waiter almost an eighty-dollar tip.

"Good morning church," Pastor Daniel roars in the microphone.

He is greeted with warm cheers and applause. Daniel stands there smiling and waving his hand to God. The congregation began to settle down after a couple of minutes.

"I know this is out of routine. I know our mass choir is ready to do their selection but I want to make an announcement to the church." Daniel pauses for a moment before he continues, "There has been many changes that has been going on within the church. You know that we were going to build a sister church in another location. But that has discontinued. My focus need to continue to be here at Abundant Overflow. I want to continue to reach the masses. As of today, we have nine thousand members and we are still growing. Most of our members are from other states and some overseas. They joined our church and watch us faithfully online and give their tithes and offering online too."

The congregation went crazy. He waves his hand telling them to settle down as he begins to pace slowly on the broad platform. "That is awesome church. And with that we have hundreds of teens in the teen church building that want to hear the gospel and get them ready for the solid food, the solid teaching that will prepare them for life. Now, there has to be a special somebody to handle teenagers."

"Amen pastor," people began to say out loud.

"Teenagers are a hand full. My ten-year-old daughter isn't a teen yet but First Lady Nicole and I are already seeing the pre-teen attitude." He began to laugh when he sees Simone cross her arms and pouts her lips. "But we have to remember that not too long ago we were once teenagers. We caused our parents grief too and it was a struggle to get us to church. But I'm glad that our teens here at Abundant Overflow want to be here. They want to come to church! And that's a great thing. We had our ministers here run teen church until we were able to find someone to take over. So, I have put in place a full-time teen pastor that I know who will continue to reach the kids, and that is Pastor Thomas Butler."

Daniel has elevated Thomas from being a Minister to being a Pastor. Everyone stood up to applaud and cheer for Pastor Thomas as he walks onto the pulpit. Thomas is overwhelmed with the accolades. He smiles brightly, showing his gleaming pearly whites. He shakes hands with Daniel, ready to take on the new adventurous assignment. Thomas changed his clothes numerous of times this morning until he decided to just wear jeans and a button up shirt. Being the pastor of a teen church, you should be relaxed just like the teens. Being in dress pants, suit and tie, can come across as stuffy.

Daniel hands Thomas the microphone wanting him to address the excited congregation. "Praise the Lord church," Thomas says in preaching voice. He has been practicing his new preaching voice all night. He doesn't want to come across too hood for the people. "I must say that I am beyond honored to lead the teen church. I have so much to pour into the youth and have so many plans in mind for the teen church. Thank you Pastor Daniel," Thomas continues as he is now looking at Daniel, "Thank you for seeing something in me that no one else saw. You poured so much into me in these last five months and I'm ready to take the church by storm along with you. I look up to you as a big brother I've always wanted. Before I came here and before I began my calling, I didn't have a family. My grandmother raised me and she went on to be with the Lord years ago. So, I was left alone. I didn't have a family to call my own. I did what I had to do to survive. But now, I can say that I have a family. Thank you for taking me in."

The two pastors gave each other a brotherly hug. Daniel is caught off guard by what Thomas said and it is tugging at his heart. "You will always be family," Daniel says to him in his ear. Even Nicole, had to wipe away some tears. After the emotional high, Thomas is off to teen church.

As Thomas enters teen church, a gospel rap group from the church is performing one of their songs on their independent album. The lights are dim and has green, yellow and red scatter lights going wild across the room with screaming teenagers. You would think you have entered a club scene. But these teens were jumping for joy, laughing, smiling, rapping along with the group and praising God. Thomas is quite impress with what he is seeing. He slowly makes his way along the side, walking toward the front, bouncing his head with the music. As he approaches the front, he keeps reassuring himself that he can do this. There is so much that he can do with this. The talent in the room is insane. Not only is the rap group on fire, but the live band is extraordinary, and there are some teens that have created a dance battle in the front. Ideas are beginning to flood his mind. Thomas has never felt so ready in his life. He has a feeling that he finally found his niche in the church.

"Alright, alright," said one of the rappers on the stage, "We need to introduce to yall our new leading teen pastor. Yall know we can't go in like we want to." Him and some others began to laugh.

Thomas know that he has to keep the same timeframe as they have in the main sanctuary. The flashing lights ceased but the lights remained dim to keep the intense mood.

"Pastor Thomas, they're all yours," he says in the microphone.

Thomas walks onto the lit platform and addresses them the way he would talk to any teenager. "What's up," he says loudly and clearly in the mic.

The teens respond with the same hello greeting back. Some teens just stood there in thought trying to figure out Thomas. The rap group began to shuffle off the platform.

"No, come back here. Where are yall going? Come back up here. You can't just start a fire then bounce."

They laugh as they head back onto the platform with Thomas.

"Alright, so this is what's going to happen. I'm going to tell everyone a little something about myself, then you guys," he says pointing at the rap group, "Are going to put on a fifty-minute mini concert, can you do that?"

The group is shocked. They were never given that opportunity to have a concert of any kind during teen church. They are beyond ecstatic.

"Are you guys cool with that," Thomas yells in the mic to the teens.

"Yeah! Yes," the teens holler back in anticipation.

"Alright, so you guys decide what you're going to do. Do you have your music?"

"We always have our music. We stay ready," the leader of the rap group said.

"That's what I'm talking about, be ready, stay ready," he says to the rap group before turning around to face the teens, "Alright, so I'm Pastor Thomas. I'm sure you guys are going to call me something different. You've probably seen me around here and there before being taken in by PD."

The teens call Pastor Daniel PD.

"So, let me tell you that I can relate to each and every one of you. I'm from the hood, the west side."

"West Side," a couple of teens chanted.

"I held down the block with my boys, while working a full-time job at a store in Cherry Blossom Mall. I was a store manager. I was a professional during the day and a hustler at night. I held down the streets and held down a lucrative store. I knew how to go straight hood," he says in a thugged voice, "Then I knew how to go proper," he says in a proper dialect. The teens began to laugh.

"But all that changed when my store closed and I was left unemployed. At the time, I was living with my girl. She held me down and I held her down as much as I could but my life felt empty. So, I began attending Abundant Overflow and joined the ministry school. From there, I got certified and was taken in by PD. My journey from there to here was intense. I lost friends who I thought was my friends. Because God was transforming me, he had to transform me from my friends. I even had to let my shorty go. She couldn't come with me on this journey. Your friends who you think are your friends, really aren't your friends. Those who are your friends now, who are there when things get rough, and keep it one hundred, those are your real friends. When you begin living the life God has for you, you won't have the same friends. Even when Jesus grew up, he had friends when he was a teenager, but when he went into the wilderness he was alone. My former friends have now become my associates. But it's all good though. I still got love for them. I may not be living in the west side anymore, I may live somewhere further away from the chaos, but I will always remember where I came from and what I've gone through to get here. So, you guys out there," as he stretches his hands to the teens, "You're going to go through some stuff or could be going through something right now, dealing with school, you breaking up with your girl or man, cheating, hustling to survive, parents, siblings, friends, or trying to keep up with the latest everything. It may seem trivial to some adults, but let me tell you, I remember what it's like to be a teenager. Being a teenager, prepares you for life. So let God prepare you. Let God help get you ready. It's going to be crazy but as long as I'm here. You got me."

The teens began to clap and roar with happiness. Even the ones who were left standing in bewilderment in the beginning are cheering. Thomas reached the teens. He is happy he made the decision to do this. He feels free. "Are you guys ready," Thomas asked the gospel rap group.

"Yeah, let's do this."

The music started up again, the shattered color lights came back on and the rap group began their mini impromptu concert. Thomas hung back, leaning against the wall on the side, bouncing along with everyone else. He gave them a couple of high fives, as the teens began to warm up to him. If he would have known teen church is this lit, he would have come to teen church to hang out on some Sundays. He sees why so many teens come here. If teen church ever existed when he was younger, he knows that it wouldn't have been as entertaining as this, but if it was, his grandmother wouldn't have to drag him to church every Sunday. And maybe he would have become a pastor sooner.

After teen church was over he collected about eighteen hundred dollars. He is surprised to collect as much as he did, especially coming from teens, but he knows that he can't keep the entire eighteen hundred. Practically all of the teens put in for tithes. He can't pocket the tithes, only the offering which he only got about four hundred dollars. That's of the one things he'll miss about preaching in the main sanctuary. Adults knows how to give extra. He just has to teach the teens how to give extra. Thomas went to the mini coffee shop that Pastor Daniel had opened about a year ago in the church, to get a small cup of coffee. Thomas is hanging around waiting for Daniel to be finished for the day. Daniel has some last minute business he needs to take care of in the office. They're supposed to be going out for dinner and Daniel is expecting to meet Jessica. But there is no Jessica. When Jessica got up from the table to go to the exit door, she returned just as quickly telling him to take her home. Thomas kept his cool on the outside but was burning up on the inside. Jessica had hurt him for the last time.

Thomas takes the cup of coffee from the young man's hand, heading back to the teen church to set up his office while he waits for Daniel and Nicole to be ready. His mind is so cloudy with frustrations from Jessica, that he bumps into a young woman who is standing behind him waiting to get her cup of coffee.

"I'm sorry, excuse me," Thomas says. The young lady had grabbed his arm to catch her balance.

"It's fine," she laughs, "I know what a good cup of coffee can do to you," she smiles.

Thomas smiles back. The young lady proceeds to the counter to order a small cup of coffee. Thomas is fighting with his decision to introduce himself. She is beautiful. He doesn't want her or anyone else see him looking at her figure that her lilac wrap dress is covering. He quickly takes a couple of bills out his pocket and places it on the counter. "I'll take care of the lady's coffee," he says.

"Thank you Pastor Thomas," she smiles.

The young man hands the young lady her coffee looking at Thomas with a smirk and gives him a silent head nod. He knows Thomas is about to make his next move with the unknown lady.

As the young woman turn around to walk away, Thomas struck up a nerve to say, "So, I know you know me, but I don't know your name," he smiles.

"Kimberly."

"Hi, Ms. Kimberly, did you enjoy the service today?"

"Yes, I did actually. Pastor Daniel's message is always on time."

"Are you a member here or are you visiting?"

"Yes, I've been a member here for about a year now."

Kimberly and Thomas began to slowly walk away from the coffee stand. Thomas is infatuated with Kimberly's smile and brown eyes. She is about three inches shorter than Thomas without her heels on which almost put her eye level. She has a smooth butter pecan complexion. She has on a hint of make-up which enhances her high cheek bones and feminine features. Thomas isn't trying to get into anything serious, especially since ending things with Jessica last night. But he can use a friend. "How do you like Abundant Overflow so far?"

"I love it," she exclaims, "Ever since I'd joined, things really began turning around in my life."

"Well, I'm glad things are going well for you."

"How was your first day as the teen pastor? Did those hormonal teens scare you," she jokes?

Thomas begins to laugh, "I couldn't let them see me sweat. But when I walked in, it was unlike any teen church I've seen and been to. The kids are able to be free and express their joy for the Lord in their own way."

"Sounds amazing."

"Actually I was just setting up my office in the teen church. Would you like to see it?"

"If it's okay, I would love to."

Thomas and Kimberly began to walk over toward the teen church extension to the building. Kimberly is excited to see another part of the church that she has never seen before. She also had a soft eye for Pastor Thomas, ever since Daniel introduced him to the church. All she knows is, he isn't married, he isn't gay and is fully into church. So, it was safe to daydream about him. She's not the only one who has eyes for Pastor Thomas. Many other single women undress him with their eyes and the talks that she over hears is downright sinful in church. What turns her on even more about Thomas is his rough-neck undercover personality. He can hide it all he wants to, but Kimberly, like so many others, can see his thug-out swag, body language and the tone in his voice. You can take the man out the hood, but the hood will always be in the man.

Thomas led Kimberly to the teen church and like Thomas, she is surprised upon entering.

"This place is huge; you wouldn't think there can be a church within a church." Kimberly is drawn to the vast underground structure. She walks toward the platform, just imagining the place full with teens. As she looks around, Thomas is straightening up some chairs and picking up little various papers on the floor. Home maintenance is the first sermon; Thomas thinks to himself. He was never anyone's butler and he isn't about to start now.

"So, what was your sermon about today, Pastor Thomas," asked Kimberly.

"Just call me Thomas. Actually, I didn't preach today. I allowed the praise and worship crew take over. They put on an impromptu concert. They're in the studio now cutting their second independent gospel album."

"Nice, maybe I'll pop in teen church one day to hear them sing."

"They're not singers. They're rappers. I don't know if you are into that kind of thing, gospel rappers."

"What," She laughs, "I grew up on Hip Hop. If that's how the Word of God has to be spread to reach the young kids, then go for it."

Thomas likes what he is hearing. Too soon to ask her out on a date so he decided on something else.

"I don't know if you have anything planned but I was going to go out for an early dinner with Pastor Daniel and First Lady Nicole. I'm sure they wouldn't mind if you come along, that's if you would like to join us."

Kimberly begins to laugh, "I'm sure they won't mind. I'm a close friend of theirs from high school. They were the ones to convince me to join the church last year when I moved here for my job."

"Really, I didn't know that. How come I haven't seen you around?"

"I've been around," she laughs, "Nicole and I hang out all the time whenever I get a chance. Simone is my Goddaughter too."

"This is interesting," Thomas says smiling, folding his arms looking at Kimberly, "I would have never known you are friends, practically family to them."

"Yeah, well you know how famous Daniel is now. People would be quick to be friends with you just because of your company and what you and your well-known friends can do for them."

"I can see that! Well do you want to join me for dinner with *our* friends? I'm sure they will get a kick out of this."

"I don't mind but what about your girlfriend Jessica?"

When Kimberly and Nicole was talking one day, Kimberly asked Nicole about Thomas. She was curious if he had a girlfriend. Nicole had told her about a girl that he told her and Daniel he was dating name Jessica, but no one has met her. They've seen her one time which was during his first time preaching at the church. Everyone found it strange that she is never around.

Thomas is thrown off that she knew about Jessica. "How do you know about Jessica?"

"A woman has her sources," she jokes.

"Ah, let me guess, Daniel told you about her?"

"No, but close, I heard Nicole and Daniel talking about her," she lies. She doesn't want Thomas to know that she asked Nicole about his love life, "I know you and Jessica was to have dinner with them today. Weren't the both of you was going to meet them before to just hang out?"

"Yeah, we never got around to that. She has busy schedules, you know. She's busy today too."

"Yeah, I know," she replies knowing that he is hiding something, "So will Jessica mind me joining you for dinner with Daniel and Nicole today? I mean, since she hasn't met them yet, I don't want to step on anyone's toes."

"No, she doesn't care. We're not together anymore, so," his voice trails off. Thomas gives a brief smile, hoping to suppress his feelings. He really wanted to make things happen with Jessica but he can't be with her since she is becoming quite nosey. "So," he says clearing his throat, "Are you ready? I can set-up my office some other time."

"What time are you to meet them and at what restaurant?"

"We're supposed to meet up about three at Lafayette."

"My, my, my, how exquisite," she says sounding impressed. Lafayette is a tad bit on the expensive side." Kimberly had gone there once on a date, only to realize that her date only wanted a "*tip*" of thanks afterwards. She knows she doesn't have to worry about that from Thomas. "Well, Thomas its only 2:00. I think we'll be a little early don't you think so?"

"Yes, but that'll give me some time to get to know you."

Thomas is interested in Kimberly and by her being close friends with Daniel and Nicole, is a major plus.

Thomas had Kimberly follow him to the restaurant so they wouldn't raise too many suspicions from the lingering church members. Thomas isn't looking to get into anything, but wouldn't turn her down if they hit it off. Kimberly is just who he needs to keep his mind off Jessica right now. He turns on his phone to check his voicemails. "Check voicemail," he commands his vehicle's Bluetooth.

Thomas never had voicemail messages before the preaching gig. Now his phone sometimes has ten voicemail messages.

"You have 12 voicemail messages. First message. 'Hi Pastor Thomas this is Pastor Derrick from Living Waters, I would like to schedule a date with you for next month to preach at my Sunday service. We spoke last month about scheduling you to come to speak. My secretary will be in contact with you to go over the logistics.'"

"Next message, 'Hi Pastor Thomas, I'm Robert Towns. I'm putting together the Preaching Mega Fest for next year and would like for you to be on a panel. I reached out to Pastor Daniel Sanders and am waiting for his confirmation. You'll be set up in a suite, car service for your entire stay and of course you'll be paid quite handsomely. I'll send you an email with the information.'"

"Next message, 'Hey Pastor Thomas,'"

"End voicemail," Thomas commands his vehicle's Bluetooth, taking a breath he says, "I'm going to need a secretary."

Thomas schedule has increased, especially since he started preaching and now that he is a full-time pastor for Abundant Overflow teen church his schedule is really going to get insane. But it's all about the money. It always was about that money and since he knows that Daniel is all about that money too, he can finally be himself around Daniel. But Thomas knows to always keep the preacher's voice on standby whenever he is talking to church people. It's all a façade. Thomas watched and remembered everything he witnessed when he was a child and as he grew up. He remembers every church he went to, they took up an offering for the church, an offering for the pastor, and tithes, an offering for this ministry and that ministry, an offering for everything. There was one church who had an auction-like offering every Sunday. They would ask people who had anything higher then two hundred dollars to line up first, then those who had a hundred to line up behind them.

They continued this until the people who had a dollar to line up at the end. But that wasn't the end of it. People who were left sitting in the pews still had to line up because they had people put something in their hand to give to the pastor. Thomas had no clue where all the money was going until one day, he saw where the money was really going. He was walking past the pastor's study room and noticed the door open. Being nosey and curious about what goes on in the pastor's office, he peeked inside and saw an open safe behind the pastor's desk filled with money and gold. Thomas could have sworn he saw a gold bar but his grandmother dismissed the idea and told him that it was a Twinkie. Thomas knew what he saw. He also saw how thick the pastor's wallet was lying on the desk next to an open Bible. Thomas wanted in but he knew there wouldn't be a chance for him to be preaching and collecting money. But here he is doing exactly what he saw and see the other pastors doing. The black church alone, globally, made a half of a billion dollars last year. And the numbers keep getting higher each year. Thomas is definitely in the right line of work.

As Kimberly is following behind Thomas, she is feeling all sorts of butterflies in her stomach. This can be her way into the society of the church. She sees the First Ladies of the church with their designer clothes, flawless make-up, fancy rides and seem as though they don't have a care in the world. She can afford all of that and more for herself. But to be in the spotlight and to have a high profile husband, has its benefits. She sees the accolades that Daniel receives and Nicole is reaping the benefits. Their love was on a whole other level before the money and now that Daniel is practically famous in the church world, he lavishes her with everything he always wanted to give her. That's why Kimberly doesn't care that Daniel is doing this to support his family. All pastors do it and he should be able to as well. There is nothing illegal about what he is doing. It's not ethical, but it's not illegal. And even if he was doing something illegal that's her friends and there's nothing she wouldn't do for them. Kimberly can't help thinking about Thomas though. She finds him very handsome and can get caught up easily with him. But she doesn't want to rush things because she doesn't want to scare him off. Kimberly knows that Nicole was a little worried about him at first. Daniel was going at Thomas full steam ahead, bringing him to the house after the first time meeting him. Daniel wanted to bring another pastor into the fold because he heard people talking about not having up-front ministers rising up at the church. People were beginning to say that Daniel just wanted all the glory for himself and that he had too much power in the state alone and now the country. People were already concerned how fast Daniel was moving up in the church world. Here is this twenty-nine-year-old man that has been preaching for only five years who has gained the attention of celebrities, the President, and international recognition. But the Bishop knew what he was doing. All of this didn't bother him because his name will forever be attached to Daniel's name. So Daniel needed to take some light off him and place someone next to him too. Daniel has always been smart since they went to high school together. Kimberly is the only one who stuck around with Nicole and Daniel after they graduated. Nicole was called an easy thot when she got pregnant by Daniel. None of the girls at the high school liked her because they were jealous of her. So, when she got pregnant, she became an easy target. But Nicole had more than just beauty going for herself. Nicole was always in the National Honors Society and graduated top of her class, but that wasn't good enough. Now look at them. Kimberly always hoped that she will find a love like Nicole and Daniel. Which means she has to take her time with Thomas. They're going to dinner as friends, but if she plays her cards right, she can be sitting next to Nicole in the front row.

Kimberly is feeling very comfortable sitting at the bar with Thomas, especially when she heard Thomas order a beer.

"Alright Ms. Kim, you know that I'm a pastor, what do you do for a living?"

"I'm a therapist. My usual clients are high risk kids."

"Really," Thomas said sounding impressed, "I know that job must be rough listening to kids who has gone through a lot of stuff."

"I have my days but helping kids mean so much to me. The kids I counsel see more things and have gone through more things than the average normal adult."

"Do you like kids?"

"They 'ight," she says laughing sipping her white wine, "Why, do you have any kids?"

"No, I don't have any kids. I would like to have one or two one day. I guess I'll be getting a lot of practice at teen church."

"I'm in no rush to have kids. I want to do a lot of traveling before becoming a mother. I have my Goddaughter and she's all I need right now."

"Have you traveled outside the states?"

"No, not yet. Not like you and Daniel. I'm still trying to make it to the Bahamas or Jamaica."

"Trust me, if I wasn't working with Daniel, traveling outside the states would be non-existent. But I have to tell you, Paris is absolutely beautiful."

Thomas pulls out his phone to show her the pictures he took while in Paris. Kimberly is in awe of the beautiful scenery and the Eiffel Tower.

"When Nicole told me that she was going with Daniel to Paris, I was very jealous. Going to Paris with your husband or boyfriend is any woman's dream."

"Maybe I can take you one day," he playfully flirts.

Kimberly looks at him and smiles before looking at the pictures again. Thomas isn't trying to move too fast, but he wants her to know that he is interested. Every pastor he knows has a First Lady. He was hoping that Jessica would have been his First Lady but that ship has sailed.

Kimberly stops swapping through the pictures when she came to a picture of Thomas and Jessica, cuddling and smiling. She notices that the picture was taken about a week ago from the date above the photo. "Nice picture of you and your girlfriend," Kimberly says holding up his phone.

Thomas takes the phone from Kimberly and places it back into his pocket. Kimberly knows he still have feelings for Jessica. She's not buying the whole "*she has a busy schedule*" excuse.

"So, what's the real deal between you and Jessica. I can tell that you still have feelings for her."

"It's not that easy to get someone out of your system like that. Jessica and I have been together for about three years. Two of those years, I was unemployed and she was the one who helped me out but then she cheated on me about five months ago. She said she felt the pressure from her family and friends to break up with me because she was supporting me while I was out of work. Well, the day I met with Daniel was the day I found her in bed with her friend. I tried to move pass it and it could have worked out but she has a problem with my new job as a preacher. She has a problem about pastors getting paid?"

"Well how else are you supposed to live? As your woman, she should have supported you, regardless of how she feels."

"I was saying the same thing. She wasn't saying anything when I had to make money hustling in the streets for my boy."

"When did you break-up with Jessica," Kimberly asked. She knows it has to be within the last couple of days from the picture.

"I told her that it was over yesterday. I took her out for dinner and she began to question me about the funds of the church. That's when I had enough. She excused herself from the table and when she came back she told me to take her home."

"Wow, that's intense. I think you still need to talk to her though. You need some kind of closure."

"I got all the closure I needed when she told me to take her home. And when I tried talking to her, it always ends with her not liking me preaching."

"Then tell me, why are you preaching? What made you decided to become a pastor?"

Thomas got quiet. Because even though she's a friend of Daniel and Nicole, he knows that he can't be too honest with her. That's all part of the deal when you become a pastor, a full-time pastor. "I was called to preach. Everyone is called to preach but there are the few, who take the initiative to preach to the people. I've always ran from my calling but God caught me. So, I began going to the ministry school at the church during the time I was unemployed and the rest is history." Thomas sips some more of his beer feeling pleased with his response.

"And she can't understand that," Kimberly asked feeding into his lie. She knows Thomas was all in it for the money too and she sees nothing wrong with it.

"I guess not," Thomas said shrugging his shoulders and drinking some more beer.

"People work for money all the time. That's what people do. How else are you supposed to live? People think that pastors are supposed to look homey and broke. Why? I've never understood that. If you are preaching and talking about prosperity, then you should look and represent it. I don't see anything wrong with what you're doing."

"Well I'm glad you do. I see why Daniel said that I have to keep my circle small. As of now, my circle just has me."

"Oh I'm sure you have more friends than just yourself."

"Nope, the guys I hung out with was about that street life. They would just mess things up for me."

"Well, then, you got me," Kimberly flirts, "As a friend of course," she jokes tapping his shoulder.

Thomas smiles at her and can't resist her charm, "You want to be down with me? Do you think you can handle it?"

"I can handle anything, you want me to handle," she said softly as she moves a little closer to him. "You know you need someone like me in your corner."

Thomas place left hand around her waist pulling her to him.

"Let's see how things go," he says, "I'll let you know if you can fill that position."

"And what position is that," she asks moving closer.

"Whatever position you're trying to fill."

Before Thomas can make a final move, he hears Daniel behind him.

"When did this happen!"

Thomas and Kimberly unlock from their embrace to see Daniel and Nicole smiling faces, especially Nicole. "Oh hey Daniel, we were just talking," Thomas laughs.

"Talking my foot, when did this happen," Daniel asks again.

"That's what I want to know because I thought we were supposed to meet Jessica," Nicole said giving her friend the look. Nicole isn't trying to have her best friend get played by Thomas. Nicole walks over to Kimberly and whispers, "Girl, what are you doing?"

"Me and Jessica are over with, so you can be easy," Thomas said to Nicole. "I was going to show up alone but I ran into Kimberly at the church. I knew you two wouldn't mind."

"Absolutely not," Daniel exclaims, "Kim is family. Just don't hurt her."

"We're just friends," Thomas and Kimberly said in unison.

"Uh-huh, sure. That's not what we saw walking over here," Nicole says.

"Trust me, we're just friends," Kimberly says.

Daniel and Nicole knew better. They knew there has to be more than the just friends comment. Nicole knows that Kimberly has had her eyes on Thomas since she became a member at Abundant Overflow. She's all for her and Thomas hooking up, but he need to be over with his girlfriend Jessica. The church doesn't need any more rumors.

"Pastor Sanders, I'm sorry to keep you waiting," the host said, "Your usual booth is available."

"Thank you."

The host led them to a booth that was located toward the back. As they walk by, many patrons are in awe to see Daniel. Walking by they heard so many 'Hi pastor, Awesome word today pastor' and just the star struck gaze. Like Daniel and Nicole, Thomas grew accustomed to it. But Kimberly feels like its new every time she goes out with them.

The couples sat down at the table with the menu facing them. Right away Daniel orders a bottle of wine for the table and a water for Nicole.

"Why would you tempt me like that," Nicole nudges Daniel.

"So have you been successful? Any news yet," Kimberly asked.

"No, not yet. We'll find out next week," Nicole said.

Thomas has no clue what they are talking about so he had to ask without hesitation.

"Successful in what? Do we need to celebrate something that's going down?"

"Hopefully so," Daniel looks at Nicole waiting for her to give the green light.

"I've been doing in vitro and hopefully I'm pregnant."

"Oh, I'm sorry to hear that the both of you was having a hard time getting pregnant."

"We have our moments," Nicole smirks off her emotions.

Without missing a beat Daniel quickly changes the subject, "So how did it go today," he asked Thomas.

"Daniel, I have to tell you. The teen church is unlike any I've experienced. It was a blast. I allowed the praise and worship group do an impromptu concert."

"Really!"

"Yes, the teens went crazy. That gospel rap group is everything. They are independent artists. They are working on their second album. You need to get them signed with a gospel label. I know you got pull."

"Hey man, that's all you. Whatever you want, it's done. I was actually talking to some people about starting a gospel label."

"I don't see why not. You are doing other big things at the church."

"Where's my Goddaughter," Kimberly asked Nicole, while Thomas and Daniel are engage in business talk.

"She's at her friend's house. They have a project they're working on for their science class."

"I don't remember doing projects in school," Thomas interjects.

"Me either. They swamp these kids with so much homework, they can't enjoy being a kid," Daniel said.

"That's one of the issues I deal with at the office. The number of kids I have coming in stressed out because of homework is insane."

"So, Thomas you know I'm going to be all up in your business," Nicole said to him squinting her eyes.

Thomas repositions himself to answer whatever question she may have.

"When and why did you break up with Jessica?"

"Nicole, why are you questioning him about his girl? Thomas, Nicole can be very forward sometimes," Daniels says excusing his wife's behavior.

"I'm just curious," she adds, "We were to meet her today, that's all. I thought you was going to settle down with her."

"No its cool," Thomas paused for a moment, "Let me just say this, sometimes you come to a point in your life when you can't rock with everyone. And I thought she would be the one who would be my biggest supporter. But she wasn't."

"She didn't want you preaching," Daniel asked.

Thomas pauses again before responding to gather his thoughts, "It's not that she didn't want me preaching. She doesn't agree with the money we make."

Daniel sits back against the booth listening to what Thomas is saying.

"She doesn't think preachers should get paid as much as we do. That's why I never had her around you. We know people got issues concerning what we do for a living. But those are the people we keep distant from."

Daniel has no words. He is happy that Thomas made the decision that he made. Sometimes you have to cut the people who are closer to you off.

"People like her are always trying to bring the church down," Nicole says.

"Especially the black church," Kimberly adds, "You can't have black preachers walking around here with grands in their pockets living in gated mansions and stuff. *Oh no!* Don't let them rise above the white preachers who are preaching the same game and living the same way. Get out of here with that."

"That's why you have me, the Bishop and other black preachers and now Thomas, who are out here changing the game," Daniel finally speaks, "We're becoming a strong force in this nation and are gearing up to impact the world. People pay good money to hear a word from God."

Everyone began to laugh. Thomas joins in on the laughter; feeling good to fit into a sector he belongs.

"Danny, when was the last time you heard from the Bishop? I tried calling his wife, but she never returned my phone calls. Is everything okay," asked Nicole.

"I haven't heard from the Bishop since he called to tell me that he wasn't going to go into the mini mall business with me, Darryl and Marshal. You know the Bishop be busy traveling all over the place. He's probably busy or he can still be sore about the contract issue. Who knows. All I know is that, he decided to turn down my offer. That's on him."

"Or he can be jealous," Kim said.

"That too, which I wouldn't be surprised. But I don't see why. He was the one that got me out here. I just took it and ran with it. It doesn't matter anyways. I don't have time to entertain childish adult games." Daniel realize that he hasn't heard from Bishop Wilkens. He even tried to reach out to him a couple of times and didn't get a response, so he would call his office. But his secretary would always tell him that he's either busy or out of town and that he would call him when he's available. Bishop Wilkens still get his percentage every Sunday and he has been getting more since membership increased. Daniel tries not to let the silence and absence of Bishop get to him, but he can't help but worry. He doesn't know what is brewing, but he has to be ready. Bishop still has the power to release him as pastor of Abundant Overflow, especially since Daniel doesn't have board members to back him up.

"Daniel, have you ever thought about doing Reality TV," Thomas ask interrupting Daniels thoughts.

"Reality TV," he laughs even more, "I'm so busy, I don't have time to watch TV, let alone be on a reality show."

"Well, they got pastors making reality shows now."

"Are they now," Daniel said smiling, calming down his laughter.

"Yes, I think that's something you should look into…more exposure."

"Sounds good," Daniel replies with the spinning wheels turning. He looks at Nicole and ask, "What do you think? Do you think we're ready for our own show?"

"Honey, I've been ready," she replies giving him a kiss on the lips.

Thomas didn't want to leave Kimberly out so he asked her the same question. She replied with a simple yes, only she pulls Thomas in for a kiss.

With all that is going on at the table, they didn't see the former Deacon Williams sitting four tables away, watching and listening thanks to a reliable tip.

Chapter 11

James 1:10-11 (MSG)

"Prosperity is as short-lived as a wildflower, so don't ever count on it. You know that as soon as the sun rises, pouring down its scorching heat: the flower withers. Its petals wilt and before you know it that beautiful face is a barren stem. Well, that's a picture of the prosperous life. At the very moment everyone is looking on in admiration it fades away to nothing."

THREE MONTHS LATER.....

"What the hell is this," Daniel yells tossing some papers at his attorney, Mr. Owens.

"Listen, you have to relax, so we can get through this."

"How can I relax? I'm in a lawsuit! My former board member Deacon Williams and the freaking Bishop Wilkens has a lawsuit out on me!"

"Did you see this coming," Mr. Owens ask calmly.

"No! I didn't see this coming! The last time I spoke to Deacon Williams was when I terminated him as a board member and the last time I spoke to the Bishop, I made him an offer to be a business partner with me, Darryl and Marshal. But he turned it down because he just wanted me and him to be partners! He didn't want to go into business with Darryl and Marshal! Why are they suing me?"

"The lawsuit states that you are pocketing the church funds, mishandling business and fraud. Deacon Williams claims that you terminated him under false accusations and for non-payments for the work he'd done for the church. And Bishop Wilkens claims that you are using the church funds to fund your side businesses and your lavish lifestyle. And because you are under his ministry, he is severing all ministry and financial ties with you. They are suing you for 8.2 million dollars for damages."

Daniel nearly collapses into his office chair. Everything has been going well in the last three months. Enrollment is up at the church, the church brings in almost a million dollars a month, the mini mall is already being built, he had a couple of business meetings with a television producer and movie director, and he and Thomas are in the process of starting a gospel label, and him and Nicole found out that she is three months pregnant.

Daniel finally sat down to collect his thoughts. He can lose everything! All the work and hustle he put into the church to support his family and lifestyle can be taken away.

"Now this isn't going to trial as of now," his attorney, Mr. Owens continued, "You have a deposition at the end of this week."

"Friday! That's five days away!"

"Listen, it's either Friday or you have to wait until the end of the month, and that's four weeks away! And quite frankly, you don't want to come to church, facing thousands of members or conduct any business knowing that you are facing a deposition and a possible trial!"

"Do you think that the word is out," Daniel asked Mr. Owens.

"I wouldn't be surprised if it is."

Daniel quickly pulls his chair up to his desk to use the computer. There is only one way to know. Daniel types his name into the search bar. This happen suddenly, without any warning.

"We need to go over some things before Friday," Mr. Owens says.

Daniel held his hand up telling him to wait. All the color from Daniel's face had gone. It's all over the internet. There's blogs and articles talking about the lawsuit against him. Of all people! The one person he thought he could trust turned around and burned him. He never expected the Bishop to try and bring him down.

"Daniel, right now, I need you to focus," Mr. Owens sat in front of him.

Daniel is gazing straight ahead, staring at a blank wall as if he is dreaming.

"If you want to come out on top. You need to work with me."

"I'm not going down like this! I'm not going down without a fight," Daniel says abruptly snapping out of his gaze. "Listen, I want to countersuit Bishop Wilkens. He's been taking money from me ever since he placed me here. I want to take him down. I know everything about him. He thinks I don't know, but I got eyes and ears in his church office too."

Mr. Owens sat back, folding his hands anticipating his next move.

"Over the past 5 years, Bishop Wilkens takes about fifteen percent from me on Sundays. My accountant Shawn, can give you the full amount. I want every last penny back from him. I take the correct taxes out of the church employee's wages and have the proof from all 5 years, whereas, Bishop Wilkens, pays his part-time employees under the table."

As Daniel is speaking, Mr. Owens took out a pad and pen and began to write everything Daniel is telling them.

"Now if by any chance you see my name on a document concerning this church building or any other document from Bishop Wilkens, it's a forgery. I never signed any documents from the Bishop. Now the name of the church is mine. I came up with the name. The church building and the house isn't in my name. So, this is what I want," Daniel says sitting forward, "Abundant Overflow Ministries and this building with everything in it will be mine. The house that my family live in will be mine. The church bought the house for me and my family, but I want the deed. I want the Bishop's private jet, beach house in St. Thomas and in Miami, and I think his net worth is 35 million. Because I have a heart, I would like to take about 34.5 million. That will leave him with about five hundred thousand dollars. I want you to rip him to shreds! Whatever you want to know I can give you a list of people in his church *and* on his payroll; they will be glad to help you, even my own mother."

"Wow, I don't think the Bishop knows what he's up against."

"See, he may have moved me and my family out the state and away from my hood, but he can't take the streets and my friends from me. I still keep in touch with friends and family there. And those who are closer to me, they set themselves up within Bishop's church. All of the administrators here are with him. I'm sure they are on his payroll too, including Deacon Williams, and the other two ladies, Sister May and Sister Barnes, which is why I fired them. I have so much dirt on Bishop Wilkens, you can send him to prison for all I care."

"This is a lot to take in Pastor Sanders. What about Deacon Williams?"

"What about him," Daniel snaps, "Do as you will with him. I don't care! He's old anyway! He can rot for all I care."

"Okay, before we go any further because I see I have a lot of work cut out in front of me, we have to talk about my fee…"

"Here's your fee," Daniel says cutting him off, "If you can get me a win, I'll give you 4 million dollars on top of your fee. And if I don't win, well you'll just get your fee before I file for bankruptcy and get thrown into federal prison."

Daniel and Mr. Owens began to laugh. "Why would you get thrown into federal prison," Mr. Owens ask still laughing a little.

"The less you know, the more you got to work with. Just get me off and I'll take care of you. You're my lawyer because you're the best in the state. Now prove it!"

"I can take that 4 million and forget about my fee," Mr. Owens says with a big smile on his face.

"Okay, then win…so, what do we do now."

"Well, your deposition is Friday, Pastor Thomas has a deposition too next week but he's not being sued. You can't have any contact with him until his deposition is over. It can jeopardize the pending case. Does Thomas know anything that I should I know? I'm going to meet with him today too."

"He knows only what I want him to know."

"Okay, so we shouldn't have a problem then. I'm going to gather papers to be served to Bishop Wilkens by Friday. Which means I have to work around the clock and I'm going to need everyone's name and phone number that you mentioned who can help you in this case. And I'll take care of the media that is spreading the story. Don't worry about that. But here is what you need to know to be ready for Friday." Mr. Owens stands up and began to slowly pace the room, "You have to be honest. But I tell my clients, to be honest means to choose your words carefully. You can say a lot without saying much. Listen to the questions carefully. If you don't understand the question, they or myself can repeat it or word it in another way so you can understand it. Don't guess. If you don't know the answer to a question just say that you don't know. If you need to speak to me privately about a question, you can do so. Don't freely give information about anyone else. That's my job. Don't explain your answer. Say what you have to say and that's it. Whatever you do, remain calm. Us attorneys can be quite pushy. You don't need to bring any documents. I'll bring everything you will need. Also whatever we discussed today, everything that you told me about Bishop Wilkens, do not tell them! The things that you told me about Bishop Wilkens are confidential. And lastly, do not speak to Deacon Williams, Bishop Wilkens or their attorneys after the deposition. Especially Bishop Wilkens because when he gets served his lawsuit papers and see that he is about to be exposed too, I guarantee you that he will try to reach out to you."

Daniel took a deep breath, "That's a lot to take in but I can handle it. Should I begin terminating some people who work here at the church? Like I said, most of them came from Bishop Wilken's church."

"No, don't rock the boat just yet. Don't make any changes until I give you the green light."

Daniel nods his head in agreement. Daniel can't believe this is happening to him. With all the other crooked preachers in this business, he has to be the one to get caught. The last thing that he wants is for him and his family going back to the hood, worse than when they left it.

After two hours, Mr. Owens had left Daniel after briefing him on some questions he will be asked on Friday. On the outside, he is keeping it together, trying to act like nothing is wrong but on the inside, he is terrified. Daniel can lose everything! He will have nothing!

Daniel pulls his beautiful, admired car over to the side of the road and places it in park. For the first time ever, he began to cry. He is feeling the embarrassment, the emptiness and loneliness. All he can do is sob. He bangs his fists on the steering wheel. He can't take the pressure. "*Trust no one,*" he remembers Bishop Wilkens saying to him. He threw his head back on to the headrest and shut his eyes tightly. Hot angry tears are falling faster from his eyes. All he can hear is trust no one. Daniel had allowed himself to trust a man who taught him everything. Bishop Wilkens had made all of this happen, the life he always wanted to give Nicole and Simone. And he is the main one who betrayed him. His emotions began to turn into anger. If he could, he would do the unthinkable, but it will only make matters worse. All eyes will turn to Daniel if the Bishop gets jumped or killed. Daniel has never thought about doing something like that in his life, but sometimes life can put anyone in a position that would make them come out of character. His cell phone began to ring, distracting him from his thoughts. He sees Nicole's name flash on the screen. She has been calling him non-stop since he found out the news about the lawsuit. He didn't want to talk to her, but he knows that there is no way to get around the issue. He quickly wipes his tears, sniffs a couple of tears back and answers the phone as normally as he can. The last thing he wants is to put stress on her and the baby.

"Hey Nicole," he answers trying to sound as if nothing has happened.

"Daniel," Nicole screams on the phone. He can hear the tears in her voice, "What is going on! I've been trying to call you all afternoon! We are being sued!"

"Yes, but it's nothing to worry about. It's not too serious. Mr. Owens was at my office going over everything. That's why I couldn't call you." He is keeping his voice calm, so Nicole can have her mind at ease.

"What do you mean it's not too serious! They froze our accounts! I went to the store to buy groceries and our credit cards were declined! Thank God Darryl was with me; he was able to make the purchase! Then we got approached by three reporters while we were walking to the car! Daniel, what the hell is going on!"

Daniel didn't know that the accounts are frozen. As much as he wants this to disappear he has to force himself to face reality.

"Listen, I'll take care of everything. I'm on my way to the house. I'm about to call Darryl and Marshal. I need you to pack a bag. I want you and Simone to stay with Kimberly until things are taken care of."

"What am I'm to do for money Daniel! I hope you had a backup plan when you decided to do all of this," she cries.

"Nicole don't worry about money. We'll be fine. Give me a call when you get to Kim's house."

Nicole hung up the phone feeling heartbroken. Her worse fear came true. She always feared Daniel would one day get into trouble about the church. She knew other pastors hated him because they weren't as successful as Daniel, but never did she imagine that the Bishop would be the one to backstab him. She quickly grabs a couple of clothes to throw inside her suitcase.

"Simone," she yells out.

Simone slowly takes her time walking to her frantic mom's call. All Simone wants to do is catch up on her schoolwork, but she's been distracted from text messages from friends telling her that her dad is in jail, or that her dad is about to go to jail because he had stolen money from the church. Simone never responded to the text messages. Instead, she was concentrating on fighting back tears and doing some schoolwork.

"Simone," Nicole calls out again.

Simone is slump in the doorway watching her mom throw clothes in a suitcase.

"Hey Simone, we're going to stay at Aunt Kim's house for a little while. I need you to pack a bag that will last you for a week or so."

"Or so," Simone silently mimics.

Nicole's mind is running a mile a minute about this change of events. She wants to believe Daniel, that the situation isn't too serious, but she can't bring herself to believe it. She notices Simone still standing in the doorway.

"Simone, I need you to pack a bag," she tells her again as she is walking to her closet.

"Is it true," Simone asked.

"Is what true?"

"Is daddy going to jail or is he already locked up?"

Nicole stops walking and turns around to see the tears sliding down Simone's cheeks.

"Those damn social media sites," Nicole says under her breath as she rushes over to Simone.

"Baby, daddy is not in jail. Daddy is fine."

"So why are people saying that he is about to go to jail because he stole money from the church," she cries louder.

Nicole embraces Simone and just held her. "Your daddy didn't take anyone's money or money from the church. There are people who are jealous of your father's success and is willing to bring him down, even if they have to lie on him." Nicole wants to believe the lie she is telling their daughter. But she doesn't know if people are lying about Daniel stealing money from the church. She saw this coming for months now. After Daniel fired the board members, she figured that will be the end of the rumors and all of that would blow away. But here it is exploding in their faces.

"So, why do we have to leave *our* house and go to Aunt Kim's house? I don't understand."

Nicole takes a deep breath wanting to shield her daughter from all of this, "Your daddy wants us to go there until he straightens things out."

"Are we going to be poor again," Simone asks her mom, looking at her hoping to hear what her heart wants to hear. She loves the life that she has now. She has bedroom that is three times the size of her old room in their old apartment. Simone loves the private school that she attends and made a lot of friends there. She has always felt out of place at her old street in their old neighborhood. Most of the kids in her class were disruptive and made it hard for the teacher to teach class.

"No baby, that's the last thing your daddy wants for us. Your daddy won't let that happen. We will just fine. You have to trust us."

She held her for a little longer before she ushers her off to her room to pack a bag. While Nicole and Simone are upstairs packing a bag to stay at Kimberly's house for a while, Marshal and Darryl are in the guest house on the phone with Daniel. They heard about the news before Daniel told them. Darryl went to the grocery store with Nicole since he had to pick up some stuff for himself as well. He knew something was wrong when both of her credit cards were declined. He wanted to chuck it up as a malfunction in the system, but when his credit card was able to go through without a problem, he knew something was brewing. Even while they were shopping, people was looking at them, and he saw some whisper to the persons they were next to. Nicole ignored them brushing it off as nothing was going on, but Darryl knew better. He automatically went into bodyguard mode. He was more concerned about getting Nicole home and getting in contact with Daniel. As soon as they got out of the supermarket, Nicole was irate and embarrassed about the credit cards being declined, that she didn't notice three reporters approaching her.

"Excuse me, First Lady Sanders, can I ask you some questions about your husband," one reporter asked.

Before Nicole can respond, Darryl barks out orders commanding them to not to speak to her and that she has nothing to say. He held Nicole tightly to him, walking her briskly to the car. Nicole immediately got into the car while Darryl tossed the bags in the trunk.

Once he got into the driver's seat, Nicole asked, "What was that all about?"

"I don't know," he says as he started the car and began to drive off, "Don't talk to anyone or listen to anything until you speak to Daniel first! People have a way of twisting s*** before you talk to the main person."

"Well, I need to call the bank to find out why was I declined. That doesn't make any sense," Nicole says as she took out her cell.

Darryl just wanted to talk to Daniel to find out what was going on. When he got to the house Marshal was on the game system as usual, oblivious to what was going on in Daniel's crumbling world. They tried calling Daniel but his phone kept going to voicemail. That's not like Daniel. Darryl and Marshal knew something was wrong. All they could do was wait for his call.

"Hello," Darryl answered abruptly.

"Hey Darryl, is Marshal there with you," Daniel ask in a husky voice. He can tell he was crying.

"Yeah, he's right here. I'm putting you on the house speaker right now." They had a house speaker connected to the house phone so they can talk on the phone throughout the house.

"Hey Daniel, what's going on man," Marshal asked, "Darryl told me what happened at the store with Nicole. We didn't want to hear from anyone about whatever is happening until we talk to you first." While Darryl and Marshal was waiting for Daniel to call them, they ignored everyone's phone calls and stayed off the computer.

"Yeah she told me too," Daniel said, "I got a big problem...," Daniel takes a long pause before he continues, trying to hold back his tears, "Bishop Wilkens and Deacon Williams are suing me."

"What," Darryl yells. Marshal places his hands firmly on his forehead, closing his eyes in unbelief to what he is hearing, "You can't be serious," he says.

"And that's not all. Their lawsuit has brought up questions concerning the funds from the church. So now there is also an investigation on me about stealing money from the church. So, they froze all my accounts until everything is cleared. I have to show them everything from the money I spend at a store to the handling of church funds."

"But you don't take *all* the money from the church! You don't reach into the collection plate and take every last dime," Marshal says.

"I know that, but they think I take *everything*. If people give it to me, I take it! It's just that simple! My family has to eat too!"

"Daniel, I'm not trying to go back to the hood," Darryl said, "We would look like straight up suckers."

"For real Daniel, what do we need to do. You know we got pull in the hood. All we need to do is make that one phone call and we can get the Bishop and Deacon Williams taken care of. And everything will be over. I'll go down for you and take the blame," added Marshal. He is always ready to take full responsibility when it comes to Daniel and Darryl. He will protect his family at any cost.

"Marshal we have enough issues going on. We don't need to add *that* on top of everything. I gave my attorney the names of the people I purposely planted in Bishop Wilkens church. I'm also countersuing him; I'm taking him for everything he owns," Daniel says firmly.

"What do you need us to do? We can take the money out the safe just in case they have people coming here to house snooping around," Marshal said.

"No, don't take all of it. Take about five thousand and give it to Nicole. Don't tell her anything about the stash of cash in the safe in your guest house. If she questions you about the money, just tell her that it came from your personal savings. I don't need her to worry about all of that. Tell me, how much did we save up?"

Daniel, Darryl and Marshal have been taking money from the church in small increments so it wouldn't be noticeable since the first day they began the ministry. Nicole doesn't know about this. She only thinks that Daniel get money from collections or donations from the church and speaking engagements. He purposely withheld information from Nicole to keep her innocent.

"We have a little over of a million dollars in cash. Let me ask you a question, do you think Thomas is a snitch," Darryl asked?

"No, this doesn't have Thomas' name on it. They are bringing him in next week for questioning. I'm not worried about Thomas."

"Well, we'll see where his alliance lies after next week," Darryl says looking at Marshal. He has in mind to pay Thomas a visit after they get off the phone. But as if Daniel is right there in the room with them, he dismisses the idea, "Leave Thomas alone! I don't need you two hot heads getting to him. If I can't have any contact with him, then neither can the both of you. All you need to do is take of a few things for me. You don't need to concern yourselves with Thomas! I'm serious! Leave him alone."

Marshal sucks his teeth and flings his arms in the air, "Why the hell do we have to leave him alone! I'm sure he knows something! And if he doesn't, we can make sure he gets the story right. You only met this dude and known him for about eight months. You can't put this s*** pass him. All of this craziness and issues with Bishop Wilkens began to brew since you allowed him all up in your business!"

"Daniel, Marshal is right. Thomas deposition can make you or break you. Let us make sure he gets the story right."

"You heard what I said! Leave him alone! All I need you to do is call the crew from our old block and let them know what's going on! We got this! This is why I always keep in contact with some of the people from our neighborhood. As long as my attorney does what he has to do, we should be good. Them and the people from Bishop Wilkens church will just get the snowball going before Bishop Wilkens knows what's going on. Now Marshal, I need you to go with Nicole and Simone to Kim's house. Make sure no one talk to them concerning the lawsuit. Whenever Nicole goes, go along with her. Stay with them until it's time to come back to the house. We have to leave the house for now until I can get the deed to the house in my name. As of now, the Bishop owns everything; the church, the house, the money in the church's account, *everything*. Darryl, I need you to stay with me."

Darryl and Marshal will do anything to protect Daniel. Daniel is family. But if he doesn't want them to get involved then they have no other choice but to let him think that they will back off.

"Alright Daniel, I'll be here when you get home," Darryl says as he gathers their belongings. After ending the call, they made their exit out their guest house. No words are spoken but they know where they are going. They have an hour to be back at the house.

FRIDAY MORNING……

Daniel hasn't eaten much since Monday. He is worried sick about today and the outcome. Darryl has never seen Daniel look lifeless and pale a day in his life. Daniel is always the strong one and here he is speechless and weak. Daniel has shed so many tears. He cried in front of Darryl the other day after he got off the phone with Nicole. He is worried sick that he had ruin his family. The media has had a field day talking about him and now other pastors maybe investigated. People are beginning to see what all the lucrative churches take in yearly and now members of other churches want an account for every dime that is spent. And this all began because Bishop Wilkens wants to sue Daniel. A powerhouse like Bishop Wilkens to sue his protégée has everyone raising their eyebrows at Daniel. It took about fifteen years for Bishop Wilkens to get to where he is, but only a few short five years for Daniel to achieve the status like Bishop Wilkens. So, it is easy for people to side with the Bishop.

Daniel is sitting in the passenger seat unable to move. The day has finally come for Daniel to face Bishop Wilken's attorneys. He couldn't wait to get this day over with. He and Mr. Owens rehearsed this day every day for the last four days. Mr. Owens interrogated Daniel on every question the attorneys will ask Daniel. Daniel is ready, but his main problem is staying calm. He would become defensive when asked personal questions about his family or his sudden interest in going into ministry. Mr. Owens told Daniel that while he is in the deposition, Bishop Wilkens is going to be served with his lawsuit papers. Everyone Daniel had reached out to in his old neighborhood and those who are members at the Bishop's church came through and provided some crucial information that will take Bishop Wilkens down. Mr. Owens was happy about the information he received and so was Daniel, but this battle is far from being over. It's a possibility that he will lose everything he worked hard for and end up back where he started, but worse.

Darryl just looks at him in disbelief. "You know what," Darryl says, "We should just leave." He starts his car ready to switch the gears.

"What are you doing," Daniel says in a dry voice, "I have to be in the attorney's office in ten minutes."

"You mind as well leave! You're acting like you'd lost! Look at you! You're all shaken up! You look like a mess! You were always this flashy, outspoken, smart guy. You never backed down from a fight."

"Who says I'm backing down!"

"You are! You're not ready to win this! So we mind as well go home, pack up our stuff and go back to the hood. You saw the hustle in church and you wanted in. So here you are, you're in! But you knew there were always snakes in the game when you first started! It's just that Bishop Wilkens was the main one you had to watch out for. You perfected the hustling thing in church. Tell me, what pastor do you know who gained close to ten thousand members, has a multimillion dollar church building with various functional workshops, building a mini mall, starting a record label, and is becoming internationally known within 5 almost 6 years in the game? Can you tell me?"

Daniel didn't respond; he continues to listen.

"No one, except you! So like you always say, you are bound to have haters, especially Bishop Wilkens because he couldn't achieve what you've done. It took him almost 15 years to come out on top. Do you think he's going to have some uneducated punk ass nigga from the hood show him out? Absolutely not! But you are allowing him to win by giving up."

Daniel knows what Darryl is saying is true, but he can't help that its taking an emotional toll on him. He went into this church game with a goal. And that goal was to make money and sustain his family. He achieved that goal and more because he treated the church as a business. If you talk a good game, you're bound to come out on top and here he is dwindling rapidly to the bottom within days. He's glad his attorney had them move the deposition instead of waiting for weeks to clear things up.

"So what do you want to do, do you want to bounce or do you want to get yourself together and win this thing?"

Daniel looks at him and nods his head. "Go inside and let them know I'm coming in. Just give me two minutes to myself."

Without hesitation, Darryl turns the car off and heads inside. Daniel is sitting in the car by himself in silence. It's been a while since he prayed. He prays before and after his sermons, but it's been a while since he had a one on one conversation. Daniel goes to open his mouth, but tears are coming out his eyes.

Daniel walks into the attorney's office with a little pep in his step. He swallowed his emotions and is ready to face the questions. His attorney, Mr. Owens is standing by the door with Darryl waiting for Daniel.

"You're cutting too close to time, Pastor Daniel," Mr. Owens said.

"I had to get myself together. I'm good now." Daniel just needed the little time to himself to breathe and prepare his mind. Daniel is good at masking things so he put on an unbothered face ready for deposition. "Are they waiting for me inside this conference room?"

"Yes, but before you go inside, I want to remind you to be careful what you say."

"I know, I know. I got this. Let's just get this over with."

Daniel walks pass him opening the door to the office ready to answer some questions. Mr. Owens walks behind him closing the door as Darryl is sitting in the waiting room.

"Pastor Daniel Sanders, I'm Mr. Kelly and this is Mr. Stic, we're Bishop Wilkens attorneys," he says shaking Daniel's hand, "And this is Mrs. Stevens, she is the reporter. She will be recording the deposition."

"Hello," Daniel says with a straight face, shaking Mr. Stic and Mrs. Stevens hands.

"You can sit here and your attorney, Mr. Owens, can sit along with you."

Everyone took their proper seats and the deposition began.

"Mr. Sanders, we are recording this deposition for legal proceedings. Do you agree to this," Mr. Kelly asked?

"Yes."

"What is your full name?"

"Pastor Daniel Sanders."

"Do you have a middle name?"

"No."

"Are you the pastor of Abundant Overflow Ministries?"

"Yes."

"How did you become the pastor of Abundant Overflow Ministries?"

"Bishop George Wilkens appointed me as the pastor about five years ago."

"Were you a member at a church in your previous hometown?"

"Yes, I was a member at Abundant Love Baptist Church."

"Who was your former pastor?"

"Bishop George Wilkens."

"What is the name of your church?"

"Abundant Overflow Ministries."

"Who are the members on your board?"

"As of now, none."

"You don't have board members," Mr. Kelly asked with raised eyebrows.

"Not at this time."

"Did you ever have board members?"

"Yes, I did."

"Why aren't they on the board anymore?"

"I terminated them a couple of months ago."

"So, you've been without a board for months?

"Yes."

"So, who has been helping the church with planning and performance of the church, financial oversight, you and your staff financial compensation, legal compliance, and maintaining the church's documents?"

"I have administrators that I trust to take care of all of those matters. I have an accountant, Mr. Shawn Davis, that keeps track of every transaction that comes in and out of the church and Mr. Owens is the attorney that takes care of the legal compliance."

"Who were the Board members?"

"Deacon Samuel Williams, Sister Esther May, and Sister Vanessa Barnes."

"Why did you relieve them from their position as board members?"

Just as he and Mr. Owens, rehearsed days prior, he responds never skipping a beat.

"They couldn't support the vision of the ministry. The vision is to help those who are in need and they couldn't support it."

"Does your vision have anything to do with the mini mall you are building?"

"Yes it does."

"And how exactly is that ministry?"

"There are thousands of people who are unemployed. So, why not create and build businesses for those who are unemployed."

"What about this record label and publishing company? We also see you have a daycare in the church as well, how are you relating these things to ministry?"

"The church is filled with so much talent, not to stereotype, but church people can sing their butts off..."

Some of the attorneys' giggles.

Daniel continues, "There aren't many gospel label and publishing companies. And those that are around, people have to go through so many channels just to get a book published or make an album. I want to cut out the middle man, so people who have the talents to sing, rap, write and dance can get their materials out there too. And the daycare is there for working parents who struggle financially." Daniel feels proud that he mastered those questions. Mr. Owens asked him those exact questions. Daniel was prepared and knew he had the won deposition.

The attorneys see the State papers in the file that Mr. Owens supplied them. Daniel can tell that the attorneys was getting upset because there is nothing to stick Daniel with concerning embezzling money. But Bishop Wilken's attorneys are just warming up.

"Where do you get the money from to finance all of this?"

"The church, the people give their tithes and offerings and we use that money to do everything that is needed for the church."

"So, how did you pay for your 2.1-million-dollar house, your eighty-five-thousand-dollar car, your wife's luxury car, and your daughter's twenty-five-thousand-dollar private school tuition?"

"I preach. I'm a full-time pastor. And the house isn't in my name. Bishop Wilkens placed me there. After pastoring for two years at Abundant Overflow Ministries, Bishop Wilkens had the church place me and my family in our home. It was told to us that the Overseer's name is on the deed to the house. The Overseer to Abundant Overflow is Bishop Wilkens."

"Can you explain this?"

The attorney shows Daniel a copy of the deed with his name on it as the homeowner. This is new to him, but Daniel has to keep his cool.

"I've never seen this before."

They gave a copy to Mr. Owens.

"Well, it has your signature."

"That's not my signature. I never signed the document. I've never made a payment to the house. I never even paid the property tax."

"Pastor Sanders, the signature matches your other signatures that are on documents that you supplied to us. So, are you trying to say that you didn't sign these documents either?"

"I didn't sign the deed to the house. Someone forged my signature."

"So that means someone forged your signatures on the documents you gave us," Mr. Kelly interrogated.

"No, you know what I'm saying. My signature was forged on the deed to the house," Daniel responds aggressively.

Mr. Owens whispers to him to relax. Daniel clenches his teeth, trying to suppress his anger.

"Okay, well, how much do you take in on Sundays?"

"It varies," respond Daniel still on an emotional high.

"Give us a round amount."

Mr. Owens interrupted the question. "My client, Pastor Sanders, can't give you that answer. You have all of the statements the church accountant, Mr. Shawn Davis, supplied from the very beginning. You also see the funds Bishop Wilkens takes from Abundant Overflow Ministries every week."

Mr. Kelly grunts silently. "How much do you make preaching at other churches or seminars?"

"It varies."

"I'm sure you can give us the highest amount you received."

Daniel thought for a moment before responding, "The most I made was about ten thousand dollars," he says lying. Daniel knows that Shawn doesn't include the amount he takes in from his personal account. They don't need to know that.

"Well how is it that you have about 5.58 million dollars in the church account but there is eight million dollars in all of your personal accounts?"

Daniel can feel the heat rising in his body.

"His accountant, Mr. Shawn Davis, gave you everything you need," Mr. Owens interjects again.

"Yes, Mr. Shawn Davis gave us all of the documents and some extras after he was served with papers informing him about criminal offense for withholding information that is valuable to the case. So, Pastor Sanders can explain the funds in his personal account."

"I prefer not to say."

Mr. Owens body language became intense. He asked Daniel if there was anything that he needed to know concerning anything, especially his finances. All Daniel had to do was give him every information. Mr. Owens hates being side-blinded in cases. His only great at what he does when his clients give him all of the requested information.

"Why did you withdraw $20,000 from your personal account about three months ago?"

"We are discussing about the church funds, not my personal funds," Daniel snaps.

"That is why we are here Pastor Sanders. Can you please answer my question?"

"It was for my wife's in vitro! We wanted to have another baby She was having a hard time getting pregnant, so we did in vitro!"

Mr. Owens wants to interject badly to tell Daniel to calm down but Daniel had already given too much information and had lost his temper. Daniel is losing this deposition quickly.

"Okay, well I'm sure can you can explain the house in Hawaii?"

Daniel froze.

Mr. Owens is even caught off guard about this new information.

Daniel couldn't speak. He knows he didn't go through with the house months ago. The offer was still on the table and the house is being considered now by someone else. And he's been stuck in a bidding war for a while. He had decided about two months ago to drop out and look for another house in Hawaii."

"Pastor Sanders, can you explain the house in Hawaii?"

"I prefer not to say."

"I'm surprised you're here today," Kimberly says to Thomas peeking her head in his decorated office in teen church.

"Yes, I started not to come but I knew it will be a bad idea if I decide not to show up."

Thomas is sitting at his desk, looking over some blogs online about Pastor Daniel. Kimberly walks into the office, closing the door behind her. "What are you looking at?"

She walks over to see the blog about Daniel. She places her hands on his head and redirects his attention to her. "I told you to stop reading those things. People are going off of hearsay. Most blogs are opinionate and the new articles can be bias."

Thomas sigh loudly, "I know, but I'm caught in the middle of this. I have to go to my deposition on Thursday. What am I'm to say, Kim? We know why, we do what we do. I wasn't expecting to get drag in all of this mess."

"We know why we do what we do, but people don't need to know everything. They are going to ask you about Daniel's spending money and the church funds, that's all. They see you as a witness and nothing else. Nicole and I spoke to Mr. Owens, so you're good. You just need to relax. You'll do fine on Thursday."

"I can't see or speak to Daniel until my deposition is over. How did his deposition go on Friday?"

Kimberly began to rub his head gently, "It was rocky. He lost his temper, but he got back on track. Mr. Owens and Nicole are quite upset about a house in Hawaii and some extra funds in his personal account. Nicole didn't have a clue about other accounts. I don't know what may happen concerning that. I'm sure there will be an investigation. So, if the worse should happen, Daniel, Nicole and Simone will stay at my house. I guess Darryl and Marshal will crash at my place too. Thank God I purchased a three-bedroom house when I moved."

"Wow, this is intense. I didn't know he has a house in Hawaii though," Thomas said shock. He dismissed what Kim said about the worse happening. Thomas doesn't want to think about that. If the worst happens, what will happen to him. He will end up with nothing too and nowhere to go.

"Yeah, everyone is shocked about that but his lawyer is looking into that and the extra funds that is in his account. Daniel said that he was considering buying the beach house in Hawaii but never signed any papers because he was in a bidding war and dropped out before all of this came about. I can't tell you too much about the deposition, but know that everything is under control. Oh and if you don't know yet, Bishop Wilkens got served with lawsuit papers on Friday. And we heard that he is pissed off. He began yelling and cursing out people in his office at the church. And fired some too."

"It's a countersuit; I'm not surprised he was upset."

"It's not just that though, Daniel is about to blow his cover. Just watch."

"What's going on? What happened?"

"Bishop Wilkens is more crooked than Daniel thought. Baby, I can't get into the details now but trust me if Daniel and Mr. Owens can pull this off and make the Bishop crack, Daniel will walk away with everything and more."

Thomas is feeling a little bit relieved knowing that there is a chance that Bishop Wilkens can lose the lawsuit. If there are incriminating evidence against the Bishop, then he has no other choice but to drop his lawsuit. Kimberly kisses the top of Thomas' head, beginning him back to reality.

Thomas smirks looking at her, "You know I missed you last week."

"I know you did. I missed you too."

Kimberly sits down on Thomas' inviting lap. He gently kisses her soft lips.

"So, when can I come over," Kimberly asked softly.

"Thursday night… you know Daniel is so paranoid he doesn't even want us talking right now. He'll have a fit if he knew you were in here."

"Which is why I told Marshal to keep a look out for me. It's not Daniel's request, it's his lawyer Mr. Owens. He knows how close I am to the both of you and he doesn't want the case jeopardized, that's all."

"How can possibility jeopardize the case being around me," Thomas says hugging and kissing her.

Nicole giggles because of his soft, tickling kisses, "He thinks I will cohort you by telling you what to say and what not to say. Since Nicole is staying with me I know more to the case than you."

"Do you know that those two, Marshal and Darryl, came to my house last week harassing me?"

"Seriously?"

"Yes, before I could open the door they barraged inside, pinning me up against the wall. But I'm not a punk. I handled both of them," he says lying. He was shaking out his mind. Darryl and Marshal are already intimidating and twice as tall as he is. Thomas was always intimidated by them.

"They thought I was a snitch and went squealing to the Bishop about Daniel. I'm not a snitch! That's not how I roll. Besides, this is a nice gig, why would I want to jeopardize this."

"Don't pay those two any mind."

Kimberly goes in for another kiss, but is interrupted by a knock at the door. They both sigh, putting their heads together wanting to just have some alone time. It's been three months since he bumped into her and they've been hot and heavy ever since. Thomas has never felt so alive in his life. He wants to use the 'L' word, but it's too soon to be throwing that around but it may just be too late.

Kimberly got up from his lap to straighten her clothes. Thomas readjusts himself before telling the person to come inside.

The door opens to reveal Jessica standing on the other side. Marshal is standing there allowing Jessica to walk inside the office.

"Hey Pastor Thomas, she said she knows you and wanted to see you. You said your name is Jessica, right," Marshal asked looking at her trying to hold in his laugher. Marshal knew who she was when she approached Thomas' office door.

Jessica can't take her eyes off Kimberly. She didn't know how to feel at that moment. Marshal and Thomas can feel the tension building up. Marshal had heard about Jessica and like everybody, he was waiting to meet this Jessica. So he couldn't pass up this opportunity to see Thomas' reaction when he allowed her to come see him. And Marshal is always down for a good catfight. He can't wait to tell Daniel and Darryl this.

"Hi Jessica, I've heard so much about you," Kimberly says extending her hand.

Jessica musters up a fake smile to shake Kimberly's hand. The two women spoke more words with their eyes than having the words come out of their mouths. Jessica's expression made it clear that she was a little jealous of seeing Kimberly in the office. Jessica always had a problem with being confident. She always compared herself to other women wondering what did they have better to offer Thomas. She never wanted to lose him to another woman. Kimberly on the other hand, her expression was very confident and made it clear that she is the new woman in Thomas' life and that Jessica is a has been.

"I can't say the same about you," Jessica replies to Kimberly's comment, "I'm Jessica, an old friend of Thomas'."

"I'm sure the both of you have some catching up to do so I'll leave you two to talk," Kimberly says smiling, now looking at Thomas.

Thomas looks at Kimberly, "You don't have to leave. I'm sure Jessica doesn't mind you staying here."

"Yeah Kim, do you know who she is," Marshal says instigating.

Thomas shot Marshal a sharp look, wanting him to be the first one out his office.

"Marshal, you really need to stop," Kimberly laughs his remark off, "I need to go get Simone anyways. We have a lunch date this afternoon."

"And I'll be tagging along," Marshal adds, "Pastor Daniel told me to stay with you."

Jessica turns her head in shock at Marshal; she is surprised that Kimberly is so close to Daniel for him to send his bodyguard with her.

Kimberly rolls her eyes, "Great. Well, since you're coming with us, you will be paying for the lunch."

"Then McDonalds it is!"

Kimberly shot him a disgusted look. She can't wait until this thing is over so she can go back to her normal life. Marshal has always been a pain since high school.

Thomas stands up from his desk to give Kimberly a hug. "Be safe. Take care of her Marshal. Don't be taking my girl and her Goddaughter to some grease pot."

"Am I on your payroll too," Marshal jokes.

Everyone began to laugh, except for Jessica. She didn't think that joke was funny, especially with the current circumstances.

"Nice meeting you Jessica," Kimberly says as her and Marshal left the office. Kimberly purposely didn't close the door behind them. She may be confident in Thomas but she isn't native either.

"Wow, I'm surprised to see you here. It's been about three months now since we last spoke," Thomas says, motioning her to take a seat.

"It has been a while," as she sits down in the chair. She looks around the plain office. She was expecting to see plaques, certificates or some kind of recognition. But of course, Thomas has only been doing this church thing for about nine months now. He has a bookcase in the corner filled with books, religious books. Jessica knows that it is only there for show.

"So what brings you here," Thomas ask taking a seat behind the desk, moving some folders and paperwork aside.

Jessica notices an open Bible on the desk too. '*Sure anything to keep up the image*', she thinks to herself.

"I decided to come to church today," Jessica lied.

"Oh ok, well, did you enjoy the service," he asked finally settling down.

"It was really good. I didn't realize how crowded the noon service can get. They had to put extra chairs in the aisles. Thankfully, I was able to get a seat."

"We get very crowded on Sundays. We have close to a ten thousand members. About eight thousand comes faithfully every Sunday, the others are online members from around the country."

"I didn't know a church can have online members from across the country. I'm used to being a local member at a church."

"The online world changed things…So, tell me, why are you *really* here? I know you just didn't come to go to church, you and I both know that. You never go to church."

Thomas knows that it is something else. He wouldn't be surprised if she is trying to be nosey about the situation that is going on with Daniel. The church was extra crowded today than usual because of the hot headline that is going on concerning Daniel.

"Honestly, I came to see you. I wanted to see how you're doing."

"I'm fine, why wouldn't I be?"

"With everything I hear that is going on, I am just concerned about you."

"I'm good. Everything is well here," he smiles.

He looks at Jessica and began to have feelings stir. As good as she is, she isn't good for him where he is in life. She is supposed to ride with him regardless of how she felt.

"I'm not going to act like what happened months ago never happened," she says, "I'm sorry we left off on bad terms. I was hurt and … I just didn't want to…"

"Didn't want to what," Thomas said interrupting her, "You've made yourself quite clear that evening. That's why I knew it was best to end the relationship. I wasn't going to make you stay when you're not happy."

"But I was happy. I was happy with you, but you know this isn't you. And know with this investigation…"

Thomas jumps up quickly to close the door. He doesn't need any church people ease dropping on their conversation.

"What isn't me Jess, huh," he says now facing her after closing the door, "This church, this suit and tie, preaching, what?"

"Everything," she snaps back, "I know you mean well but you can't go down this road."

"If you came by here to see how I'm doing, I'm doing great. But if you came here to try to start talking about what I shouldn't be doing, you can leave."

"Thomas, I'm just concerned that's all. I still love you."

Jessica's eyes begin to tear. It hurts her to see him with another woman. Thomas still has love for Jessica and he always will but he knows the decision that he made was for the best.

"Jess, I will always love you but we are going in two separate directions right now."

"I showed up at Lafayette that Sunday. I was going to approach you but I saw you with the girl who was in here," she says speaking about Kimberly. "I started to approach you anyway but then I saw Pastor Daniel and his wife walk up on the both of you before you…," she pauses, hesitating to know the answer to the question, "Was you talking to her while we were together?"

"No, but I don't see why that's any of your business."

"For all its worth, I'm sorry that I pushed you away. I tell you this," she says finally standing up getting ready to leave, "I learned not to listen to my family and friends concerning my relationship, depending on the situation, of course," she chuckles, "But as much as this hurts, you are right. We are going down two separate paths. Even though I don't support this *hustle*, I'll be around if you need me or if you need to get some things off your chest." She purposely used the word hustle to get a rise out of Thomas.

"That's the thing, this isn't a hustle. This is becoming my life."

"Sure," Jessica laughs, "I get it. You have omitted the word *hustle* from your vocabulary."

"It was nice seeing you," Thomas says opening the door.

"Thomas, I was joking," Jessica giggles.

"I'm glad that you find this a game. I don't get you. You come here out the blue wanting to see me, you try to play down what I do but then tell me how much you love me and how you'll be there, but then you turn around and sh...," Thomas catches himself when he realizes where he was and a teen walking past the door, "You need to go."

Jessica smirks a little and walks past him.

Thomas knows Jessica is up to something, but what? He didn't sign up for all of this, but this is better than having bullets flying past his head and running from goons because they want to rob him of Chris' money after he makes a drop. Thomas has been on edge since he was told to appear at an attorney's office. He hopes that this will blow over. He then remembers that Kimberly had told him that Bishop Wilkens is more crooked than expected. He never met the man, but he knows he is a man you don't want to cross now that he sees what he's trying to do to Daniel. Before he is able to pull information on Bishop Wilkens, he is interrupted by another knock at the door. He lifts his head from the computer screen.

"Hey Brother Miguel," he says forcing a smile.

"Pastor Thomas, are you going to come check out the sound system that was just installed in the new studio?"

"Yeah, here I come," he says getting up from his desk.

Surfing the web on the dirt on Bishop Wilkens has to wait. Daniel put Thomas in charge of the new studio they built, gearing up for the new record label. One way or another he is going to make his money.

The day finally arrived for Thomas' deposition. As much as Thomas tried not to think about it, he couldn't. He spent the last three days working at the church, making sure the set-up of the studio was going smoothly, keeping track of incoming orders and keeping tabs on the tithes and offering that the teens gave on Sunday. He took his money from the offering and had Shawn, the accountant, deposit the tithes into the bank account that is just for teen church. Thomas has already preached about the meaning of tithes and offerings. Simply put, the offerings are for him or whoever is ministering that day and the tithes go directly to an account just for them. That money is used for the building of the studio, parties they would want to have at the church, workshops, etc. Thomas had about five hundred teens the first Sunday he became the new teen pastor. That number has almost doubled. There are about nine hundred teens now. Thomas knew how to get the kids come to church. Get them excited about things they want to do at church and do it. And opening their wallets is easy. He tells them that each person can put in two dollars. One for tithes and the other for offering. Thomas can easily bring in over a thousand dollars every Sunday. Four or five thousand tax-free dollars a month. And that doesn't include the salary he gets from the church itself since he is now full-time.

But all of that can be gone just as fast as he got the position. He thought about his new Brownstone townhouse and new car, fancy clothes, eating at five star restaurants and having the best of everything. It can all be taken away. Without the hefty income and the incentives, he can be back in the hood. Then his thought went to Kimberly. She wouldn't want to be with him without the luxury that comes with this. She wasn't with him or seen him when he was penniless and running small time drops on the streets. Jessica was the only one there. This began to infuriate Thomas even more. If only Jessica would have supported him and was on board with everything, then he wouldn't be feeling so on edge with everything. Mr. Owens had spoken to Thomas over the phone and told him that Bishop Wilkens attorneys are going to question him about his knowledge on the church finances and about Daniel's spending habits as well as his own. Thomas was already informed about that from Kimberly on Sunday. But when Mr. Owens asked Thomas if there was anything that he needed to know about, Thomas quickly said no.

Mr. Owens had then hesitated and spoke carefully again, "Are you sure, there is nothing, absolutely nothing, I need to know about?"

Thomas began to sense a hint of doubt within himself, "No," he replied slowly.

"Okay."

Thomas knew Mr. Owens was caught off guard by Daniel's house in Hawaii but there was nothing he could think of for Mr. Owens to be aware of. Since Thomas is just a witness, they would use his testimony *if* they go to trial. Sometimes these things can blow over. Thomas has been so busy and on edge he has barely eaten or slept. Thank God he really wasn't required to be at an engagement because he wouldn't know how to function. But before going into the attorney's office, Thomas is sitting in his car, trying to relax.

To waste time since he's there almost a half an hour early, he takes out his tablet to look up information about Bishop Wilkens. The first thing that caught his eyes was the first couple of articles that was a day old about Bishop Wilkens countersuit. Thomas clicks on the article and began to read about the countersuit Daniel has on the Bishop. Surprisingly, Thomas became aware that the Bishop has had two other churches who had small civil suits against him about eight years ago concerning finances. So, this isn't the first time Bishop Wilkens has had an issue with one of his churches. The article said that a source close to the Bishop said that Bishop Wilkens is extremely angry and has been on the phone with his attorneys to find ways to scrap the lawsuit. But it was too late because he now has an open investigation on himself. The Bishop even reached out to Pastor Daniel, but never got a response and Bishop never came to church on Sunday, and had cancelled all speaking engagements thus far. Thomas also read that Daniel is seeking close to 35 million dollars in damages in the lawsuit.

"Where in the world does Bishop Wilkens have 35 million dollars," Thomas says out loud.

Thomas is engrossed. He wants to know just how crooked Bishop Wilkens is. What Daniel is doing is small compared to the Bishop. He quickly pulls up Bishop Wilkens wiki bio. He notices that Bishop Wilkens has 3 Phantoms, a private jet, three yachts, 5 multimillion dollar homes. "How can a pastor have all of this," he says out loud. He sees that the page was updated about a week ago. Thomas knows that Daniel must have his hand in this somehow. Thomas never created a social media page and now he wishes that he did because he knows everyone has to be talking about this. Kimberly couldn't tell him much, but she told him enough for him to look up the Bishop. Thomas sees that Daniel wants to leave the Bishop dirt dry. Thomas feels like he is caught up in a turf war between two kingpins.

Thomas is distracted with a tap on the window. His heart nearly skips a beat. He sees Mr. Owens standing next to his window. Thomas rolls his window down trying to break a small smile, "Hi, Mr. Owens."

"Hello Pastor Butler, you're early."

Thomas is use to people addressing him as Mr. Thomas or Pastor Thomas so to hear his last name with a title made him cringe on the inside.

"Yeah, I rather get here early than to wait at home watching time move slowly."

"Well, you can come on inside since the both of us is here. We should be able to get started earlier since the both of us is already here. I never had a client beat me to a hearing before."

Thomas nods his head in agreement. He clicks off his tablet and got out the car. Thomas' stomach is in knots with each step he takes. Before going inside, he pauses at the door. It feels like his body is shutting down. Thomas has never been so scared in his life. Everything relies on him. No matter how thigs are beginning to look bad for Bishop Wilkens, Daniel is still being investigated and Thomas can still lose everything he hustled for.

"What's wrong Pastor Butler," Mr. Owens asked.

Thomas is kneeling over feeling sicker. Mr. Owens is use to his clients feeling like this before a trial, but he never saw a witness react like this before. Thomas' reaction is making Mr. Owens worried. He doesn't know if there is something that Thomas knows that can make Daniel lose this case. He has enough surprises for now.

"Do you need medical attention," He asks.

"No", Thomas replies silently, "I'll be okay."

"Well you don't look okay," Mr. Owens impatiently responds.

Mr. Owens looks at his watch to check the time. They have fifteen minutes to be in the office. He decides to wait until Thomas composes himself. Thomas nerves has overtaken him. The pressure feels unbearable but he managed to stand up to face Mr. Owens. Thomas' eyes are a little red as if he was crying, "Mr. Owens can I ask you a question?"

"Sure what is it?"

"Is it true, that since I am a witness that my testimony at this deposition will determine the fate of Pastor Daniel? Does everything fall on my testimony?"

Mr. Owens knows that everything rests with Thomas, but he doesn't want him to know that because it can jeopardize Daniel winning the case. The only witness Bishop Wilkens has against Daniel is Deacon Williams. Surprisingly, the former board members, Sister May and Sister Barnes, denied any wrongdoing by Daniel. So with new information Mr. Owens had just received prior to arriving at the law office, he decides to put Thomas mind at ease.

"No, Pastor Daniel will be fine. I'm not to mention this but Bishop Wilkens is now under investigation with the turn of the countersuit. Because of that there is a possibility he may withdraw his lawsuit against Pastor Daniel. Just answer the questions directly and things will be fine…you'll be fine. Bishop Wilkens is going down fast," he says with a big smile on his face. Within a couple of months, Mr. Owens knows that his reputation as a high stake attorney will be on everyone's want list. He can start his own law firm with the nice bonus he'll get from Pastor Daniel just for winning the lawsuit. His mind is on winning. As long as he doesn't have any more slip ups like Daniel's house in Hawaii, this case would be a definite win for him. "So you don't have to worry about messing things up for Pastor Daniel," he concludes.

Thomas said okay and proceeds into the building. They are greeted promptly by the front receptionist. Thomas has never set foot inside an attorney's office nor had to deal with them. He looks around the simple office expecting to see attorneys walking around in a lavish expensive office with walls made out of glass. That's what happens when your reality relies on what's on the small and big screen. There are a couple of side offices with doors closed that had the attorney's names etched on the gold plate on the door. Thomas looks at Mr. Owens who appears to be right at home with his briefcase tightly held in his left hand. This is his usual playground and Thomas is a rare visitor. They are approached by an older white man who is wearing a black suit with a blue shirt and tie underneath. Thomas can tell the expensive taste of this attorney has because of his black wing-tipped shoes. He can smell the hint of richness, but see other mixed emotions written on his face.

"Good morning, Mr. Owens and Mr. Butler," the attorney spoke, shaking hands with them. Mr. Owens knows about the change of events concerning Bishop Wilkens, so he is well aware of the underlying nerves Mr. Kelly is experiencing. When he shook his hand, the moist glands of nerves gave it away.

"I'm Mr. Kelly, Bishop Wilken's attorney," he introduces himself to Thomas.

Thomas doesn't say anything. It isn't nice to meet him given the circumstances.

"You're just a little early but we can get things started if you are ready. But if you need time with Mr. Butler, we can wait for a couple of minutes," Mr. Kelly says to Mr. Owens.

"Yes, we're ready. We don't need any more time," Mr. Owens replies. He knows that Mr. Kelly wants to prolong starting the deposition.

Mr. Kelly turns around to inform the receptionist to send the other attorney and deposition writer and recorder to the conference room. Mr. Owens and Thomas follows Mr. Kelly to the back of the hall that has a large conference room. Once inside, Mr. Kelly shows Thomas where to sit. Thomas sits down trying to relax. Mr. Owens walks over to him lowering to his level to whisper, "At any time you don't know an information just say I don't know. I'll be sitting across from you and will interject if I need to, okay?"

"Okay."

"Alright, now just relax."

Mr. Owens walks away heading to his seat. Thomas began to relax and waits for the other attorneys to come into the office. He can't believe how he reacted before coming into the building. He doesn't want Mr. Owens telling Daniel how much of a punk he was before coming inside the office. Thomas began to think how Daniel faced his deposition last week. He was probably calm; he's thinking to himself. Daniel always appeared unbothered excepted when he was at his house to talk to him about being the new teen pastor. But that was only because Nicole was sick. Thomas caught a glimpse of Daniel's sermon on Sunday on one of the many televisions they have in the church. He even appeared unfazed then by this whole situation. You would think that he would have had another preacher preach for him on Sunday, but he handled everything on his own. Pastor Daniel is one powerful man to face the church, days after being hit with a public lawsuit by a church giant like Bishop Wilkens. The media was having a field day with this. The reporters and paparazzi was allowed to come into the church, but they had to leave their cameras and equipment inside their vehicles, and they weren't allowed to interview or talk to the members of the church concerning the lawsuit.

The other attorneys began to fill into the conference room. Thomas notices one attorney walk briskly over to Mr. Kelly to whisper something to him. Thomas is paying close attention to Mr. Kelly's face. He wants to know the secret too. Why couldn't it wait? But no avail, Mr. Kelly kept his poker face.

Everyone takes a seat and began the deposition.

"Good morning, Pastor Butler," Mr. Kelly says, "This is Mr. Stic, Bishop Wilkens other attorney to my right and to my left, this is Mrs. Stevens. She is here to record the deposition. Do you have any questions at this time?"

"No, I don't have questions."

"Okay, then we can get started." Mr. Kelly motions to Mrs. Stevens telling her to begin recording. "Can you please state your full name with title?"

"Pastor Thomas Kendal Butler," he answers calmly.

"How long have you been a member at Abundant Overflow Ministries?"

"For a couple of years."

"I need an exact number."

"I would say about four years now."

"And during those four years, what was your services at the church?"

"I was just a member, then I enrolled in the church's ministry school."

"I see, so you became a pastor through the school at the church?"

"Yes."

"Did Pastor Daniel Sanders tell you to become a pastor or bribe you?"

Thomas silently giggle, "Absolutely not. I became a pastor by my own doing."

"Before you were a pastor, what was your line of work?"

"I worked at a clothing store. I was the manager until the store closed. Then I was unemployed until I followed the calling God had been tugging at my heart to do."

Thomas knows he gave a great response because he sees a slight smile on Mr. Owens' face.

"I understand that you go with Pastor Daniel Sanders to many retreats and conferences, as well as, his trip to Paris. Did you notice any frivolous spending?"

"No."

"I'm sure you went to the malls with Pastor Sanders on some down time from preaching. Did you see him buy anything outrageous or any expensive clothes?"

"No, not at all. The only stores we would go to are the usual department stores."

"Do you know how much the church brings in every Sunday?"

"No, I don't."

"You're a full-time pastor, how much do you get paid?"

Mr. Owens interjects, "Pastor Butler doesn't need to respond to that question."

"Mr. Owens, I assure you, this question has been approved by the pending judge who will be hearing the case."

"If there is a case," Mr. Owens snaps back.

"Pastor Butler, please answer the question," Mr. Kelly continues aggravated with Mr. Owen's remark.

"I get a salary of seventy thousand."

"That's a nice salary for a beginner pastor. Were you ever making that much as a manager at a clothing store?"

"No."

"How much was your salary as a manager?"

"I made about fifty-two thousand a year."

"It must be nice to enjoy being able to enjoy the lavish lifestyle. You've flown to Paris, eaten at five star restaurants, living in a Brownstone house and you also purchased a nice luxury car. I say being a pastor has its perks."

Thomas see Mr. Owens twitch. Both he and Thomas has no clue where Mr. Kelly is trying to drive Thomas to. Thomas doesn't enclose the perks to just anybody. People on the outside of the church always wants to know, but only the few knows.

"I'm just doing the Lord's work, that's all," Thomas responds.

"Sure you are. Tell me, do you know a Jessica Sampson?"

Thomas froze.

Mr. Owens facial expression became tense. Who is Jessica?

"Yes", he hesitated a little.

"Who is she to you?"

"She is an ex-girlfriend."

"I see, how long were you in a relationship with Jessica Sampson?"

"I don't see how this is relevant to the case. But I was with Jessica for about three years."

"Did Ms. Sampson come with you to some conferences?"

"No."

"What about the trip to Paris?"

"No."

"I'm sure you took her out with you, Pastor Sanders and his wife before?"

"No, I haven't."

"Why? Why not bring her around your pastor? Your boss? You were in a serious relationship with her for three years, why keep her away from the church and Pastor Daniel?"

"I have no comment."

"But you indulged her with your new found fortune Pastor Sanders gave you, right?"

"I have no comment. My personal life has nothing to do with this."

"Are you sure about that?"

Thomas is sitting there motionless. His mind is now wondering what he said to Jessica. He never included her into the dealings at the church. He never told her what was going on and why they are really preaching. He knows and Daniel knows that it's all about the money but that isn't Jessica's business. Then it occurred to him. Why did Jessica show up Sunday unexpectedly? What was she trying to look for? After three months of no contact, she suddenly appeared.

"I repeat; my personal life has nothing to do with this. Ms. Jessica and I has been over with now for about three months. And before then, things were rocky between us, especially after I caught her cheating."

Mr. Kelly's mouth drops open and the other attorneys' slumps in their chairs in defeat. Now it's becoming clear. They must have gotten to Jessica to get her input. Only to have it backfire in their faces.

"Yeah, she cheated on me and that was before the trip to Paris. So, she's just a bitter ex-girlfriend."

The attorneys last plan has dropped. Mr. Kelly is upset that Jessica failed to tell them that this could put a dead-end in their plan to bring Pastor Daniel Sanders to trial. All Jessica wanted to do was help her uncle, Deacon Williams.

Chapter 12

Matthew 7:15 (NIV)

> "Watch out for false prophets. They come to you in sheep's clothing, but inwardly they are ferocious wolves."

THREE MONTHS LATER…

"So to conclude my sermon for today, I want to leave you with this," Daniel says turning off his tablet, "What's meant for you is for you. God has prosperity written on everyone's lives in this place. You will have people try to take it from you but what's meant for you, is for you. And sometimes you have to fight a little harder or *dirty* but you'll get what's yours. As many of you know, the last couple of months has been crazy. But I'm here to tell you that your pastor is still standing."

The congregation roars with applauses. Daniel is standing there taking in the cheers and whistles. Nicole is standing in her usual spot with a pregnancy glow, smiling at her husband, giving him a sly wink.

Daniel continues as the congregation settles down, "The lawsuit was dropped as fast as it came but the war was still on. Many people were affected by that and the media had its field day but we, I, came out victorious! There is a megachurch on the west coast, there is a megachurch in the south and now we are the megachurch on the east coast!"

The congregation roars once again. "We are now a family over nine thousand!" The congregation roars even louder. Daniel is just standing there letting them release their excitement. He finally lifts his hand up to settle the crowd. "What's meant for harm for me and my family, it turned around for our good. I just want to say thank you. Thank you for sticking around with your pastor. We lost some members and that's okay because we gained so many more in place of them. We are looking for a new church building in the area that can hold our nine thousand family members, so everyone can come together at the same time under one roof. Nicole, can you come up here sweetheart."

Nicole made her way up the pulpit with the assistant of Darryl. She takes Daniel's hand smiling like the perfect First Lady she is.

"I love this woman so much. We were high school sweethearts and eloped as soon as we graduated high school. We got married in the courthouse. Our parents flipped out, didn't they?" He looks at her smiling as she kept saying yes and smiling too. "In two weeks we will be celebrating our ten-year anniversary, and we wanted to share some exciting news with you. Instead of going away for our anniversary, we decided to stay here and have our vows renewed with the wedding that my wife deserves. And we would like to invite our church members."

The congregation began to go crazy. Daniel and Nicole looked at each other and playfully giggle. "Now we can't invite everybody, but, we will be sending invitations to people. We want to share our special moment with family and everyone here is family." He looks at Nicole, "Do you want to say anything," he says trying to give her the microphone.

She laughs and rolls her eyes as she takes the microphone. "My husband knows I'm not the public speaker," she laughs, "But since he wants to put me on the spot, I mind as well share it all. As many of you know, Pastor Daniel and I are having a baby." The congregation began to clap and cheer loudly, as she rubs her six-months pregnant belly. "But, but, that's not all," she raised her voice in the microphone to speak over the applauses. The congregation began to settle down once again. "We are expecting twin boys!"

Everybody went crazy. Daniel is overwhelmed with the surprising news that they are expecting twins. He can't contain his excitement. He began to jump up and down, running over to the band to give them high fives.

Nicole and Daniel decided to share the news with the congregation today since it's the first day of filming their reality show. But Daniel had no idea Nicole was carrying twins.

Daniel finally composed himself. All he can do is hug Nicole. This is the best news he's heard since Bishop Wilkens dropping the lawsuit, making a public apology and trying to make a fifteen-million-dollar settlement with Daniel. See, Daniel was much smarter than Bishop Wilkens. He purposely didn't flash the money he gets from the church to avoid matters; such as being investigated. There was nothing they could find to pin on Daniel and hold him accountable, not even the house in Hawaii that Bishop Wilkens try to push off on Daniel. Bishop Wilkens was the one who was in a bidding war with Daniel, he purposely withheld his name. After winning the bid, Bishop Wilkens had someone put the house in Daniel's name and forge his signature. Bishop Wilkens is facing a slew of charges. And he is looking at doing a couple of years in the federal prison. If only he left Daniel alone, he could have continued to go under the radar. Bishop had taught Daniel everything he needed to know about making money from the church. Daniel took the advice, but he wasn't into screwing people over like Bishop Wilkens and some others. **He wasn't into selling fake blessing oils, fake bottles of miracle waters, towels and swamping people's emails and mailbox to persuade them to give to the ministry**. Daniel did what he did best, he used his gift of gab. Say the things he knows people want to hear. The things all preachers need to know how to do. And they will have people running up to the altar, dropping money on the pulpit, attending and paying to go to every conference, convection and gospel show. Daniel was also more business minded than the Bishop. He wanted to make money in other ways besides just preaching in the church. He was very attentive to the other successful and prominent pastors who had lucrative side businesses. The mini mall was just a start. Daniel wanted to tackle the music industry. That's where he knew he can make the most money. So when Thomas brought up the suggestion of starting a record label, Daniel was already in. Everything that Daniel did was under the radar so it wouldn't bring suspicions. Bishop Wilkens put it past Daniel. He knew how hungry Daniel was, but he didn't know that he hungered for more. Daniel's greed in the church caused him to be successful, whereas Bishop Wilkens greed caused him to lose everything he worked for.

Daniel gave a little farewell benediction and heads out the sanctuary with Nicole. They stopped to say hello and chit chat a little with some of the members. They know that it will look good for the cameras. They have three cameras following them around while Thomas has two cameras following him in teen church. Daniel and Nicole took the elevator to his office. Once inside, he can't resist grabbing Nicole again, hugging her excitement. The camera crew continues to film.

"When did you find out you're pregnant with twins," he asked looking at her.

"A couple of days ago, I went to the doctor's office for my appointment. And we heard two heartbeats. He did an ultrasound to make sure and we have two small baby boys. I have a video of it at home. Kimberly came with me, since you were out of town."

"Well, give me all of your appointment dates because I want to be there." Daniel usually goes with her to all of her appointments, but he was busy going to conventions and appointments at Mr. Owen's office concerning the case. All the heat is finally off of Daniel. His accounts are unfrozen and he got everything that he asked for in the lawsuit. He didn't need Bishop Wilkens private jet, so he sold it and donated half of the money to charity and the other went to the investment of the mini mall. Daniel now has over twenty-five million dollars in his personal account because of winning the lawsuit.

Daniel and Nicole walks into his office still taking about her surprised news. As soon as they walk into the office, Daniel began kissing Nicole and telling her how much he loves her. The cameras in the office are still recording while the crew is watching and smiling. Darryl knocks on the office door before entering.

"Since when do you knock on doors," Daniel jokes, looking at Darryl.

"Since you have cameras following you around, I don't want people to think that I don't have home training. You are supposed to knock before you enter an office."

"Home training? Really," Nicole jokes back.

"Hush," Darryl says then looks directly in the camera, "Ladies, I'm single and am actively seeking a good Christian lady."

"Man quit playing," Daniel laughs and pushes Darryl playfully, "This isn't a find a date show."

As soon as he said that, Marshal came walking into the office with a suit and tie on. Everyone began laughing. The last time he wore a suit was at Nicole and Daniel's wedding and Daniel had to pay him just wear one. Marshal is standing in the doorway watching everyone get a laugh at his clothes.

"What do you have on," Darryl asked, "You didn't have that on this morning."

"Yes, I did, I changed my clothes when I got to church."

"So, that's what was inside the bag," Darryl said still laughing.

Marshal waves his hands at the three of them and walks fully into the office. The cameramen pane the cameras from top to bottom. They can't stop laughing either. Here is Marshal with a body of a bodybuilder wearing a suit, nearly busting at the seams. Daniel wants the reality show to be natural and real like his life really is. Darryl and Marshal are setting the bar really high. The producer is already talking about giving Darryl and Marshal their own show. Daniel had signed a contract to record for seven weeks with fifteen thousand per episode. Darryl and Marshal signed a contract too with ten thousand per episode. Thomas signed the contract too with ten thousand as well.

Thomas is very eager and excited to be on a reality show. After their conversation about three months ago about doing a reality show, Daniel didn't hesitate to talk to some people he knew who can pull those strings. When word got out that Pastor Daniel was interested in doing a reality show, the phone wouldn't stop ringing and the calls kept coming even more when the lawsuit went public. It was a no brainer for them to do a show, especially when Bishop Wilkens dropped the lawsuit. Deacon Williams had to dismiss his as well. Mr. Owens had informed Thomas about Jessica's family relationship to Deacon Williams. That had explained the reason why she was very adamant about Thomas not preaching and her questioning him about the church's finances. As soon as Jessica found out that Pastor Daniel was training Thomas to be a full-time pastor alongside him, she called her uncle, Deacon Williams, to find out if he knew Daniel's motive. She knew Thomas and knows that Thomas is far from being a pastor. She accepted him going to church on Sundays and going to their Bible school to do something with his time, but never go into ministry full-time. Then her antennas really spike when his lifestyle changed. After her mother was taken advantage of by a crooked pastor, she wanted to take them down, even if it meant she had to take down the man she honestly loved. It killed her to see Thomas with another woman; she wanted Thomas to be out of the church hustle so they can focus on getting things right between them. When she found out how close Kimberly was to Pastor Daniel and his family, she knew she didn't stand a chance. After Daniel's, lawsuit was dropped, her uncle couldn't get a dime from Daniel. He wished he stayed in the office with Sister May and Sister Barnes. Daniel kept his promised and kept them on payroll and gave them an advance after the lawsuit was dropped. Jessica tried calling Thomas to apologize but Thomas never answered her calls. Thomas didn't care if he never sees or speak to her again. He never thought that Jessica would ever betray him. For one thing, Thomas was glad that he listened closely to Daniel's instructions when he told him to never tell everything about the church and what they do to anybody. The more Jessica pried, the more it made Thomas resist her. Thomas knew something was up but never assumed that she wanted to bring him down. Thomas loved Jessica but he quickly fell out of love with her. It was as if God was actually trying to protect him from being burned by her. Thomas is just thankful that he missed that bullet.

Him and Kimberly has been going strong since day one. She has been by his side, supporting him, ever since. Thomas is happier than he's ever been. The teens in teen church has increased by two hundred. Thomas was worried that members would leave and take their teens with them, but that wasn't the case. The teens loved how Thomas present his message to them and the street edge that he brings to the pulpit. Thomas finds himself relatable to the teens. He was hesitant at first, but he began to find his place in the teen ministry. That's where he belongs. He speaks to about nine hundred teens every Sunday. Thomas has the largest teen church in the east coast.

Thomas walks off the pulpit amped about his message to the teens. He and pastor Daniel keep their sermons parallel so hopefully it can engage in them having conversations with their parents. But today, Thomas went off topic and talked to the teens about sex before marriage. "This is what I will tell you, if you are going to have sex, then you need to be safe. Wrap it up! There is so much protection out there to protect you from falling into sex traps. Now clearly the Bible says to abstain from sex until marriage but if our free will is willing you to do the latter, be safe then. Don't have a sex trap mess up your purpose in life."

Thomas slap some high fives and brotherly hugs after service. The cameramen follow him as teens began to swarm him just to be seen on the reality show. Thomas is no fool; he knows that's all it is. Everybody wants to be on TV.

"Yo Pastor T, your sermon was lit today," a teen said.

"'Ight, thanks man. I know I'm going to see you Friday night at the after school party?

"Yeah, yeah, I'm a come through. I may bring shorty too."

"'Ight, I'll see you Friday then, son. Stay blessed," he says giving the teen a farewell hug.

He can see Kimberly standing toward the back, waving at him. He smiles and waves back. He knows he has to get to Kimberly and head to Daniel's office. Everyone is meeting in his office in the scheduled first episode. That's the only thing Thomas has to get use to in the next couple of weeks, being on a set schedule, and not being able to mess around with Kimberly. Because the world will be watching, there is an image he and Daniel has to uphold. But Kimberly still comes over to Thomas' house every late night when the camera crew leave. Thomas finally approach Kimberly giving her a hug and walking toward the back elevator Daniel had installed so he can easily access his office.

"You've done an excellent job, Tommy," Kimberly says holding his hand.

"Yeah, I went off topic today but it's needed to be said."

The cameramen are surrounding him and Kimberly.

"Are you able to make the after school party on Friday night," he asked Kimberly.

"I want to say yes but I may have a late night. But I can meet you a little later," she replied.

"Okay."

They proceed to get into the elevator heading to Daniel's office. Last year during this time, Thomas was just the usual unemployed guy, trying to make a name for himself, and now here he is on a reality show, with a hot girlfriend, banking more money he's ever made in a year, and becoming a popular teen pastor. Kimberly always reminds him that he can be the first popular mainstream teen pastor. So, that's something Thomas wants to achieve. To team up with Daniel to start off will be great. For one thing, Thomas knows that he doesn't have to worry about Daniel turning into a Bishop Wilkens. Thomas knows that he is a different person from the Bishop.

The elevator opens the door to the empty admin floor. Kimberly and Thomas heard the producer inform one of the cameramen on the walkie talkie in Daniel's office, that they were getting ready to walk into the office. Kimberly and Thomas are making small talk as they walk to Daniel's office.

"Can you talk about Marshal's clothes," the producer instructs to Kimberly and Thomas.

As if on cue they change their conversation to Marshal's suit.

"Did you see Marshal in his suit today," Thomas asked.

"You know I did. How can you miss someone as big as him in a suit?"

Thomas opens the door to Daniel's office, entering with smiles and laugher.

"Hey man," Daniel says to Thomas giving him a hug, "Tell me, did you tell Marshal to wear a suit and tie today?"

"Absolutely not," Thomas begins laughing.

"Marshal didn't even wear a suit and tie to the prom," Kimberly snaps.

"Look, I did you a favor and took you to the prom because nobody asked you," Marshal shot back.

"You took Kimberly to the prom," Thomas asked surprisingly.

"Yeah, he took me to the prom," Kimberly responds crossing her arms.

"Now, I have to see those pictures," Thomas began laughing harder.

"There aren't any pictures! I refused to take pictures with Marshal while I was all dressed up and he showed up at my house in jeans and a polo shirt."

Everybody began laughing hysterically again.

"At least I wore a polo shirt," he shouts back.

Marshal and Kimberly always had a love and hate, Martin and Pam relationship. Like Thomas, everybody gets a thrill when the both of them go back and forth.

"Alright guys, let's chill," Daniel says wiping his tears of laughter, "Is everybody set to be here on Friday?"

"Yeah, I'm here," Darryl says.

"I'm coming in early to make sure everything is set for the artists," Thomas says.

"Awesome, this is our night to promote and introduce the gospel artists we have here at the church to the neighborhood. Thomas, we have a meeting on Tuesday morning with the attorneys to finalize some paperwork with our new record label."

"'Ight, 'ight, maybe we can have the artists sign their contacts on Friday," Thomas says.

"Maybe, but we can't rush these things too quickly. If we come out prematurely, there will be no growth."

Thomas agrees with Daniel is saying. He is just eager to get to work and start business. Daniel always see what Thomas is doing and appreciate his eagerness. After Thomas did away with the fakeness and became real, Daniel knew he was the right one he chosen.

"So, I heard there are some pastors who aren't happy that you're taking some of their members," Marshal says, "After that whole lawsuit, and the Bishop business being out there, many pastors aren't liking you too much right now."

"Yeah, we need more protection on Friday. There is a protest that is going to be led by some pastors in the area. They are supposed to be here on Friday night protesting at the after school party," Darryl adds.

"Why are they protesting at the party," Nicole asked.

"Because I preach the truth. The things that are in and out of the Bible. Anytime someone feels threaten, they have to make their voices heard."

"Especially haters," Thomas interjects as he holds Kimberly around her waist.

"Especially haters," Daniel says in agreement, raising his voice, "There are many haters that comes with being popular, especially in this industry. This is why there are a few select pastors that can qualify to be with the elite. We, the elite, are about to take the whole church thing to a whole new level. Just watch."

Excerpt from *Forever a Church Vixen*:

When their wives made their surprise appearance at the hotel, me and Veronica went to with Bishop Randy and Pastor Maurice, our playtime was over. Except mines, was just beginning. You see, First Lady Lena made me an offer that I couldn't refuse. She knew her husband Bishop Randy had a problem keeping his penis in his pants. She didn't want to give up on their lavish lifestyle or their marriage for the sake of their two kids. So, she gave him to me. She told me that if he is to have a mistress, it should be me and not the other sloppy women in the church. She feared that the other hungry lust-filled women would ruin everything for them. But not me. I have my own money, career and relationship to protect. This arrangement is worth all the mind blowing sex Bishop and I take part in. Raymond is good for lovemaking but this girl need that back breaking, hardcore full-throttle pounding. And Bishop Randy pulls out on all the stops. He doesn't know understand why Lena never questions him if he comes home late. He doesn't know about the arrangement me and his wife have and he doesn't need to know.

To catch up read *Church Vixens*.